DUCK BLOOD SOUP

Mystery Writers of America

DUCK BLOOD SOUP

Joseph Molea, MD

Mystery and Suspense Press
San Jose New York Lincoln Shanghai

Duck Blood Soup

Mystery and Suspense Press
an imprint of iUniverse, Inc.

For information address:
iUniverse, Inc.
5220 S. 16th St., Suite 200
Lincoln, NE 68512
www.iuniverse.com

ISBN: 0-595-21843-1

Printed in the United States of America

For Barry

Who, had he not been born,
I would have dreamt into existence,
So rich is the impact of his character
To my imagination.

Author's Note

Though the events in this book bear some similarity to those of a certain segment of my life, the characters and happenings are creations of my imagination. Any resemblance to real people or events would be a coincidental effect of the creative process. The story portrays a disease whose effect on behavior is quite predictable. The characters are composites, to be sure, of many individuals. In creating such characters, I have drawn freely from the experiences of many suffering colleagues. I have adhered only loosely to the pattern of my own life. To this extent, and for this reason, I ask to be judged, not as an autobiographer, but as a writer of fiction.

Acknowledgements

Many thanks to those people who helped make this novel possible: Thanks to Robert Lubbers at *Saskatoon Literary Agency* for representing the manuscript. Thanks, also, to Bobby Christmas of *Zebra Communications* and Grace Hope from *A Writers Excellence* for critiquing early drafts of the book. I am indebted to Paul Samulson, my editor, for asking the right questions and getting to the heart of the main characters, and to the rest of the editorial staff for putting the project together with such clarity of portrayal. If there are any technical errors in this book, they are all mine.

Also, I would like to convey my gratitude to the following physicians: to Dr. Joseph Van De Water for the privilege of practicing surgery, to Dr. Alvin Watne, for teaching me the two essential things needed to be a successful writer (a pencil and a pad of paper), to Dr. G. Douglas Talbott for teaching me how to live one day at a time, to the late Dr. Roger A. Goetz for teaching me to make the hard decisions, to Dr. Donald Dwyer for always giving me a second chance, and to Dr. David P. Myers for helping restore my professional reputation.

I owe a special debit of gratitude to my clients and colleagues at *HealthCare Connection Inc. of Tampa, Florida* and the community of recovering medical professionals for living the lives that provided me such rich material to write from. Special thanks to the members of the *Atlanta Writers Resource Network* [now defunct], and its' former director, David McCord, for sharing their work, enthusiasm, candor, and confidence with me. Thanks most of all to my wife, Heidi, without whom any book would be inconceivable, and, of course thanks to mom and dad.

Prologue

"Dreaming with morphine after an operation, I believed the night climbed through the window and into my room like a second story [man]…[He] had the dirty color of sickness and had no face at all…"

—Jimmy Cannon, sportswriter

*T*he mode of flight always changes. It's an airplane one time, a helicopter another, or, some type of contraption that shouldn't be airworthy at all, some aeronautical fabrication of my dreaming brain. The sensation of flight is amazing. I am filled with it. I watch myself flying these airships. I am flying. I operate the controls. The machines fly low and slow, close to the ground, more like drifting paper airplanes.

It dawns on me that I do not know how to fly.

I just linger there, in my dream, and let myself lose control. Then, the air stops pressing up against the control surfaces. It's not a bad feeling, crashing to the ground in one's dreams, falling, with the ground coming up at you fast. It's a scary feeling, but not bad.

You might think, "Why wouldn't he wake up from such a dream with a gripping fear of crashing to his death? Why doesn't he sit bolt upright, heaving and sweating in his bed?" I don't know, nor can I explain.

"You've had a seizure."

The words form themselves in my mind like smoke rings leaving the pursed lips of a tycoon. They seem inserted into my brain from somewhere outside myself. The sensation, not unpleasant, is one of troubled sleep, perhaps, or, awakening from a dream.

"You've had a seizure."

The words have no meaning, but, they fascinate me as they coalesce like clouds in the sky of my mentation, then dissipate into vapor: The incomprehensible smoke signals of an unseen messenger hailing from a mountain top far, far away. Through the haze I see a drink, a Manhattan, perhaps, judging from its color, siting in a plastic cocktail glass on the table before me; a magazine, *Scientific American*, I think, rests in my lap. My seat rocks back and forth.

These things I remember.

I remember having trouble reading. The words are just lines on a page full of jumbled type. Illegible characters wiggle like earthworms writhing on a paper bag, annelids desperate to escape the hook. The din of track-rails under my seat and the seashell sound of human whispers form the sound-track for my vision.

This is not the end; neither is it the beginning.

Then it dawns on me: *I've had a seizure. Jesus.*

Light envelops me like a luminescent shroud: a veil through which my consciousness ascends, brilliant and beautiful, back into the world. Yet, the whole process is some how annoying. The brilliance of the lamps assaults my eyes. Surgical lamp design considers the surgeon's comfort, not the patients. My stinging eyes make this all too clear: I am the patient. These particular lamps pack extra photons, exotic physical species, into bundles, neither particle nor wave, and yet both at the same time, having no mass but tremendous energy, that collide with my exhausted eyes. The malapropos weight forces my eyelids shut. Then my mind, set adrift on this turbulent sea of artificial sunshine, sinks back, like a battered raft, below the waves on a cool ocean of sleep.

New faces appear each time I rouse. Each voice tells the same story; helps me pull the details of my adventure together. "You'd been traveling," they say, with smiles, with frowns. "You arrived at the Thirtieth Street train station here in Philadelphia last evening, a Thursday, on the return leg of a trip from Philadelphia to Baltimore and back. You fell out in the parking lot, some kind of fit. When you collapsed a friend, an attorney friend, brought you here. Do you understand?"

"Yes," I say, but I have no idea.

"The electrical waves of your brain became disorganized." A disembodied head floats above me. Hands orbit this unholy satellite making the point. "The waves spread over the cortex, the higher centers of the nervous system, like an electrical storm. A Gran Mal seizure, it's called. The brain, the organ of consciousness, fails. We don't know why this happened. Not yet, anyway. Had your seizure not broken when the Valium was administered you might have died. Do you understand how lucky you are to be alive?"

I nod. It seems like the thing to do.

"In a seizure the body burns up all the glucose in an uncontrolled fashion leaving none to nourish the brain. We suspect you suffered no permanent brain damage, a fortunate circumstance. No clear precipitating agent could be identified either. This type of seizure is called 'reactive'; it occurs when one suffers—how shall I put this—*exposure* to a noxious substance."

"Noxious substance?"

"Noxious, you know, like drugs or alcohol, some type of toxin. We may never know the nature of that substance—unless, of course, *you* have some idea?"

I shrug.

"A large amount of narcotics was found in your blood."

Again I shrug.

"This may have contributed to the seizure."

Another nod.

"I see, well, the good news is it may never happen again. The bad news is it may happen again tomorrow."

Laying on my back, my head strangely full, I feel like an over-filled balloon about to pop. Everything inside me presses out. The feeling is hard to explain, like something from a Pink Floyd song. My mouth tastes of choral hydrate, medicinal and sweet. My eyelids bounce off each other. I peer out through snake eyes, mere slits in my face. Like mother used to say, "Two piss holes in the snow."

Then it dawns on me. *The Narcotics. They know about the narcotics. They don't know I'm a doctor, though, not yet anyway.* "Where am I?" I say, and startle at hearing my own voice for the first time.

"Our Sister of Saint Nicholas Hospital Emergency Clinic in Center City, Philadelphia," they tell me. "You are safe," they tell me.

Safe, I think, *Bullshit.*

The smells, more than anything else, convince me of where I am, the acrid odor of sodium hypochlorite solution, Clorox, and other disinfectants that linger, like death clinging to a corpse, keeping the bugs from jumping up and overrunning the place. Death, like bacteria, never leaves a hospital. Death hides, pressed further and further down by the well-meaning staff who labor, like mourners, adding to the mounting layers of rotting flowers, cut and piled high on each new grave the dead leave behind.

Twenty-four hours of my life, recorded in charts, reflected on electronic monitors, sketched on EKG test strips, passes through my own consciousness without registering. Productive time to be sure, full of CT scans, EEG's, brain scans, EKG's. A friend, Vincent Buddy, visits me, but I do not remember that. Post-ictal slumber is all that penetrates my memory. My name is Rocky, like the fighter from Falls Church, Massachusetts, Rocky VanSlyke. I am a resident physician, a surgeon, training up in Germantown at All Saints Hospital. I have been a surgeon for just over four years. This is something I know that they do not. Most of what they know does not interest me. The drugs interest me, or, should I say their comments about the drugs.

"Do you remember anything?

"Yes."

"Do you remember your name?"

"Yes. VanSlyke, Rocky VanSlyke." My eyes fill with tears. Somebody places a hand on my left shoulder, a disembodied hand. It communicates much: pity, maybe, or understanding in abundance. The voices continue to speak, more to each other then to me. These must be the medical students and residents making rounds on an interesting case. I can imagine them ploting: *Hey, the doctor who 'O.D.'ed is in Room 320; lets go check it out.* When the lips pause I ask, "Reactive?" It's the only word I can muster, the only thing I grasp from what they are saying.

A voice answers, commanding in tone. "Well, as you know, *doctor*, the cause of a new onset seizure in an adult is a brain tumor until proven otherwise."

That must be the attending; Oh shit, he's figured it out. "Yes, well, I haven't had my neurology rotation yet."

"I see, well, a diagnosis of 'Gran Mal seizure, reactive type' simply tells us you do not have a brain tumor. It means we don't know what caused the seizure."

"You said they could be recurrent, these seizures?"

"That's correct."

"What's the likelihood of that?"

"Not likely." The voice pauses. "Unless you are, well, *exposed* again."

"Exposed?"

"Yes, exposed to the precipitating agent."

The drugs, you idiot. He's talking about the drugs, my mind screams. Then my eyes close and I feel the air rush past me.

CHAPTER 1

The first time I ever shot up Demerol—main-lined it, I mean—still seems like yesterday to me. Strange. I did not enjoy my first experience with IV drugs anymore then you, an earth person, would have enjoyed the moody October shades of winter that filled my apartment that evening. A chill, like death, settled on everything.

Vince shot up first, then sat, steak faced and sweating, as he fumbled with the syringe, struggling to get at some more of "the medicine" as he like to call it. It's not easy to aspirate drug from the vial. When I asked if I could help he said, "Yeah. Open a goddamned window."

I turned on the air.

So, on the brink of winter I became like Richard Milhouse Nixon: cooling the frigid air so I could start a fire. No matter that the fire was in my veins, so hot even the windows—had they opened to the autumn night—could not have quenched it. A moot point in any case; in my old place the windows were nailed shut decades ago. *Fuck it*, I thought, *If Kennedy liked Demerol so much that he didn't care if it was "horse piss," Who am I to argue? The hole in my soul must be a least as big as the hole in his back was.*

These thoughts overtook me as I presided over Vince's desecration of the paraphernalia. This part of the ritual made me sweat.

Watching some fat slob fumble with drugs and needles and vials, seeing his thick stubby fingers contaminate the syringe, watching the needle come off in the stopper of the vial, watching all this just to get a taste for myself, made my stomach flip. Medicine is an art. Finesse draws medication into a syringe as much as suction. Of course, I could have done all of this myself in a heartbeat, but Vince liked to fiddle. He took forever to perform this simplest of medical procedures, things I could do in my sleep. Watching him was good for me in a sense, it atoned for my sin: letting a thief in the temple. I might have smote him with the Staff of Aesculapius, driven him from this holy place. Instead I let Vince use me. But, I also used him. You see, we deserved each other.

❋   ❋   ❋

All Saints Hospital, where I train to be a surgeon, nestles between the pointy-ass skyscrapers of center-city Philadelphia and the flat-faced street people who huddle outside the abandoned mansions of Roosevelt Avenue in the upper Northeast side. Vince personified such extremes in my mind: the sublime and the ridiculous. As the hospital attorney he was a mentor of sorts. He was also a criminal. He haunted me. It's hard to explain. It's a yin-yang kind of thing (heavy on the yin). Karma incarnate. My own suspicions aside, There seemed to be more to him, more history, more motive, then anyone knew. There were just too many coincidences to explain when he was around.

People talked in whispers around him. Someone would notice him whispering in someone else's ear, pulling another one aside. A real politician. Oh, I did some checking; you bet I did. I was a bit simian about it all, perhaps (hear no evil, see no evil, speak no evil), but not a complete idiot. Had I paid more attention, maybe, or had I had any shrewdness with things of the world, my life might have been different. To be honest, it wouldn't have mattered, anyway. Not at the time.

For the better part of four years, Vince touched every part of my life, my education, my world. Promotions, awards, special recognition, Vince made sure they came my way. And, he made sure I knew they came by way of his influence. Weather they did or not, who can tell. My good fortune was connected to his taste for good drugs. Maybe I really was as good as I thought. Maybe not. In retrospect, his insinuations into my affairs seemed to happen by design.

Using drugs with him slowed things down for me, delayed the passage of time and my graduation into adulthood. Things moved too fast for me in those days. This much is obvious: I stuck needles in my arm and loved the drugs he taught me to use, I loved them more than I loved myself. Had I been a different kind of person, who knows? Somewhere, maybe things worked out. If you believe Stephen Hawking we all exist in multiple universes.

❦   ❦   ❦

The light was otherworldly.

The harlequin lamp in the corner of my flat made Vince's face look washed out, overexposed, like an X-ray picture, something from *The Outer Limits*, or *The Twilight Zone*. The light rays hit him dead on, square in the jowls. Shadows casting about over the dents in his temples, on the edges of his brow, made him look like a bleached skull with candles in the eye sockets: the last remnant of a human sacrifice. My vision blurred as I watched him—he was taking so long. I squinted harder. The shape of his head changed, a lump of Silly Putty. The roundness of it, the color of the skin, made a mask of his face, a big, huge jack-o-lantern of his head. He wore no make up to cover the palor, although that might have been nice. He just may have been dead, now that I think about it. When he saw me smiling at him, he said, "What the hell are you looking at?"

I shrugged and looked away. *Fuck him*, I thought. *He's such a good attorney; let him figure it out.*

"What the hell are you smiling about over there?"

"Just waiting for you to get finished", I said through the kind of grin my mother always referred to as "shit-eating". "What's with you? You're all thumbs tonight"

"Yeah, well, give me a second—ouch, goddamn it!—It's almost ready."

Jesus, the things I put up with for a fix.

      ❀   ❀   ❀

The administration at All Saints ignored us residents. We were invisible to them most of the time, as were the patients, the other invisible entity. Once a year, though, when it came time to attract new resident physicians to the hospital—the next crop of indentured servants—they made a fuss over us. There was a luncheon and an assembly. "You fellas—I include the women when I say that—WEEEEEE-POP-SCREEE—goddamn P.A. system, Um, Hem, you fellas are the ones that need the help," one of them would say, the administrator or one of his lackeys. It doesn't matter which one. The electric voices funneled through microphones from the battered lectern all sounded the same. Manipulation screeched from the speakers like static. Feedback blared, at regular intervals, over the public address system. "It's your responsibility to paint the program in the best light."

Surgical training survives on this kind of mind control. George Orwell would have had a field day with the All-Saints administrative staff. He would have called the book, *Funny Farm*. "Some doctors are more equal then others."

When I interviewed, I wanted the job at All Saints so badly I could taste it. I would have taken the position if it had been in a veterinary clinic. (It's not as far fetched as it sounds. In the Army, the veterinarians take over for the battalion surgeons when the surgeons get killed in battle.) Surgical training is surgical training: plug the leaks; stop the bleeding. It's training reserved for the physician elite. "When you're done with this program , son, you'll be able to sew cobwebs to flatus!"

Nice work if you can get it.

Then, at five A.M. on that first day, driving down Kensington Avenue in the dead of summer, past the abandoned relics and burned-out cars, I realized my terrible mistake.

With a gasping breath lodged in my throat I made the left on to Second Street, palming the wheel for speed. My other hand kept me from gasping as I struggled to get the top up on my convertible without stopping the car. The shadows of abandoned row houses, the empty lots, the streets filled with paper and glass, the silhouettes of abandoned cars, the smoldering trashcans, and the boarded-up windows gave the neighborhood the surreal look of a horror movie set. *I'm on the set of the Omega Man*, I thought, *No, the Night of the Living Dead*. The crack-addicted skeletons waved their bony come-ons at me, selling all they had left of themselves for one more rock of cocaine.

Mother of God, what have I done.

These people were sent by God, according to my professors, to teach me the practice of medicine. After they were beaten, shot, raped, or neglected to the point of inanition they came.

When the student is ready, the teacher will appear.

All Saints Hospital, all two hundred beds of her, amounted to a typical community hospital in an urban-ghetto neighborhood. Nothing special. The purr of late model German imports, break-lights glowing as they slowed to hail the crack venders and prostitutes who lived around there, provided the mood lighting. Dope dealers replaced the hustle and bustle of Italian and Jewish immigrants who scurried back and forth to cobblers and tailors on Lehigh Avenue at the turn of the last century.

All Saints was the typical inner-city infirmary.

Jesus, Mary, and Joseph.

Ready or not, there I went.

❀   ❀   ❀

The long hours of my residency substituted for life, hot showers for sleep, coffee for meals. It worked for a month or so. No booze during the week, either. Lots of drinking on the weekends. Not really enough, though. Normal things lost their appeal. Anhedonia it's called. I asked Zack once, "Is this all there is"? Zack's my pal, my senior resident. It was a rhetorical question from the student to the master. I never expected him to answer, but he did. He rubbed his chin and squinted one eye. "No. It gets a lot worse."

"What?"

"Well, the death has a way of settling on a patient's skin after the person has gone."

"What the hell are you talking about?" I had no idea what he meant, not back then, anyway. Zack was senior to me back then. He took a leave of absence. Personal time. When he came back he was a year behind me and changed. For now, he was the master.

"Nothing, never mind. Forget it. Let's go smoke a cigarette."

"I don't smoke."

"Oh, right, right."

Good Ol' Zack. I liked him even then.

Depressed thoughts about dying, about not waking up one morning, popped into my head within a month, or maybe two of my start date. Now, when I posed the same question to Vice, "Is that all there is?" Well, Ol' Vince, he nodded; he just reached in his bottomless pocket and pulled out a pill. "This," he said with a flourish of the ghostly disc, "is all there is."

"What the hell are you talking about"

"Have you ever tried one?"

"A Percocet? Now, why would I do that?"

"Hell, you prescribe them for other people. Don't you think you ought to know what it does to you, its effects and all?"

A reasonable enough suggestion: rational, justifiable.

So, I took the pill. Percocet. Maybe a Codeine pill or two. Half, at first, then the other half. Ten minutes later my life changed. As that pill dissolved I changed. Something happened; something good. The elusive feeling of that pill seeping from my gut into my blood, gave me the first hint of that lily-white-peace that imagined a wonderful career, beautiful woman, and unlimited happiness. It lasted twenty minutes. A wonderful nugget of peace glimmered in my chest from then on, every time I took one of those pills.

And, the Demerol worked even better.

Believe it or not, I hated needles as a kid. Psychiatrists would say I suffered some lingering trauma, I suppose, some shock from seeing my father stuck so many times. That's Just psychobabble bullshit. I didn't much mind sticking needles into *other* people, for example. I kind of enjoyed it on occasion. Accessing a vein when the nurses blows it gives one a sense of satisfaction. The idea of sticking needles into myself just never appealed to me. Not even after I'd been doing it for months and months. It's not like one day I woke up and said, "I know, I'll stick a needle in my arm!" No, I did it on a dare, just to prove something to Vince.

"Nobody likes needles," Vince said brushing me off. "Who likes needles?" He laughed and shook his head.

Fuck him! If I think about it, I never really liked him.

Our relationship did become far more fundamental then friendship after that. A weird symbiosis existed between us, like the orange and yellow clown fish swimming through the black tentacles of a poisonous sea anemone. His personality stung other people, but I didn't feel a thing. Not at first. The danger eluded me at the time. His poison failed on me, at the beginning. That changed. Subtly, like The Amazing Kresskin or the magician, (What's-his-name? Copperfield?), I let myself be manipulated by Vince, mastered by his post-hypnotic suggestion, faked-out by his extra-sensory perception, shaken by his inner voo doo, his peculiar vibe. *When I count to three you will open yours eyes and not remember a word I've said.*

Vince seduced me like a thirteen-year-old virgin. He turned me out like a cheap whore. I knew it later, but not at the time. In the beginning, I wanted no part of the drugs, I just wanted to impress him, show him I had the balls to do them. *Forget about the needles,* my mind told me. Cases of people hooked on the needle, just the needle, itself can be found in the scientific literature. "Needle romancing" it's called, when one falls in love with the sting and burn of beveled metal slipping under the skin. I wanted no part of that. In the end, though, I injected myself on a dare, to prove something to Vince, to prove something to myself, nothing more. Just now I can't seem to recall what that illusive something was.

The pills? Well, hell, they were just pills.

A 22-gauge insulin syringe delivers exactly one cc, 100 milligrams of Demerol, into whichever superficial body cavity you choose. The pressure one exerts against the plunger creates a pocket, a weal under the skin, a space in the fat, a cavity in the muscle, a pinhole in the vein. Vince shot into the vein in his arm. I chose the muscle of my thigh. No specific reason. The thigh is a huge muscle, as good a place as any to violate if one is intent on violence. The skin of my leg, prepped with alcohol, pinched between my own fingers, heaped up in a pile between my thumb and forefinger to keep the needle away from a nerve or a blood vessel, looked blanched and white. Vince didn't prep his sting. Bang! He stuck his arm like someone throwing a dart at a board or playing pin the tail on the donkey. No sterile technique. No tourniquet. No doctor could ever do that. Bad technique breaks the spell. Bad technique is bad ju ju. It angers the spirits, stirs up infection, promotes necrosis. So much of surgery is ritual.

My thigh ached after the injection, but that was all I felt. My mood did not change. Minutes of pain passed with only that lousy throbbing in my leg to oscillate with the lightness in my head. Then, when the Demerol kicked in, I felt disoriented and nauseated. My perceptions shifted back and forth, like an elevator door opening and closing. My head became a hard-boiled egg, an over-filled balloon. Different parts of my psyche exposed themselves to all the rest in an endless series of shifting feelings. Anger, fear, love, hope, despair, guilt, euphoria passed by my consciousness like a slide show stuck on continuous play, a Wurlitzer Juke box flipping through an endless row of 45s, searching for something by Sinatra, *The Best is Yet to Come*, maybe.

"I must be missing something here," I said, or, maybe I thought it. It's hard to tell looking back.

"You need to try it I.V." Vince said, that I'm sure of.

He filled the prescriptions I wrote for him. As long as I kept writing prescriptions, Vince said he'd pay. He came through with the Demerol, all right, as long as I kept writing those 'scripts. Once I did shoot the stuff I.V. I went up fast, one hundred milligrams at a pop, four times the normal dose. I went up from there.

One hundred twenty-five milligrams

One hundred fifty-milligrams.

One hundred seventy-five.

One thousand milligrams at a sitting wasn't unusual. Two hundred milligrams at a pop teased me after the first four months. A lot of Demerol, veterinarian doses. Enough to cause one hell-of-a seizure.

I wasn't there yet; like I said, I didn't like needles.

❧   ❧   ❧

"Drug addict," Karla said, but it came out sounding like, "drug-attic." "Drug-attic, drug-attic, drug-attic!" like a little chant.

Drug-Attic: a place in the home designed specifically for the storage of drugs.

Jesus, Mary, and Joseph.

She went on like this, after I'd been doing what I'd been doing with the drugs for a while, whenever I lingered in the bathroom, or, peered too long into my shaving-kit at the wrong time of the day.

"Drug-attic," she'd mutter under her breath, "Drug-attic, drug-attic, drug-attic," if she detected the tattletale sound of any pill bottles rattling.

I'd laugh. "Karla Trenton, the chanting nurse."

"Rocky VanSlyke, surgeon junkie."

"Hey, hey, hey now, ease up, will you?"

"You're the one who'd better ease up, buster. You're chewing those Percocet like you would M&M's."

"Look, don't make me go through this again."

"Poor baby."

"You, of all people, should know what it's like."

"You're the one who wanted to be a surgeon."

"I'm gonna go home."

"Why? What's wrong."

"Nothing. I'm tired of your shit and I'm gonna go and get some rest."

"Go where?"

"To my place."

"Don't go."

"Don't fuck with me, then."

"Don't go, please? I'm sorry. I won't tease you any more. I was just kidding. You know that. Please don't go. I'll go rent a video and get some Chinese food, okay? Don't go. You can relax. I'll leave you alone?"

"Okay."

Karla and I met one night early in my training when I was the junior surgical resident on call for pediatric surgery. "Junior," as in, not much good to anyone. She caught my eye as I passed the nurses station on my way back from the pediatric intensive care unit at about 3 AM.

"Who's that?" I asked Zack, the senior resident walking with me. We weren't pals yet. That would come later after he returned from where ever he went and was working for me. Now I was working for him. He had just helped me establish IV access on a three-week-old infant boy who needed a new liver. He placed the IV through the soft spot in the tiny head.

"Karla, I think her name is." Zack spoke but it might as well have been the voice of God. Who else could stick a needle into a baby's head and get away with it? The spell broke, though, as he sucked air in through his teeth with such violence and greed that the very act of his inspiration seemed sorted. "Szzzit." The sound was all the more vile to my ears for my having already fallen for this woman.

"What's that supposed to mean?" I demanded defensively.

"What?"

"All the, the—" My hands filled the vacuum between us with absent minded gesticulating, "—the sucking sounds. What's with all the sucking sounds? Do you know her?"

"No, but I've heard stories, man," he said, lowering his voice, narrowing his brows, and leaning forward. He clasped one hand over my shoulder. *!Muy Caliente, hermano!*"

"Hot? That means 'hot', right? What do you mean by hot? Do you mean 'hot', as in good, or 'hot' as in bad?"

"I mean 'hot' as in I'll bet that *puta* lets me take her temperature with the tip of my tongue, *hermano*." He patted me on the front of the shoulder with the back of his hand. "What do you think?" Then he stuck out the longest tongue I've ever seen and licked the tip of his own nose. "Just like that—right up her ass."

"Ugh," I groaned, grimacing and grasping my gut. "You have *got* to be some kind of sick Gene Simons mutant." I gave Zack a shove.

"Gene Simons? Whose Gene Simons?"

"You know, the bass guitarist from the group KISS, the one with the huge tongue? Never mind." I hoisted my thumb back toward the nurses' station. "Is she seeing anybody?"

"Some geeky medical resident. Nobody to be concerned about. You need to get over there right now and start talking that stuff up, man. I'd do it myself, but my wife has been all over me lately about the broads, so I've got to cool it. Go on man, but if you score you have to tell me all about it."

"You're sick."

"Go on, man. I'll even dictate the procedure note on the kid." He returned the shove that propelled me toward the nurses' station.

"Jeez, I can't pass that up," I said, looking back over my shoulder. At the nurses station I shuffled some papers around until I caught her eye.

"Well, hi there!" she spun around on the balls of her feet, running shoes squeaking. She sported an angelic smile that seemed unnatural at that hour no matter how sincere it might have been. "How may I help you?" She bounced on her tiptoes, ready to get on to her next patient.

"Help me?"

She pointed to the papers and forced a second, broader smile.

"Oh, ah, oh, yeah, well—"

Recognition flashed across her face and her smile tightened into a sly grin. "I see, well," she leaned over and scribbled something on one of the papers. "If you're not doing anything this weekend why don't you come down-the-shore?"

"Oh, ah, jeez, well, I don't know." I cleared my throat, "Are you having a party or something?"

"Nooo, I'm going to be there all by myself." She stared at me for a second, her smile broadening. "Here's my number. Give me a call," she said. Then she was gone.

She liked to tease me.

She never believed me addicted. The comments were hyperbolic humor. She even filled scripts for me a few times. Whenever I wrote her a prescription for her birth control pills, you know, or for antibiotics, I'd slip in a prescription for my pain pills and no one was the wiser. Professional courtesy, *quid pro quo*.

So, we met that evening, there in the children's hospital, with the sound of crack baby hip-hop, bleating IV pumps, and cardiac monitor R & B riffs forming the music of our romance. In addition, from then on, she was more then a nurse, she was an exotic dancer, tan and pretty, gyrating as she called me to her floor in the middle of the night. After that, answering the phone in the on-call room seemed less bothersome.

"Hi. Sorry to wake you, she would say. We need your help with a central line on three West. Can you come?"

Of course I could. I always could.

What are the advantages of dating a healthcare professional? Well, for one, healthcare professionals understand the stress of the profession: how it works on you, brakes you down, plays on your mind. They also understand that if you work hard you must play hard. They almost never mind drug abuse (as long as you treat them right, and, I always treated Karla well). Oh, one more thing. The quid pro quo I mentioned is simply this: you cannot leave, no matter what. The unspoken understanding is they chill, you stick around. If not, all bets are off. Yet, as nice as Karla treated me—she never gave my any serious trouble—I never entertained heavy marriage considerations. I did not want to get married. I might have, anyway, but that's beside the point.

The thought of marriage crossed my mind one evening when the wind blew cool off the ocean. That summer wind came blowing in off that Jersey shore, right on through the screened-in sun-porch of the three room cottage—her family called it a "beach house"—over the frosty beer bottles strewn in front of me, and effected my thinking like a lyric from the Sinatra Ballad of the same name. That third beer hit me just right, the pills kicked in and I almost asked her to marry me right then and there. But, my pager went off, and I had to go into the hospital, so, I never did—thank the good Lord—and it's just as well. At times like that one forgets the hangovers and the boredom, the pain of it all.

Anyway, before I lost my mind and did something stupid, Karla changed. Not that it mattered much. I was hooked on junk and dependent on her. We'd been seeing each other a few weeks, I guess, when I figured it out: the whole puking thing. Her breasts pressed against her sweaters, tense and sexy, which kept me pretty distracted for a while. Her bosom, and the way her hips jutted toward her flat tummy, reminded me of an hourglass filled with sand. She sifted past my hands when I turned her over, laid her down and pressed myself against her. I was used to the way she looked in the light and felt in the dark: a Barbie Doll, but softer, of course, and warmer; "fully functional" as they say in those ads for inflatable companions.

She did not stay that way for long, though. Her figure lasted, um, about a year. At the most. Later she still looked okay, I guess, but less girlish. The thin, sallow, willowiness that attracted me to her slipped away. She still attracted other men. Their comments and glances never stopped. Once she began to put on weight neither of us believed the things I said anymore. "You're not fat," I lied. I was a walking commercial for hair-color, a promotion for a fad diet. "Baby, you look great." She would glance at me from the bedroom half squeezed into a dress or a pair of jeans a chipmunk smile of satisfaction blooming on her face. Then she would notice me noticing the brownish edges of her teeth, where the acid from her stomach bathed the enamel away and her smile would be gone.

At first she explained her frequent visits to the ladies room as if it were an occupational hazard. "I must have picked something up from the kids at work," she toyed, "You know how easy those kids pick up a bug. Like vermin; then they pass it on to everyone who gets with in four feet of them (Tee hee)." Did I understand what really went on? How could I? Karla ate everything. For awhile I thought it was me, that I was eating the stuff or seeing packages of food that were never there

"Hey, what the hell happened to those Doritos?"

"What Doritos?"

"The ones I bought last night at the convenience store, when I bought the beer."

"How should I know? I told you, I don't eat that junk. Maybe you finished them last night. You were pretty drunk. Maybe you got the munches in the middle of the night and finished them."

Am I losing my mind? Maybe. Maybe not.

The truth of those mysterious disappearances came to light one day as I staggered back from the beach, sunburned and groggy from one of my frequent thirty-six hour vacations. Out of the hospital at seven A.M. after a Friday night on call, a couple of Percocet for the road, on the beach at Long Beach Island by Nine A.M., drink until nine that night, up at seven and do it all again. I heard her as I grabbed another wine cooler from the old Frigidaire. It was only another step or two to the bathroom.

She expected no audience. The door stood open. Karla, my beautiful Karla, sat on her haunches, her naked breasts pressed against the cool porcelain, fingers reaching down her throat. Bone rattling sounds tore out of her as she wretched. Her guts blew, drenching her arm with vomit. This hellish sight held me as spellbound as any sight of the ripped body cavities I saw at work, spilling their contents on the floor of the ER had. *My paper shoe covers*, I thought and looked down to check my feet. By now, her ferocious humping and vehement head bobs, were all that was left of the fit.

"Karla," I whispered, "Baby, Jesus Christ, what's happening?"

She swung around, her hand still planted in her mouth, and muffled a startled scream. Her lips looked like they might fit around the thick end of a baseball bat as her fingers hung from her mouth. She gazed at me for a moment; Her look was so dazed that I dropped my wine cooler thinking I might have to revive her.

Before I could take a step, she crawled across the floor to where I stood and began tugging my trunks down. In stunned silence I let her sopping fingers grope me; pull on my throbbing cock like the handle of a broken candy machine, reluctant to give up the goodies. She took me into her mouth, up to the hilt, and recaptured the hypnotizing rhythm from moments ago

Pieces of stomach contents collected in my pubic hair and the smell of vomit and bile clung to her. I gagged, fought the urge to vomit. By now, her starved gulps had soften to a gentle suckle, a child at her mothers breast, and I realized that I had ejaculated with out experiencing the orgasm. She kept on working until she had sucked me dry. It became too painful for me to tolerate any longer and I pulled her head away. She collapsed, twitched out her own orgasm with her other hand, her cheek pressed against my leg, my hand holding the side of her face, supporting her as best I could.

After a moment she looked up and pointed at her mouth. "Can I have something to wash this down?"

The capsized wine cooler rolled around on the floor close by, so I reached over and handed it to her. She pressed the bottle against her face for a moment, and then she took a swig.

"Thanks." She handed the bottle back. "Want some?"

❧   ❧   ❧

Vince stared at me.

The engine purred the way Cadillac engines do. He sat there with the doors locked. I stood out in the rain and stared back at him like an idiot as the windshield filled up with raindrops. When I tired of all the nonsense, I pounded on the window with my fist. Bending down, I glared at him. He made the "what?" sign with his hands.

"Open the fucking door!"

He flapped his hands up and down in feigned excitement.

"Cut the shit and open the door!"

The lock clicked and I got in. "Jesus Christ, what was all that about?"

Vince ignored me and turned on the radio.

I stared at him

"What?"

I reached over and turned it off. "Cut the bullshit."

He scratched his head, rubbed his hand all around on top, and chuckled long enough to aggravate me. "These are yours. I've already drawn them up."

As I took the ten syringes from him, each filled to the "one cc" mark, I noticed that the sleeve of his shirt was already rolled up. There was blood on the cuff.

Relax, I told myself, *he's just fucked up*. When it dawned on me how many syringes I held in my hand, I wondered to myself, *What am I going to do with all of these?*

I needn't have wondered.

This is how it worked: The car phone rings. This is not unusual. If you are an older pharmacist, the storeowner, let's say, or the manager, you fill the 'script without a call. It's a sale. But, if you are young, or new at the job, or you want to keep some Demerol for yourself, then you call. You dial the number and it rings. You start to get nervous; *real number*, you think. I answer by identifying myself as the doctor. You compare my name to the name printed on the prescription. It's the same. I sound serious, maybe even a little put out. Not angry, just aloof. *The doctor's on his car phone*, you think. *This had better be good.* You're more nervous now. You don't call the doctor for just anything, not when you're holding a legal 'script with a D.E.A. number on it.

You identify yourself. You are calling to confirm a script for injectable Demerol. I ask you to describe the customer. You relax. I may be curt, but I make sure you sense that I understand; this is collegial. You describe the middle-aged, balding, obese man standing before you who could be anybody. I confirm that, yes, that is my patient and that the poor, moon-faced, bastard suffers from kidney stones. That's believable. I am to meet him at my office in twenty minutes to administer an injection. It is late, and I would appreciate it if you could expedite the prescription. I don't say so, but my voice sounds tired. Maybe you think I could use a rest. Can you expedite it? Of course you can, you say, and thank me for my time. I hang up before you have a chance to confirm my office address, but you are not about to call me back. You look at the patient and smile. He does not look to be in pain, but that does not concern you. You know that pain from a kidney stone is crampy, colicky pain, it's called. It comes and goes.

You also know Demerol is a synthetic narcotic and will not only kill the pain, but will also relax the smooth muscle of the ureter, the tube from the kidney to the bladder, and help the stone pass. You give the prescription to the patient, and he pays you the twenty dollars. Demerol is cheap. It's been around a long time. You make seventeen dollars profit. Six hundred percent mark up. Maybe you know that Demerol was marketed as a non-addicting substitute for morphine in the '50s. Maybe you don't. Even if you do you could care less right now. You notice as you hand the medicine to the patient, that he is getting red, beginning to breathe heavily. You think that maybe he's about to have another attack. You are happy to see him leave the store, even in a suspicious rush: an ambulance call is not going to get you out on the store any earlier. You don't know that the man is craving. You couldn't know it's just that (or, could you)?

What happens next?

I drive to a gas station and get into the car, with that same fat, balding man, the one who has taken the moon for his face. He hands me the syringes as I have described. Ten and ten. That's the deal. I write the script, he pays for it. I'm the one with the medical license. I've already paid, he says, and I believe it.

Smooth.

For a moment, I felt far away. Through the windshield I watched the gas station sign as it looped around and around. The reflection of the colors from the revolving neon sign bounced red and blue beams off the driver-side window. The colors behind Vince's planet-sized head looked like some cosmic spectacle in an alternate universe. The blinking sign reflected in the exact spot on the windshield where my own eyes stared back at me like a face in the glass marquee of a huge pinball machine. It's a game, I think, Pull the plunger. Let it fly. What the hell, in for a dime, in for a dollar. IM, IV, what's the difference? Maybe this is it. Maybe this is all there is. Up goes the ball, up my arm and out through my ears. The steel ball bounced here and there, in my head, in my chest. I felt it. I watched the lights flash and heard the bells ring from outside myself. Then I felt the burning. The first shot. Aaah...

Tilt.

My eyes closed, and I laid my head back on the seat.

This is what you think: in a dark funeral parlor you sit before a casket, uncomfortable in your new little outfit. Heaven and hell flash through your mind. All your relatives died just like this, they all died too young of "heart attacks." You remember that someone in this very room explained how all your uncles died shoveling snow off their driveways in Cleveland. That's not how this woman died, however, the woman in this casket. Goodness, no. The neighbors whisper words like "alcoholic" and "drug addict" when they think you are out of earshot. You don't recall whose funeral this is.

Was it your funeral, Mom?

You hear a voice in the back of your mind, "Drug-attic, drug-attic, drug-attic," it chants, like that, inside your head. You push the needle past the skin again. You like the sting; you hate the needle, but love the sting.

You're now about the same age as when this woman, the woman in the casket, died.

What a shame.

       ❀   ❀   ❀

This is how it feels: after the rush, you feel almost normal, happy, like a child waiting for Santa on Christmas Eve, except with a headache and an odd, metallic taste in the back of your throat, maybe a hint of nausea. Then, you're exhausted. Nirvana, right. It barely lasts twenty minutes. Less then two hundred milligrams left.

Later, when it's all gone, when you have found your way home and you are alone in your apartment, you just want to sleep. You're afraid to sleep, alone in the dark, but you want to sleep, so you pretend. You lie on the couch with the television on. The drone should help you to doze off, but it doesn't. You can't focus on the picture. You watch the blue and white flashes on the wall. It's easier. Then, you startle; you wake up with your muscles cramped and twitching for not having changed position in hours. An uneasy sleep, at best, if you can even call it that. In the morning you are still exhausted. You stay in the shower as long as you can. It doesn't help.

Now you're late.

You have a vague sense of impending doom that sticks to you like the lingering reek of a sour towel across your face or the stench of wet dog fur on your hands. You swallow aspirin with your coffee to try to shake the fog away from your brain, but it does nothing for the headache and makes your nausea worse. You make a promise never to do this to yourself again. Never. Then you think of how much better you'll feel when you do.

Then, you go to work.

Now, would you ever suspect, as you meandered in the direction of the tall gentleman standing next to the flesh that used to be a human being, the doctor in the sweat-spackled scrub suit, the surgeon, the first person to smile at you since you've walked into the hospital, as if all the insanity and chaos might be okay, as if you belong here? Would you ever suspect what he, the chief surgical resident, does with that needle and syringe sticking out of his pocket when he gets home?

I pilfered medical supplies all the time. Just about everybody did. Needles, syringes, suture kits, you name it. One never knew when such things would come in handy.

CHAPTER 2

"*I*t's a stab wound to the chest, I think."

"You think?"

"It's a stab wound to the chest."

"That's better. What's the ETA?"

"About five minutes."

"Okay. See if you can get the paramedics back on the horn and see if you can get more detail about the mechanism of injury: what he was stabbed with; the direction of the thrust, you know…"

"Uh-huh. I'm writing. Go on."

"Current vitals and call the OR. We may get a chance to crack this suckers chest."

"Uh-huh."

"You ready to rock and roll?"

"Uh-huh…Oh, ah, what? Oh, sure. Anything else?"

"Yes, there is, now that you mention it. Stop writing. It slows you down."

"Uh-huh."

"One more thing."

"Yes?"

"Relax."

"Yeah, right…*Click.*"

Interns remind you of how far you've come. They are also more work. You almost always end up doing everything twice: once to teach them, and once to do the work. After I called the ER nurse to make sure I had accurate information and had everything ready for a trauma code I got up off my bed in the on-call room and washed my face. No time for coffee. The wall clock read 2:14 A.M.

"See this?" I pointed at the blood spurting from the man's chest.
"Yes"
"That's called pulsitile blood flow. What does it mean?"
"Ah, that he's got an arterial injury?"
"Well, if it was in his leg I'd agree with you. Look at where the wound is."
"Just left of the xiphoid; under the rib cage."
"Yep. This guy's got a stab wound to the heart. Were taking him up stairs. Everybody? Listen up! We're taking this guy to the OR. I need ten units typed and crossed and get me thoracic surgery on the phone. Put on a glove and stick your pinky in the wound."
"What? What for?"
"To stop him from bleeding to death before we get him up there. Just do it. Save the questions for later." The kid looked at me. "Listen," I said, grabbing the intern by the scrub suit and pulling him to me, "questions are okay, just not now."
"Okay."
I turned to the nurse anesthetist. "Tony, what's his pressure?"
"Well, looky here. It jumped right up to a hundred when your sidekick stuck his finger in the dike."
"I love it when a plan comes together."
"Fuckin' A."
In fifteen minutes we had his sternum split. I put a purse string suture around the intern's pinky that plugged the center of the wound. "When I say 'go', you pull your finger out, okay?" He looked at me. "Ready—go." He pulled out his pinky finger and I tightened

the suture, but not before a jet of blood six feet long shot across the room. His heart stopped twice before we finished, but once the bleeding stopped his pressure came up to normal. We put a couple of felt pledgets in the heart muscle to reinforce the original suture and closed the chest. We were closing the skin by the time the attending arrived.

"Any bleeding in the belly?" Dr. Waterman, the rotund chief of surgery, said poking his head through the door from the hall way.

"He's got a little nick in the liver, but it's not bleeding; we lapped him to make sure."

"Spleen's okay?"

"Yep."

"Nice job. Make sure you get an echo-cardiogram to check his heart valves and keep him on antibiotics, like forever, right?"

"You got it."

"Thanks a lot, Rock. Really nice save. I'm going home."

"Thanks."

"Oh, and Rock?"

"Yes, Dr. Waterman, sir?"

"Are you okay? Your hands are shaking."

"Ah, shit," I said, stopping for a moment to stretch my fingers, "Too much coffee, I guess.

C. Calvin Waterman touched the side of his nose with one of his enormous fingers—fingers so large that it was a never ending topic of conversation how the man ever tied a surgical knot–furrowed his brow and huffed, "Um, well—"

"I'll cut back."

"I've spoken to you about this before."

"I'll cut back."

"Okay; and Rock?"

"Yes, Dr. Waterman." I exhaled, my voice dripping with feigned exasperation.

"That is, hands down, the best use of an intern I've ever seen."

"Thanks," I said and smiled, but the intern couldn't see me, not with my mask in place. The rest of the team saw his forehead redden and chided him with "atta boys".

        ❦   ❦   ❦

My shift ended on a quiet note. Not a creature stirred anywhere in the house. Zack Sweeney was in the cafeteria by himself, as usual, drinking a cup of coffee, and palming a photocopy of an article from some surgical journal. Today he was palming a copy of the *Philadelphia Inquirer*.

"Zack, that new intern, what's his name?"

"Can you believe this? The police are forming a special task force to investigate fraudulent prescription writing!?"

"Zack?"

"Let's see, blah, blah, blah, blah, oh, here, 'Detective Frank Degrase of the Philadelphia Police Department who heads the task force, a consortium of state and federal agencies, says that the growing number of illegal prescriptions in the Greater Philadelphia Area is posing a treat to public health.'"

"ZACK?"

"Huh, What?"

"The new intern?"

"What about him?"

"What's his name?"

"Tim. Tim Newburg, I think. Why?"

"Because he's all over the place down in that ER. He can't grab his own ass with two hands at the same time."

"He's not so bad."

"Yeah, well, I just talked him through a stab wound to the chest and I though he was going to have a stroke."

"So, he reminds you a little too much of that shy intern four years ago who was afraid to stick needles into a baby's head, huh?" Zack looked up from his paper and grinned.

"Cut the shit. I've got to get him up to speed fast or we'll all be up all night wiping his ass for him."

"He'll be okay. I'll spend some extra time with him." Zack was the senior resident on call for that day, the guy just under me, which I always found ironic given how things had started out. Zack waited for me to tell him about all the patients he would be responsible for while I was away, a procedure known in the business as "signing out." I liked signing out to Zack. He understood how important it was to know about the patients. He always made himself available. "Always make yourself available for sign-out," Zack taught me when I was still a young intern following him around. I always had. Now he was practicing what he preached. I like that about him.

Other residents might be anywhere when I went to sign out. I'd have to beep them or page them overhead. It might take me an hour or two to find them and get out of the hospital. Not with Zack. He was always in the cafeteria at 6 P.M., drinking coffee or reading the paper.

"Weeell," he said, shaking his head again, "good luck, there, Detective Degrasse! You'll probably end up arresting half the medical staff and a lot of little old ladies." He pushed a bowl in front of him aside with the paper. "It started out to be some really lousy chili. So, I fixed it up, you know? I added a little salt, a touch of black pepper, a dash of paprika, and lots of Tabasco." He smiled. "Now it's the worst damn bowl of fucking chili I've ever tasted. Want to try it?" He lifted a spoonful.

I shook my head and put my hand out to stop him. "Don't even kid about that shit. I'm out of here. You want me to tell you about these unit players?"

"No, I don't." He was being honest. "But, go ahead." He took out a pen and paper.

Old man Zack had me by a couple of years but trailed me in his training because of the time he had been away. He took his "sabbatical" as he called it for reasons that had never been clear to me. He had a reputation as a hard worker and all the residents liked him. Everybody liked him except the attendings, who, on the contrary, hated the man for reasons I never understood. Looks could be enough sometimes. Tall and too skinny, he walked as if his arms and legs hadn't been attached to his body quite right, like he might come apart if he stopped too fast or changed directions suddenly. To see different parts of his body heading in different directions at one time as he came around a corner, or entered a doorway unnerved people. Scrub suits, never the cleanest garments to begin with, were always stained with, blood, iodine, or some unrecognizable substance. Zack's, on the other hand, might well be stained with the remnants of a healthy meal or axle grease. He wore the things everywhere.

"Now That shit's over with," he said as he stuffed the list of my patients into the shirt pocket of his scrubs, just under a stain, "Let's you and me go for a smoke." I hesitated. "Come on. Karla can wait another seven point five minutes." He smiled over his shoulder. He was already up and on his way to the glass double doors at the back of the cafeteria, the tap dance of his Bruno Maglis on the highly polished linoleum floors keeping time with the syncopation of his dangling limbs.

Zack lead the way out to the dark night of the courtyard with the glow of his cigarette ash. He lit one for me. I'm not a smoker, but I accepted the cigarette he offered, and took a drag. Zack exhaled long and hard. "Man." When I didn't react, he went on, "Man, it's going to be a long night."

My hand ran over the top of my head and extended the reach up into a stretch. "Aren't they all."

The way the smoke wrapped itself around his voice made Zack's words more potent somehow.

"Something up with you?" There it was.

I shrugged, took another drag, wanting to wrap my words up too, wrap them in smoke so they would float. Zack looked down at his cigarette, turned it over in his hand, then stuck it back in his mouth.

He had that squinty, one-eye-shut, James Dean slant to his head when he spoke again. "You just don't look happy, man."

"I'm happy." The words dropped between us like lumps of coal.

"Um. Something up with Karla?"

"You know. You know how it is," I said, answering a different question.

"Yeah, I know."

But, I knew he asked about something else, something deeper.

Placing the cigarette in my mouth, I imitated Zack, and held my hands up in front of me in a gesture of "Who knows?" Before Zack said anything else, his beeper went off and I thanked God. I jumped, but Zack didn't notice.

"Shit." He stuck his cigarette back in his mouth and reached around to unhook the little plastic box from his scrub pants. His cigarette ember made lines in the dark that looked like art: Picasso's drawn with a penlight. "Can you believe that the kids actually go out and voluntarily buy beepers? Jesus, if they only knew..." He pressed the button on the side of the beeper, and held it up to his eyes. Through the space in his teeth around the cigarette came a sound like, "Puck."

"Fuck is right." I put a smile in my voice.

He shook his head again, flicked his cigarette into the dark and headed for the glass doors.

"Fuck," he said again, "It's the ER Gotta go, man. I'm outta here."

"Go." I said. "Get outta here." For a moment I just sat there in the dark. Zack had time to skitter across the cafeteria floor and disappear before I moved a muscle. My heart beat a hard, fast, primitive rhythm. *It's the cigarette,* I told myself, *that's all.* I reached around and turned off my beeper; I had made it one more day.

❦   ❦   ❦

After I left the hospital I stumbled around the dark garage until I found my car, a task too monumental not to become dangerous for someone in my mercurial state of mind. In the dark, my key chain transfigured, each key appearing the same and none fitting the lock, like one of those impossible puzzles one encounters in novelty shops on the boardwalk in Atlantic City. After a period of hood banging, foot-scuffing frustration one of the keys slipped into the lock and I was in the car cranking the ignition. The knobs on the expansive chrome dashboard of my ancient Chevy made the lights as easy as Braille to find. The car was a death trap (they don't make dashboards like that anymore). The stereo, an after-market Alpine, thoroughly modern and more than ample, looked out of place, shining transcendent blue against the yellow of the sparse instrument panel. Smooth jazz sounds came from the black, plastic speakers.

The stereo was worth more now than this old, beat-up, 1968 Chevrolet Impala, Super Sport, the only possession I had left that belonged to my father. The odometer read just over eighteen thousand miles when I turned it was cherry, but still in good shape, having spent so many years garaged and unused after my father lost his legs. No one drove the thing after the shooting, not until my father died, but I sat in the driver's seat of that car almost everyday when he was passed out or sleeping, dreaming of the day when I could drive it; dreaming of the day when he would be gone and the car would be mine.

The tires, burning a little as they chirped off the apron and out of the parking lot, and chirped again as I punched the gas and turned too hard trying to head north. Four hundred cubic inches of steam twisted two hundred horsepower and a four/eleven gear ratio gave her enough torque to put a lot of road behind her really fast. I loved that car. Lehigh Avenue filled up with the resonance of the duel exhaust booming off the abandoned buildings as I passed.

The back of my throat and my lungs felt full.

The lingering tingle of nicotine in my brain reminded me of the sex.

Then, my car phone rang.

"Hey," Vince said.

"What's going on?"

"Nothing. I called the switchboard and they said you weren't on call tonight. Thought I'd give you a ring and see if you were going to stop by on your way home." His voice came through in snatches. It mixed with static and another conversation the phone had captured from the cell: a woman laughing, or someone screaming. I couldn't quite tell. I thought of Karla.

Vince came back again, said my name.

"I don't know, I'm kind of tired." He knew I'd come over. I hated that he knew.

He laughed, "We can fix that!"

"I'll bet."

"Besides, Karen's in from Villanova, and she wants to see you." I heard laughing and commotion in the background, snippets of, "Dad," whispered, and "DON'T LISTEN TO HIM," shouted through a covered mouthpiece. He always found a way to make my visits seem innocent.

"Okay."

"Got your pen with you?"

"Always."

"Where are you?"

"Roosevelt. By the bridge."

"See you in ten minutes."

He hung up.

The woman's laugh faded in again, just before the air went dead.

CHAPTER 3

I am looking at a book.

My bedroom door is closed to keep my parents out. Forests of dark green and yellow plants, leafy and moldy, growing up from the dark ground of the printed words jump up from the pages and fill my walls and the floor, building a forest to protect me from the out- side world, the chaos of parents' lives. Color drawings, black and white photographs, line the pages. Sketches labeled "fig." followed by a number decorate the margins and give captioned information that, to me, is almost incomprehensible. Deadly nightshade, Madagascar periwinkle, Pacific yew. Plants with such exotic names they make me dream of paradise, along with the names of the medications that come from them, fill each paragraph. Their names, their little pictures, fascinate me, but I don't understand.

The title of this magical tome is *The Encyclopedic Textbook of Modern Medicinal Plants*, by Sir Ian W. Hathaway. Two-thirds of my mother's name, written in perfect cursive, stands in the left uppermost corner of the front cover, just above a faded black stamp that reads, "Sister's of St. Joseph's Hospital School of Nursing." The address that accompanies her name I do not recognize. The book belongs to Louise Kilmer, someone I do not know. I know Louise Kilmer VanSlyke. She is my mother. Who is this other woman, a woman who sat in the library of the Sisters of St. Joseph's Hospital School of Nursing, her long hair hanging down, the jungle in her mind hanging down around her, filling the floor around her feet, the walls, the ceiling over head with images of dark green and yellow plants, enticing her to steal away with the magic book, to write her name in the top left hand corner of the front cover, to try and make it her own? I am too young to understand the idea of my mother as a child, but not too young to understand the impulse to steal this marvelous book before me. All day long I remain in my room gazing at this book, then, before I go down stairs Supper, I scribble over her name and write my own.

It must be Sunday.

❦   ❦   ❦

"Do not adjust your set. We control the horizontal; we control the vertical. We can blur the focus or sharpen it to crystal clarity. You are about to begin a journey from here to…the Outer Limits."

I think it was "the Outer Limits."

It may have been "Twilight Zone" or "Night Gallery," who knows. Something about a doctor's back medical bag from the future. The medical instrument kit from the year 2450 falls into the possession old Dr. Full, a retired physician and drunkard expelled from the medical association for milking patients. The instruments virtually operate themselves. The discovery of the black bag restores Dr. Full's self-worth and dedication to healing. A street-wise woman, Angie, realizes the value of the medical instruments and their origin. Through blackmail, she forces Dr. Full to accept her as a partner. When Dr. Full decides to donate the instrument kit to the College of Surgeons, Angie murders him. Later, while demonstrating the safety of the medical bag to a patient, Angie plunges the scalpel into her own neck, confident it will do no harm (a great marketing technique.) Meanwhile, authorities in the future learn that the medical bag is missing and deactivate it just before Angie's demonstration.

She slits her own throat.

By the time the police arrive, the contents of the black bag have already rusted and are decomposing

Fascinated, I lay on the floor, gazing, contemplating. It will be many years before I find the short story, "The Little Black Bag," by Cyril M. Kornbluth, the cleaver science fiction story centered on the doctor's black bag. The story illustrates how the black bag is an enduring and powerful symbol of the medical profession and healing. The tale employs the bag as a symbol to raise interesting questions about the role of the physician in society and the nature of healing: there is clearly more to doctoring then technology and skill. The story foreshadows future technological advances that threaten to reduce the role of the physician to a mere mechanic. While the author portrays a future brimming with scientific discovery and dazzling technology, it nevertheless seems to be a society bereft of common sense, a society I will inhabit.

Yet, the child that I am can't help but think, *What if I had found the bag?* Imagine: In an instant, I am the most wonderful surgeon in the world! Over one shoulder, my glance catchers my father dozing in the chair. Over the other shoulder, I spy my mother reading the evening paper. What if? I think and keep my revelry to myself. It is better this way.

As I turn back to the screen my mother speaks breaking the spell, "Wake your father and tell him to go to bed."

"No. I don't want to. You do it. I'm watching the story. Were you ever a nurse? Why does he have to go to bed anyway? It's early."

"Do as I say, mister, or I'll…"

"You do it!" A feeling flutters around in my chest, like a moth caught inside a lampshade as the show begins again. "Mom, you do it. I want to watch this. Did you go to nursing school? There's this book—"

"Don't you talk back to me! Don't you dare talk back to me you little…Are you talking back to me? You wait, Mister. You just wait!"

So, I wait. I watch and wait.

❦   ❦   ❦

"Hi," Karen blushed as she answered the door.

"Hi, yourself." I stepped in.

Karen, a stone beauty, had shoulder-length, raven black hair with highlights of blue flashing through it. Shapely and slender, she made my heart ache every time I got within several feet of her. I knew Vince, knew how he thought. Set up visit, a fishing expedition. Use Karen as the bait. I looked into her eyes, saw the two little portraits of myself staring back, two little bald men smiling too hard, staring back. I thought about it for a moment, then I said, "Where's your dad?"

"He's in his room but, don't go yet, I want you to stay and talk to me." She pulled on my left hand, rubbed her hands over my knuckles, and looked up.

"I have to talk with him for a minute; I have to talk to him about something at the hospital."

"But don't you want to talk to me, just for a minute?"

"Sure I do! You're the reason I came over. Just give me a second, okay? I'll be right out." She pouted. "I promise I will."

She knew bullshit when she heard it. She accustomed herself to it. Any relative of Vince's would know to do that. She'd be angry, but all the more eager for the next visit. It couldn't be helped.

"Come in." His voice came from behind the bedroom door when I tapped. "Come in you sorry bastard."

The knob turned in my hand and I poked my head in. Vince lay in his bed watching the soundless television. He Lou Dobbs on "Moneyline" like Rain Man watched Judge Wapner: He never missed the show, never. Vince, an idiot savant when it came to money, was crippled in almost every other area of his life. He scribbled numbers on scraps of paper, like secret messages to himself, and then he threw them away. A marvelous display of obsessive-compulsive behavior.

"Doctor!" Vince never took his eyes off the screen, "Tell me all about it; all those lives you been savin' while I've been propped up here waiting for you." He scribbled more numbers.

"Four hernias, three gallbladders, and a colon," I said. "That gunshot wound that's been trying to die since last Saturday will probably transfer to the ECU tonight."

"ECU?"

"Eternal Care Unit."

"Shit! Who's on call?"

"Zack."

"Jesus, God!"

"You need to lay off him, Vince."

He talked politics nonstop. His job obligated him to consider the liability of just about everything. Malpractice. The whole debate always pissed me off, because there is just about no way to explain to a non-physician, or an attorney, what it is like to have to make snap decisions when you're in the thick of it, decisions that can cost people their lives. It's hard enough in the middle of the night thinking you might kill somebody without hearing about how much it might cost the hospital in the morning.

I wanted to say, "Tell all your buddies up there in administration to come down and spend a night doing what Zack and I do," but I didn't.

"Who's that dope gonna kill tonight?"

"Come on, Vince, give the guy a break! Everybody fucks up."

"No, you come on, Rock. If that family ever has an attorney look at that chart, the one where your pal broke the old guy's ribs, we might as well just sit down and write the check. I don't give a shit what Dr. Rage told the family."

"But it's okay for your pet heart surgeon to set patients on fire?"

"That was different. It was an accident."

"An accident! It's an accident to ignite the alcohol you just doused on a patient with the spark of an electric cautery?"

"He put it out."

"Jesus, Vince."

"It's different."

"It's only different because Dr. Cash, (his real name) is the biggest money maker the hospital has! But, mark my words, the first time he has to stay up all night long taking care of his own patients in the ICU, instead of Zack doing it, or me, he'll be headed down the road to whatever hospital has enough slave labor to supply babysitters for his fucking disasters."

"Touché."

"Doctors are human, Vinny, and human beings fuck up."

"You don't."

"I meant other doctors."

"Oh, so now you're not human? You're superman, I suppose?"

"Fuckin' A right."

"So what's the difference between you and mortal humans like your buddy there?"

"Humans feel fear."

"And you don't?"

"I have the cure."

"Ah," he said, laughing, "Ah, ha."

"So, where are they?"

"In the top drawer of the dresser, and it's about time for another prescription, now that you mention it." He always made it sound like my idea.

"I left the pad in the car," I said, "I'll write it on the way out."

I'd been writing Percocet for Vince prescriptions for years. He just asked me for a 'script one day, after one of those dinners, I think, or a trip to the theater. He said he had taken Percocet before. I could save him a visit to his own doctor if I could just write him the prescription, just that once. It would save him the forty bucks for the visit.

What the hell, I thought at the time.

The Percocet in his top drawer Vince takes like aspirin, two to four a day. Vitamin "P" we call the pills now. I take them too. I'll feel better in 10 minutes.

❧   ❧   ❧

As the hospital corporate attorney, Vince was at the hospital all the time. "I have but one client: All Saints. All others beware." Something he'd ripped off from one of the Godfather movies. He said shit like that all the time. The whole phrase, engraved on a bronze nameplate, sat at the front of his desk. Everybody knew him. He interviewed members of the medical staff for malpractice defense. Quality assurance stuff. Quality assurance is usually a nursing position, but at our place, Vince did it.

❧   ❧   ❧

A lot of people haunt the memory of that first blurry month of my residency. A lot of faces in the hallway. Vince, the first person to remember my name, is the first person of whom I have a clear recollection. Even at the time I figured there was an angle.

"You're VanSlyke, aren't you? Dr. Rocky VanSlyke?"

"Who wants to know?" I asked. He intimidated me. The size of him, the color of his suit, everything about him freaked me like a Republican nightmare. He came on like a used car salesman selling something I didn't need. He was F.O.S., just like a dozen abdominal x-rays taken of the nursing home patients I had seen and assessed for acute abdomens that day, none of whom had acute abdomens, but all of whom where just as full of shit as this guy. And, also just like the nursing home patients, he just kept coming. Nothing slowed him down.

"Rocky VanSlyke, the new hot shot surgical resident that the whole hospital is a-buzz about, from Alabama, right?"

"Georgia. And you are?"

"That's right, Medical College of Georgia!"

"Yes, and you are?" Now I was pissed off. The senior resident was waiting for me to do a procedure on a patient in the ER. My beeper went off. End of the shift, a grueling thirty-six hour shift, and here I stand with this guy blowing more smoke at me then a steel mill, disingenuous as hell. Just like a fucking attorney. Not that I had much experience with attorney's. I hadn't had any. In fact, I hadn't been a doctor long enough for anyone to sue me for malpractice, but I had heard all the stories. I had been in the hospital long enough to hear the jokes.

"Oh, you're busy. I'll let you go, get back to work." He shook my hand, backing away.

"And you are?" I said a third time, following him, rather insistent.

"Vincent Buddy. I'm the hospital attorney."

So you're Vincent Buddy, I thought.

Vince called me later on that day, before I left the hospital, and invited me to dinner. I didn't feel like eating. I wanted to sleep, being so drag-ass tired, but my curiosity got the better of me. The office of the Chair of the Department of Surgical Services was in the tower of offices adjacent to All Saints Hospital. The lights on the eighth floor in the wing that housed surgical services were always a blaze. No secretary sat at the desk in the outer office of the Chairman of surgery and the door behind it stood open "Dr. Waterman, can I speak with you for a moment?"

C. Calvin Waterman—the "C" was for Clarence a name you dare not utter if you hoped to be a surgeon—dipped his bald head even closer to the document he faced, peered over his half spectacles from behind his massive walnut stained desk, and waved me into his office with the butt of a Monte Blanc fountain pen. "Speak."

This is a one, fat, man, I thought. *This is the fattest person I have ever seen.* His starched white coat with his name and the words "Vascular Surgery" tattooed in cursive over his left breast pocket seemed to hold his flesh in place. When I approach his desk, I first noticed his fingers, like a bouquet of maduro-cigars clutched by tiny hands. "Well, sir, I've been invited by a Mr. Buddy—"

"Good God-in-Christ, are you mixed up with him already?" He said pulling off his glasses between a Churchill and a Robusto and pitching them onto the desk in front of him. "What the hell did you do, kill somebody?"

"Well, no Sir. You see—"

"Christ Van—Van, what the hell is your name?"

"VanSlyke, Sir."

"Christ, VanSlyke, you've only been here a month and already you're killing People? Killing people is for the chief resident and guys like me, understand?"

"Yes, sir, but—"

"Interns are to be seen and not heard, is that clear?"

"Yes, sir."

"They speak when spoken to, got that?"

"Yes, sir.

"Now, what the hell happened?"

"Well, Mr. Buddy invited me to go to dinner with him, some business dinner for the hospital, and I wasn't sure if it as appropriate."

He put on his glasses, folded his thick, black fingers, leaned forward on his elbows, and peered back over the rims of his spectacles. "He invited you to dinner."

"Yes."

"And you're not sure what you should do."

I saw where this was going and lowered my head.

"Are you hungry, Dr. VanSlyke?"

"Well, sir, now that you mention it."

"Do have anywhere else to be?"

"No, sir."

"Well, then, I guess if I were you, I'd go."

I could feel my cheeks getting red. "Yes, sir, thank you. Sorry to have bothered you."

I was halfway out the door before he called me back, "Oh, VanSlyke?"

"Yes sir?"

He was waving a five-dollar bill at me. "Give this to Mr. Buddy and him he can kiss my black Ass."

"Sir?"

"He mentioned you might be by. Enjoy your meal."

"I will. Thank you."

Dinner at the Chart House turned out to be a negotiation for a CT scanner the hospital wanted to purchase. A free meal, for Vince, gave new meaning to the phrase, "*Carte Blanche.*" For example, in this case, the invitation that had been extended to him by the company selling the machine extrapolated, in Vince's mind, to mean me or whomever else it might strike his fancy to invite. He invited me to go places, to expensive lunches or on weekend junkets, events to which he was invited in the course of business—perks, to the obvious cha-grin of the unwary host. He had no shame. I felt embarrassed, but I got over it. I knew my time would come.

The looks on the faces of the sales people from the German man-ufacturer of the CT scanner said they agreed with me that I had no place being there. They got hit up enough for legitimate perks, I'm sure, so they let it slide. An average looking man named Stan, and a stunning woman, blonde I think, with the longest legs I had ever seen, stood and offered, as I recall, as close to a cordial greeting as they could muster under the circumstances. I couldn't muster the energy to give a shit if they liked me or not. Stan in his ridiculous three-piece silver-gray sharkskin suit, which seemed to match his hair said, "I see we have the same tailor," pointing at my scrubs. Everybody chuckled as we sat down.

Vince introduced me. He left the impression that he and I had known each other for years.

The sales people nodded bored as they could be with this useless introduction.

"Now, Mr. Buddy, as I was saying," the woman said. "The hospital would be responsible for—".

"Just hold your horses there, young lady. Let the doctor order his meal. He's just finished a long shift, and he needs to take some nourishment."

In the silence you could hear a fly fart. These people weren't used to such treatment. As I found out later, not many of the people Vince dealt with were.

Vince said to me, "What're you drinking?"

"Water'll be fine, with a twist of lemon."

"Hey, Miss," he called out, loud as a bull horn, over his shoulder, "Could we have a Wild Turkey over her for the doctor, on the rocks with a twist?" He made a gesture to me. I nodded, just to get it over with. She came over.

"Give her your beeper. You're happy to get rid of that thing, I'll bet," he said, smiling, in control.

It wasn't necessary. I was no longer on call, but I just smiled and handed over the beeper to the beaming waitress.

Then, Vince turned and faced the sales people; "I've asked Dr. VanSlyke to take time out of his busy schedule to be here with me in case I have any clinical questions. I don't know a thing about the clinical aspects of this contraption."

"We've had studies run at the University of Chicago," the blonde started up again.

"Young lady," he waved his hand, palm out, flailing in the air in a gesture of *no mas*. "I wouldn't understand that stuff if you sang it to me." The sales people looked around, their battle plan in disarray, their momentum bogged down in the blustery weather of Vince's personality. For a brief moment the mood sagged. The tide had turned. It seemed they'd been at it awhile, and, like me, were about to surrender. The sale was now secondary to cutting their losses, conserving their resources to fight on another day. The woman leaned over the table, shoulders sagging, and eyes cast down. The man loosened his tie and focused a blank stare somewhere over Vince's head. Vince watched, took note, analyzed a dramatic pause I would come to recognize as the moment before he pounced, went in for the kill. I'd even anticipate it after a while, developing my own perverse voyeuristic blood lust. We made a pretty good team after that, a regular Butch and Sundance.

"Dr. VanSlyke?" Vince began again, when he was convinced he had everyone's attention. They looked up, stunned at the sound of his voice. A smile, born of my bourbon, bloomed across my lips. "How many CT scan studies did you order today?"

"Excuse me?"

"How many CT scan studies did you order today?"

My face scrunched into a caricature of a reflective expression and I rubbed my chin. I looked up, and then I looked down. When I caught the eye of the woman, I laughed. Yep, I was drunk. "I'm sorry what was the question again?"

"How many CT scan studies did you order today?"

"Two," I said holding up three fingers.

"Routine or emergency?"

"Emergent."

"And how long did it take you to get the results on the ones you ordered?"

Waving him off with my free hand, I said, "Only one of the studies got done, due to the backlog at Germantown hospital. That's the hospital with the scanner. We have to refer them, as you know. It'll be two or three days before we see the results."

"Is that delay acceptable to you?"

I took another drink and wiped my lips on the back of my hand. "Acceptable? No, it's criminal."

He turned and looked at the sales people who now seemed to be staring at me. Their mouths wide open.

"How many would you have ordered if you had a machine at your disposal?"

"Four more, routine."

He took a moment to reflect. He rubbed his chin and digested the information. "Sounds like—like the hospital needs a CT scanner. Shall we proceed?"

Both the sales people looked at each other, back at me. I smiled at the woman.

"Let's let the doctor eat his meal, first," Stan said.

"Doctor, would you like another drink?" The woman said touching my knee under the table. "You must be exhausted after such a long day."

I could not believe my ears. And when I felt her legs cross in my direction under the table I thought I would lose my mind. She brushed my leg with her foot. Her pumps dangled off the toes of her right foot; up and down; up and down.

"Go ahead, doctor," she said, low and breathy, leaning forward, "Have another one. You look like you could use it." She touched my knee again with her right hand, moved it up my leg almost to the groin. She smiled and tilted her head.

"You don't know the half of it, lady" I said, as I tried to calculate a twenty percent commission on a couple of million dollars. Two hundred thousand? Something like that.

Vince leaned back, smiling. So much for dinner. *There's no such thing as a free lunch*, I thought, and smiled back. This is how it works. In retrospect, I believe this whole outing he engineered just for me, an object lesson designed to teach me the potential inherent in playing along.

      ✤   ✤   ✤

When I came back in with the prescription pad, Vince leaned out of his bed, peeked around me, to see out the door. He motioned for me to close it. As I did I saw Karen sitting in the living room, two fingers supporting her pretty face, one in her mouth, staring straight ahead, unblinking, at the television. I shut the door.

"We should write for some Demerol." He used the plural form.

I was stunned. "Demerol?"

He made a face, like I knew exactly what he meant. "You know what I mean," he said, "You know exactly what I mean. We should try and get some."

"Demerol tablets are no more effective then Percocet,"

He shook his head. "Not tablets, Injectable."

"Injectable?"

He nodded and put his finger up to his lips.

"Injectable Demerol!?" I said, incredulous.

Vince motioned down with his hands, then made the "shush" sign and laughed.

"No way," I said shaking my head. "No fucking way."

"Okay."

Making hand motions myself, now, I waved him off. "No way, I said. I'm not writing for anything injectable."

"All right."

"You'd never get it filled, anyway. Who the hell would fill that?"

"You write it, and I'll have it filled in 15 minutes."

"Bullshit."

"Ok."

"Who the hell's gonna fill it? What pharmacy is going to have injectable Demerol sitting on the shelf?"

"Small ones. Ones that have to compete with the big chains by stocking things the big chains don't have. The ones that survive by charging you dollars for things that cost pennies because they know it's an emergency, and you can't get it anywhere else."

"Bullshit."

"All right."

"I don't even know how it's packaged."

"Here." He pulled an old copy of the Physicians Desk Reference from his bed stand and handed it to me. The cover of the current one was red and this one was blue, blue, and tattered. The information changes very little from one edition to another. "I always keep an old copy around, just in case," he said and sneered.

"'Just in case' what?"

"Just in case, oh, you know. This and that. Just in case...Oh forget it. Here."

I looked up the reference, just for kicks. Demerol. Merperidine. It comes packaged 3 different ways, ampoules, tubex, or multi dose vial; 2 different strengths, 50 mg/cc and 100 mg/cc.

"What, ampoules?"

He shook his head no. "The pharmacies don't fuck with vials; vials are too clumsy and people get cut on the caps when they break them off to get at the drug. That's for the hospitals. The pharmacies only carry the multi-dose vials."

"What, fifty mg/cc?"

He shrugged. "You get twice as much in the same volume of the other one."

"One hundred."

"That's what I'd do."

"And you really think you can get this filled?"

"Sure."

"How the hell do you know all this shit?"

He shrugged again and laughed, "I just know."

I wrote the prescription, shaking my head all the while. "I'm just doing this on a dare, you know, because there is no way in hell you're gonna get this filled. It's a one-time thing."

"Of course."

❦   ❦   ❦

Doctors are salespeople. Ask any surgeon who's convinced a woman to sacrifice her breast to a mastectomy when lumpectomy and radiation is an option. Lawyers are taught salesmanship; it's a part of them. It's in their blood. Lawyers are better at the art of negotiation. Doctors act cold-blooded, but it costs them.

❦   ❦   ❦

Like a naughty boy who skipped school by feigning illness in order spend the day in bed eating cookies and now realized that, with the hour so late the time was passed when anyone would notice if he were out and about, he could go and sneak some more, he said, "Let's go for a ride."

On the way out, Vince patted his daughter's head and said, "Honey, we'll be right back." Another fib. She knew it, too, as well as I did and did not bother responding.

"Good night," I said to the sliver of light that disappeared through the crack in the door as I shut it behind me.

"The car phone might ring," Vince said, but it never did. I drove back to my condo. The red lights gave me an excuse to burn some time; I lingered at stop signs. My mood was edgy, tense, and sexual. Fear mixed with anticipation. The night rolled out before me on ribbons of red taillights, zoomed past me on blades of shining white headlights, and streaked my windows with rainbow neon storefronts. Waves of light broke on the hood; moonbeams and garnet flooded my windshield, then passed over me, a luminous wave rising from an onyx sea crashing in the dotted lines trailing behind my car in the rearview mirror. Rain fell, then it stopped.

When I arrived home, I couldn't bring myself to leave the car. Waiting for Vince there in the parking lot, in the dark, I started to feel better, almost excited, a sensation that didn't seem to fit. Enough time had past to assure me he had blown me off again; he had gone somewhere to hoard the drugs for himself. That's odd, I told myself. I should be pissed! Then I remembered going to Vince's dresser, taking the two Percocet from the top drawer, and swallowing them dry. This was typical. After taking the pills I would forget. When the euphoria came, arriving like a lover sneaking up from behind, wrapping her arms around me, covering my eyes, I would be amazed and wonder to what I owed such good fortune. The pleasant illusion attached itself to whatever activity occurred at the time. At the moment, sitting here in my car, alone in the dark, I wondered why a doctor, or anyone else in his right mind, would consider doing anything else.

"Let's go." I heard a voice say out of nowhere, and I jumped.

Startled, I looked toward the voice. Vince shouted at me from the passenger side. He looked different, more ruffled or something, more plastic. Maybe his shirt looked rumpled with his left sleeve rolled up. Was he wearing a tie before? Had he just pulled up alongside me and put the window down, hung his left elbow out the driver's window, cool like, with that cuff of his undone like that.

"Here." He held the glass vial with the purple label toward me. The metal cap was already peeled away. I put up my hands to stop him and looked around.

"What the hell are you doing? Are you crazy? What do you expect me to do with that? Jesus, put that shit down, will you, before you get us both arrested!"

He laughed, threw his head back and guffawed. Big joke. "Oh," he said. "You can cut people open from stem to stern, but you can't draw up a little Demerol…"

"Not in the parking lot." I chuckled, but I didn't think him funny. I felt self-conscious, a little scared or embarrassed. That would change.

"Well." He pulled his arm back in the window, "Well then, let's go inside and get situated."

❧   ❧   ❧

He sat on my couch and fished through the bag of tuberculin syringes. That lamp with that green dancing harlequin, the one with the black spots and gold trim, illuminated the walls, the furniture, and our faces with yellow light, like the fading colors of an old photograph. The glimmer stuck to everything, like a memory sticks to the brain.

He took out a needle and drew up the Demerol.

"Here." He handed me the syringe, straight up, with the cap on it. He smirked, still a little sarcastic, but more excited.

I looked at the syringe in my hand. One c.c. One hundred milligrams. He stared at me for a moment longer, then went about his business. Setting the syringe on the table next to me, I stood up and unbuttoned my pants. I had to drop my pants to give myself the injection; at least I thought I did.

When I did the shot of Demerol, the sting to my skin surprised me. Startled, I flinched just as the needle entered my skin. I froze. Vince sat in the same place, but he had stopped what he was doing to watch me. I had not wanted to gasp, hadn't wanted to appear unsophisticated, but I knew I had recoiled from this latest violation by the satisfied look on Vince's face. I must have gone white, but I'm sure I was the picture of yellow jaundice in that light. Gathering my courage, I pushed the plunger, hard, with my thumb, and felt the ache of the liquid forcing its way into me, filling the muscle, like water filling a balloon.

My eyes closed and a jet passed over, someone going somewhere, disappearing. The Demerol took a long time to kick in. A lot of waiting, putting pressure on the site, sitting there with my pants down. I didn't open my eyes. Vince's breathing told me that he had done his shot, too. When the drug started to work, I felt my own breathing change. I just kept my eyes closed.

Getting caught, someone knocking at the door, or the phone ringing, never crossed my mind. Oh, sure, I worried that someone might page me, but I worried about that all the time anyway. That guy in the unit might go bad. Zack might need help. Anything could happen. But, later, when I came to, I knew, maybe for the first time, true paranoia. My skin was warm and moist; I was lying on the floor.

Maybe I pulled my pants back up, checked to see I had buttoned my fly in the mirror. I straightened my hair. I had only passed out for maybe a minute.

CHAPTER 4

"Get away from me," she sobs. "Get away from me, you son-of-a-bitch."

My father, opening and closing his hands, pumping his fist, says nothing. He is a boxer without a punching bag, a soldier without any rules of engagement. My mother buries her face in her hands and turns toward the kitchen sink. In a moment, she'll start doing the dishes, I think, like nothing's happened.

"Lou," he tries, "Lou, honey."

"Don't honey me, you bastard. Not after this."

My father stands in his uniform, dirty, just in from the field. An alert. Something to do with the Cubans or the Russians. "I have no idea what the hell you're talking about. I've been living in a fucking tent for two weeks! All I do is worry about you. I think about you constantly when I'm away, you and little Rocky. I can't wait to get home, and then, when I do—"

She turns on him fast, face contorted, a mask. Her hands are up, recoiling from him, as if from a flame, then attacking, fingers bent forward like claws. "The only reason you're allowed back in this house, you bastard, is because I bore you that child. And I can't be a mother and work, too. But, you! You just go gallivanting off with your army buddies to drink beer and chase woman."

He moves toward her, to comfort her, to explain. It's no use.

"Leave me alone," she says, and pushes by him, retreating to the bathroom, slamming the door.

This is new. There have been other outbursts, but none like this. Something's different. Something else is wrong.

We stand in the kitchen, my father and I, but he is alone with his thoughts. He appears confused for a moment. I can see his mind racing. Then the confusion in his eyes melts into resolve. His jaw sets like stone.

He begins checking drawers and cupboards. The refrigerator. I know what he's looking for.

"Dad?" He looks at me for the first time. I point to the garbage. He goes to it and finds the empty, a clear bottle with a red and black label. He looks at the bottle, then back at me.

"How's my baby boy?" He says, smiling for the first time. He picks me up. "Did you miss your daddy?"

I smell the pot roast, the carrots mostly, half dished out, sitting on the counter. I smell my father's sweat and dirt from the field as he swings me back and forth in his arms. The first whiff makes me feel hungry, warm and secure, but then I'm sick to my stomach. I start to cry.

From the bathroom, I hear the medicine cabinet open and close. He stops swinging me and stares at the bathroom door. My father puts me down and says, "Be a good boy. Go watch television"

I leave, like a good boy, and go.

The living room is dark, but the television is on. I hear the crackle, see the light, blue and white, a bubble that fills the room. Already I feel safe. My favorite pillow, one from the couch, is missing, but I am safe anyway in my cocoon of light. I will not move.

The bathroom door opens. Footsteps and the tinkle of silverware on the kitchen table follow. More footsteps, heavy this time and the door closes again. I hear the shower. I change the channel to a real station.

Later we all sit down to dinner. The pot roast falls apart; it's so overdone, splayed around like old brown rope over a swamp of onions and boggy carrots, *ropa vieja* the Cubans call it. Through dinner my mother is calm, She almost appears normal, happy. My father is quiet, serious, but the irony gets the best of him. "Two weeks in the field training to kill the bastards, then I have to come home and eat their food." His skin still burns red from the hot shower. His black hair is thinning, but it's cut so short that it doesn't matter. They reach for the butter dish at the same time, which leads to a little tug of war. He lets go of the dish but smiles. She offers it back to him. He notices the difference and does not care why.

Truce.

"May I please be excused to go watch 'Dr. Kildare?'"

"Yes, you may," she says, still looking at my father, her eyes wide, "Put your dishes in the sink, now, go on and be a good boy."

In the bathroom I left the door open. Leaning over the sink I peered into the mirror, and thought about my parents. Turning my face from one side to the other, it became clear that, despite the way I felt, nothing about me had changed. My shirt held a funny crease. My hair looked flat. I tried to straighten again, but gave up. *Why should I?* My right cheek looked red, a tight checkerboard pattern remained, an imprint from the rug, marks like those left by a pillow when you've slept too hard with your mouth open and drooling. *Nothing to worry about; these creases will go away.*

As I stepped out of the bathroom, I found Vince still sitting on the couch fumbling with the bag of syringes.

"Forget it," I said as I moved past him to the refrigerator to get myself something to drink. "Want a beer or wine cooler or something?"

"What?"

"It's late. I've got to go to bed. You want something to drink?"

"But we've got a whole bottle of this stuff left."

"You can have it."

"Okay."

"You want something to drink? This is your last chance."

"No," he said," Fuck, no," and kept on with the syringes.

I watched him for a minute as I opened a beer and took a swig. I shook my head. "I don't see what the big deal is with that shit."

"I told you, you have to do it IV."

"Yeah, well, you can just have it."

"All right."

"Leave me some Percs, though," I said as an afterthought.

"As many as you want."

"How 'bout six."

"I think I have four."

"Four's okay."

"How about just one more shot?"

"You do what you want." I shook my head, "You do what you want, but I'm done. You can have it."

The phone rang. Vince prepared his next fix. As I picked up the phone, I heard the glass fall, hard, against the lamp, the one my mother had given me. He struck it with his flailing hand. An OD of some sort, I imagined, judging from his lack of body control. He looked dead but his chest was still moving. I never worried about him.

"Rocky?"

"Hey, Karla."

"What was that noise?"

"Nothing. I dropped a glass in the sink as I was picking up the phone." I looked over at Vince again and watched his chest heave.

"Oh. Well, I was just checking to see how you're doing tonight, if you've had to go in or anything."

"Nope. It's been pretty quiet."

"Is Vince over?"

"Just leaving." The needle still stuck out of his arm.

"Tell him I said 'hi.'"

"I will."

"If you want me to, I could come over?" A question.

"Come over if you want," I said, and then, "I might still get called in."

"It's okay." She sounded lonely, hopeful, almost pathetic.

"If I'm not here, the key will be under the mat."

"See you soon, I hope."

"Me, too. Bye."

"Bye."

When I turned around Vince moved, startled, and collected his things.

"Time to go."

❧   ❧   ❧

A couple of weeks passed before I could muster the courage to take Karla up on her initial invitation when we first met in the hospital, after Zack egged me on. I made excuses.

"Oh, ah, I remember. See, the problem is that I'm taking trauma call this weekend."

"Uh-huh."

"You know how it is."

"Um."

"This schedule sucks."

"I know."

"Well, I'll call you, okay?"

"Okay."

Things I thought she'd believe.

The day I finally mustered the courage to go to the beach, she met me at the door with a kiss. She was naked but for three swatches of colorful material covering the important parts, and three pieces of string holding the ensemble together.

"Do you like my green bikini?" she said, bouncing on her toes.

Bikini? I suppose it was in a minimalist sense. She stood on her tiptoes, leaned against my chest, and touched her lips to mine as if we had known each other for ages, as if we were lovers. She caught me flat-footed for a second. My hands hung at my sides. If I were a cynic I would have called her actions cold and calculated. Instead I gazed into her eyes, the color of blue algae. They stood wide open, held me there long enough to feel myself getting hard. Then, bang!

The door slammed behind me.

She acted as though nothing passed between us with the kiss, then turned and showed me around the place. She suggested I change in the bathroom. When I returned, the air on the porch where she sat felt both cool and warm at the same time, like an ocean breeze over a sun-warmed beach. Her stare disarmed me for a moment, left me playing with the waistband of my trunks, feeling self-conscious and insecure.

"Ready?"

I forced a smile. "Ready or not, I guess."

"That's right. Ready or not," she said and took my hand. We traipsed out the door, across the street, and down one hundred feet to the beach. Later, I walked that route many times in my sleep. Karla read books that day. We listened to music from a boom box, Luther Vandross. I found out later he as addicted to heroin. Ironic.

These things we would do many times, over and over again during our time together. A movie once in a while, but nothing more social than that. Her friends? She never mentioned any of them. It was as if she had no life before me. Her parents made her feel uncomfortable. I never understood why. Her parents? Her brother's and sister? Forget about it. She might as well have been hatched from and egg. She hated her father for God know what and belittled her mother for no apparent reason. We didn't visit them very often.

"Look, my father's a butcher who developed a bad heart condition at a young age. His doctors controlled his symptoms on medications for years until they stopped working, then surgeons implanted a pacemaker, an internal defibrillator, and a new heart, into his chest, in that order."

"So, is he okay or what? Is he still alive?

"The pacemaker kept his heart beating at a reasonable rate, and the defibrillator administered a shock whenever it stopped or went too fast. The shocks startled him. He would stare off into the distance like a man seeing a vision."

"Jesus."

"He'd say stupid shit like, 'Did anyone else hear that?' or, 'Is it lightning outside?'"

"God Almighty. How long did that go on?"

"Most of his adult life. A nineteen-year-old-boy made a new heart available to him one Saturday night when the kid was killed in a car crash."

"Hey, how come so much attitude about the old man? It sounds to me like he was really sick."

"Oh, he was sick, all right. He became the family babysitter and spent a lot of time home alone with his 'young daughters.'" She said this with a flirtatious wiggle of her hips and a touch of the back of her head." Then her mood changed. She began to sulk.

"What about your mom?"

"My mother. Ha! What a joke," she said turning her back to me. "My mother became the 'breadwinner.'" She made little hash marks in the air with her fingers, as if she were clawing at the air when she told me. "She took nerve pills to deal with the things 'Daddy' was doing to her 'daughters' when she went to work."

"What! Are you saying, that your father, your father—what, took advantage of you?"

"Just forget it."

❧   ❧   ❧

Karla loved my apartment with its wide windows, painted walls and color scheme, gray, with matching wall-to-wall carpets,

"I like it here. It's so bright and new."

My place, with one or two modest exceptions, looked like a comfortable office. More often my living space resembled a bad display in a good furniture store. I never liked the pad much.

We both liked the cottage, or, beach house. Not the house, so much, but being at the beach. The place possessed a charm that transcended all understanding of its humble construction. A coastal pad, complete with old board games with missing pieces and seriously mismatched furniture. The house stood not forty feet from the beach. A yellow sign at the end of the street, bent cockeyed by some aggressive beach goers desperate for parking, announced that the pilgrims of the sun god could drive no further. The dead-end sign and a fifty-gallon garbage can framed a breach in the dune, a path to the sea, the other end of the rainbow. We talked of living in the place, someday, when we could afford it, with the rest of our lives neatly tucked away.

❧   ❧   ❧

After Vince left, I straightened up a bit and turned on the television. I found the first few drops of blood on the arm of the couch where many more would collect, far too many to explain away as a wayward stitch in the fabric.

"Fuck!"

I hurried and cleaned the spot with cold water. As I finished my beeper went off. I pushed the button to check the number—the hospital. I called.

"Your man with half a lung is trying to die," Zack said when I called. Thought you'd like to know."

"Who's the attending?"

"Barrister."

"Well, I'd better eyeball him, at least. Barrister's a prick. You know how those guys get."

"Yep. That's why I called. See you when you get here."

I put on a clean scrub suit, washed my face, and left my key under the door for Karla on the way out.

When I got to the hospital, the guard propped the door open for me with his left foot so he could keep smoking his cigarette. "Hi Doc." The smoky wind whistled through his teeth. "Working late, huh?" he said and smiled as I slipped by.

"You know how it is," I said, though I doubted he did. *What the hell could he have to smile about*, I thought? *What the hell does he know about it?*

"Did you strip the chest tube?" I leaned over the bed and checked the breathing tube on the half-a-lung guy.

"Yep," Zack said.

"Any clots?"

"Nope."

"Pluravac still bubbling?"

"Yep."

I listened to his lungs, then checked the settings on the ventilator. "He's going to die. It's a shame, too. It was a nice piece of surgery. He should have died on the table."

"Yep. Sorry to drag you all the way in here for this."

"Don't sweat it. I'll call Barrister."

The way trauma patients were assigned, attendings rotated on a schedule for administrative purposes. Residents managed the patients, a system as old as Twentieth Century Medicine. Harvey Cushing, the famous neurosurgeon, complained bitterly of having to

manage William Stewart Halsted's Patients and he had no way of
knowing that Halsted, the father of American surgery, was off getting
high on morphine. The system worked well most of the time, until
something went wrong. Then, everybody scrambled to keep his ass
out of a sling. I found it prudent, therefore, to let the attending know
what went down, in case a run-in with a disgruntled family member
turned into a lawsuit.

"Good Job," Barrister said when I called, "Excellent; I can always
count on you, Rock."

After making the call to Dr. Barrister, on my way out of the hospital, I stopped at the nurses' station on Four West and picked out a
chart at random. I dialed the number of the all-night pharmacy at
University Hospital and asked to speak to the pharmacist. When she
got on the line, I explained:

"Hi, working late, huh? Ha-ha. Listen, I'm the resident at All
Saints caring for, ah, Mrs. Gorky and her attending wants her to have
a preparation of Benelyn cough syrup with Dalaudid, 5 mgs. /cc., but
our pharmacy closes at midnight. Could you mix some up? Sure?
Well, great. I'll be right over with a prescription to pick it up."

The Pharmacy happened to be on my way home.

CHAPTER 5

A photograph taken by a news photographer for the *Army Times*. My mother wears a sleeveless dress with an empire waist that makes her look pregnant. The style is pure sixties. Her hair is cut short, Twiggy style, so is the dress. She looks young, attractive, and wholesome. In the picture she steps back, fanning the hem of a wedding dress the train of which spills off the table she stands behind, a display for the camera. Carol Merrill, Vanna White.

There is movement in the picture, fluid, candid. She smiles, but her mouth is open as if giving an explanation. Her legs are long and shapely, like a ballerina's.

A Kodak moment.

It is clear why the editor picked this shot.

The caption: "Soldier's wife heads drive."

Why have I never seen this picture before? It rests in a box of papers, at the bottom, the kind of box a child dare not go through until some reason for familial curiosity arises the kind that sits on the top shelf of a closet, over in the back, undisturbed, moved around once or twice a year to get at the Christmas decorations, until a parent dies.

It sat there for years.

My eyes dance over the picture. I recall something that a science teacher said to me after a teacher conference in seventh grade. I look away, somewhere between my eyes and where the red spots fade into the yellow paint on my parents' bedroom wall.

"I didn't realize that your mother was so young!" Mr. Lecher says, in my memory.

I smile but fight the urge to go all the way and bare my teeth, growl.

"She's really attractive. Your father's in the service, isn't he? How long has he been away? Is she coming in for her parent teacher conference? Please remind her to come and see me soon."

I can still see his letching face, the hungry smile.

Back in the box, the article reads, "Louise VanSlyke, along with keeping the home fires burning for her husband 1st Sgt. John VanSlyke of Bravo CO. 1-34 Armor, and caring for their son Rocky, will head a drive to restore old wedding dresses for thrift stores in the local community."

Why don't I remember this?

In the picture, somewhere, on the floor maybe, or, around the corner, waiting while the shutter snaps away there must be a child; if only I knew where, maybe then I'd remember what was going on at the time. *Where am I during all of this?* Maybe I am in school with Mr. Lecher asking me stupid questions instead of teaching. Seventh grade. When my father is gone.

We live in an Army town in Georgia, a quiet little place, percolating with tension. I feel it, stinging, even as a kid. The tension burns, like chronic sunburn on the back of the neck, like the knowledge that this place is not my home.

Home.

❦   ❦   ❦

My parents grew up on the historic Love Canal, just this side of Niagara Falls. They called it "home" as far back as I can remember. Both sets of grandparents lived there. My parents first born child, their only begotten son, yours truly, was born there. The poisoned waste from Union Carbide, Anaconda Brass, American Cyanamid, Auto-Lite Battery, and Occidental Petroleum used the abandoned canal as a dump. A poisoned slurry collected waiting to be pumped by The Hooker Chemical Company into the remnants of William T. Love's cursed ditch. The canal was designed to divert the Niagara River from it's course and energize the industrial revolution outside Buffalo. Later, Hooker covered it over with a clay cap and topsoil, making it pretty for city officials and the Niagara Falls, New York Board of Education. They bought it and built the Ninety-ninth Street Grammar School.

My grandparents never moved from there, even after people started getting sick.

My parents danced with the devil. A courtship over the fire rocks at the Love Canal ignited their love affair. By the time the scourge of the leaking chemicals hit, the Army had taken my father and my father, in turn, had whisked us away. For some years after my parent's death, their dancing continued to affect me, the fire rocks danced in my blood, too. Something deadly infected my life from that rocky beginning, and whatever the substance was, it got my parents first, long before the nastiness ever got me.

Our move to a small Army post near Augusta, Georgia, to a 300-acre site on the Savannah River, was to be our move to a simple Southern life. Simple Southern life. Simple? Army life, for all of the camaraderie, is anything but simple. It confuses dependents. Our arrival on post resembled a trip to Disneyland: everything looked so clean and orderly on the surface; something must be going on underneath. Army life left me with the sickening sense that I'd paid dearly for the privilege of standing in line. Men and women marched by in starched uniforms, a parade of pomp to prepare them for the circumstance of war. My father was there to prepare for war on the nuclear battlefield.

My mother hated the assignment. "They're making plutonium here, for Christ sake, for thermonuclear bombs!"

"Who told you that?" my father said, hushing my mother. "It's a god-damn ecology laboratory."

"They've got five production laboratories and two chemical separation plants. What kind of an ecology laboratory has that?"

"They do experiments."

"Yeah, you know what experiments they do? General Clawson's wife couldn't wait to tell us at the new recruit reception. In one experiment, two persimmon trees were injected with radioactive calcium. Web worms were placed on the trees to feed.

"So?"

"So, you know what this is?" She shook something squiggly in his face. "It's a Web worm; I picked it off your son's head."

"Give me that—Jesus."

"Sixteen loblolly pines were sprinkled with strontium-90 fall out. They're irradiating hardwood trees with gamma rays."

"Honey—"

"They're injecting radioactive iron, zinc, and iodine into fucking field mice, red-winged black birds, sagebrush lizards, and yellow-bellied slider turtles."

"Honey—"

"They're sticking wires of something called tantalum up the asses of salamanders and feeding radioactive houseflies to spiders.

"Honey, you shouldn't be talking about that stuff; besides, it all safe or they wouldn't be doing it."

"Safe! This house is full of fucking spiders."

"Don't be ridiculous."

Oh, my mother joined the PTA and the woman's auxiliary of the Noncommissioned Officer's Association and sang in the church choir. She tried to be a good sport for my old man.

"They're all a bunch of kiss-asses. Those biddies would do almost anything to get their husbands promoted."

She talked about the radiation when she drank.

"They'd suck a colonel's radioactive dick if it'd get their husbands promoted. What hypocrites. I can't stand these two-faced backbiters. I hate it down here. Everybody acting all prim and proper as a magnolia blossom to your face, but can get those hopped skirts hiked up fast enough when any swinging dick who out ranks their husbands comes calling."

Men? Well, now, they were a different story all together. Men, they were an all-together different thing. She liked the men in the army just fine; she liked the uniforms. She smiled when she talked about the men, especially when she was drinking. There were plenty enough men around in the army, but even all them weren't enough to keep her happy.

"If it weren't for your father and all his patriotic bullshit we'd be out of here and back up north in a New York minute. Fighting for freedom; doing our part—ha! You can have it. That's all your father's idealistic bullshit."

She wanted out, she said. She missed my father, she said, hated it when he was in the field because she got stuck at home with me. She drank more when he was away. The drinking made her lonely. The loneliness made her crazy; the men made it tolerable she said.

During the Cuban Missile Crisis, when President Kennedy explained the clamor and asked what we could do for our country, my mother was right there asking not what the country could do for us.

"Listen to what President Kennedy says, Rocky," She said through her tears. The president is talking about your daddy."

I listened.

Good evening, my fellow citizens. Cuba....Within the past week, unmistakable evidence has established the fact that a series of offensive missile sites is now in preparation on that imprisoned island. The purpose of these bases can be none other than to provide a nuclear strike capability against the Western Hemisphere...

I strained at every word, but I couldn't understand any of it. How did this involve my daddy?

This secret, swift and extraordinary buildup of communist missiles is a deliberately provocative and unjustified change in the status quo, which cannot be accepted by this country, if our courage and our commitments are ever to be trusted again by either friend or foe. The 1930s taught us a clear lesson: aggressive conduct, if allowed to go unchecked and unchallenged, ultimately leads to war.

I have directed that the following initial steps be taken immediately...

A black and white television picture of the President could say things to make a mother swoon and cry.

The greatest danger of all would be to do nothing.

After that, the soldiers disappeared from town. They went away, my father along with them. More came, different ones, mostly from the north, looking young and scared, out of place in a southern town. They looked like I felt. I don't remember any of their names, the ones that slept over. I ignored them. I knew, in a while, they'd be gone and Dad would be back.

Every day for months there were new faces on Main Street, in the stores, in and out of our front door at night and in the morning, crew cuts and blank faces, already corpses. Newspaper reporters from Savannah and Augusta stopped people on the street, acted puzzled, and asked about the missiles, the hustle and bustle. "What's all the hubbub?" they asked.

Avery warned, "Do not talk to the press!" Avery's father is a major. He is my best friend.

I wouldn't talk to anyone. "Loose lips sink ships!" That's what my Dad said.

In school, we had air-raid drills. Duck and cover. The papers speculated Atomic War. My friend, Avery didn't care. Sometimes, when Avery and I were not smoking cigarettes or stealing penny candy from the country store, we would sneak a beer from my mother's stash and, after we were drunk, we would sneak into the post chapel. After we pulled each other's pants down and finished our grab-ass desecration, we said prayers for our fathers. Avery led. "Colored people in the south are big on prayers," he said, then he began, head down, fingers intertwined:

"Our fathers,
Who art locked away somewhere,
Fodder for the atomic fireball,
Hallowed be your names…"

Avery was colored. His family knew how to pray.

"That fuckin' Kennedy ordered a naval quarantine because he don't have the balls to call it a blockade," Avery said, on the way out the door of the chapel. He tipped up the beer can, squinted one eye, and peered into the punctured can to see if anything remained "A God-damn, fuckin' blockade is what it is. How's that Jive-ass, honky, bastard gonna grant the Negro his civil rights when he don't even have the balls to stand up to the Russians?"

I shrugged and tipped my can up, mugging Avery, then squinted my eye and peered inside my own can.

"The greatest country in the world can't invade an island ninety miles off the coast of Miami full of nuclear missiles?"

I shook my head in disgust, "Sheesh."

Later when the missile-loaded ships turned back we got some more beer and went back to the chapel. "Well, now, Mr. Kennedy, let's just see how well you do with Dr. Martin Luther King!" Avery said, holding up his beer bottle to the raw sienna light of the stained glass to see the level of the amber liquid.

I held up my bottle. "Let's just see," I said, squinting my eye.

Our fathers came back, but now and again their units would be placed on alert, staging to depart for Vietnam, or someplace else just as exotic. Air-raid drills at school would remind me of Avery's prayer and how well it had been answered.

"Did you see the newspapers, man, talkin' 'bout how there must be room on the planet for all nations to co-exist. Sure. Right. Let 'em visit Selma; let 'em visit Montgomery."

I tried not to think too much about the things he said.

Avery had a sister, an onyx beauty with beautiful, shiny, black skin and big brown eyes. I forget her name. We used to walk down to the pond together and throw stones. She taught me to skip them, how to find the flat ones, how to snap your wrist just right to make them cut through the air and bounce off the green water, to count the times they skipped, even the few stuttered skips at the end before they sank below the surface. Sometimes we threw stones at the ducks we saw floating on the pond and watched them fly up in the air.

The keys were not under the mat when I got back home. "Karla?" I said out loud at the door and tapped lightly with my knuckles. A rustle behind the door betrayed her presence. The door opened a crack, then all the way, cleaving the darkness of the hallway with a shaft of light so bright I had to squint and look away. She stood behind the door, her head hovering over the edge at such an unnatural angle that she appeared more like the head of a jack-in-the-box, pendulous on it's spring, a disembodied face, then a woman. She'd be naked, of course, behind that door, expecting me to be enticed, not expecting my true reaction.

"Hi."

She'd never know the difference.

Her overnight bag lay on the floor, in the corner, her clothes spilling out. The reflection of her chubby thighs, distorted even more in the window across the room, begged me to look away. "You're going to catch a cold," I said as I brushed past her.

"Not if you warm me up, I won't!"

"Here."

Playful, I tossed her a sleeveless "Penn" sweatshirt, with big, red, block letters I'd left draped over the back of a chair, "This should warm you up."

She giggled; she'd embarrassed me again without knowing why, an occurrence, which never failed to delight her. I let her carp. Sometimes it's easier for me to pretend.

"Wow," She said with unrestrained sarcasm and held up the sweatshirt, she struck a pose, a caricature of fashion model, "What a great idea."

As quickly as I could, I turned off the lights and headed for the bathroom. After a couple of quick swigs and gags of the cough medicine I had pick up at the pharmacy on the way home, I went back to her. Her perfume, Chanel, I think, reminded me of something I couldn't quite get a handle on describing, and her hair felt full and thick, though it smelled as if she hadn't shampooed it in a day or two. Her skin, smooth and warm, pulled me in as I put my arms around her. Now, in the dark, now that the medicine warmed my belly, I felt better. She dropped her arms and stood there, surrendered, close to me, inviting me. The curve of her ripe breasts, the pout of her growing belly, the thin wet spot below the mound of black, curly, pubic hair trimmed short, felt like intoxication.

I looked down at the floor.

The drone of an airplane flying over caught my mind as I floated away. The whining sound of the engines faded in and out, oil and rumble, the distant thunder of an approaching holocaust. The sound faded as I touched her from behind and reached forward to feel, again, the spot where she was melting.

❋   ❋   ❋

When I got back to the hospital the next morning, I went to the unit and found Zack. He sat at the nurses' station, his chair swiveled around backwards, leaning against the counter. He read a chart as if it were a newspaper, flipping pages, scanning the lines, searching for some topic, more out of habit than any great interest. "Let's go have a cigarette," he said, cheery, when he saw me. On the way out, he stopped by the bed of a patient with tubes hanging out of him. "Hey, show me how you unclogged that chest tube again."

"Here." I showed him. He looked over my shoulder as I stripped the tube, then we moved on.

"Wow, great. Is that all? I kept going over it in my head last night, but I couldn't shake the feeling I was missing a step. Hmm, well," he said, shrugging, "I couldn't figure it out for shit, last night. I must have tried for two hours."

"It's the suction, pal. It's all about the suction."

"I knew it had something to do with sucking; when you get down to it, all patient care sucks."

"You got that right," I said, "That's why doctors invented nurses." We both laughed.

"Jesus, you're ornery in the morning."

"I'm not kidding. I did this rotation in Great Britain during my senior year in medical school—"

"No shit?"

"Yeah, it was great. You know how they run clinics? The surgeon comes in his suit coat and tie, sits down at a desk with a tape recorder, the nurse takes off the dressings, brings the patient in, the doctor takes a look, dictates something like, 'remove sutures; place steri-strips; return in two weeks for wound check,' the nurse takes the patient out, removes the sutures, places the steri-strips, dresses the wounds, and that's it. The doctor never even gets his hands dirty, unless he's operating, of course."

"You've got to be shitting me!"

"I'm not, and guess what happens at three P.M.?"

"I can't imagine—she blows him or something?"

"Everything screeches to a halt and the nurse wheels in a cart so they can all have tea."

"Tea! Jesus H. Christ."

"I swear to God. I saw it with my own two eyes. Imagine, a place where they actually believe that someone with twenty-five years of education might be wasting his or her time doing scut."

"Imagine."

In the cafeteria, we grabbed some coffee and headed for the picnic tables. He handed me a cigarette. My hands shook badly. I patted my pockets as If I didn't have a match hoping he would light the cigarette for me.

"I'll never be able to light this fucking thing let alone do any surgery. I either need more sleep or more drugs, I can't quite figure out which."

Zack held out a burning match, and I leaned my head forward and lit my cigarette without too much trouble. It was a shot in the dark and I thought for half a second he was about to light my eyebrow but then I smelled the sulfur and burning tobacco and knew the cigarette was lit. The smoke spread out before me like the pleats of a Japanese fan. The first drag made me feel dizzy and I thought I'd puke, but I didn't. The cough medicine had unsettled my stomach for hours afterward. "It's the sugar in the syrup," Vince said when I told him. I drank almost half the bottle the night before.

You were drinking cough medicine like soda pop, you idiot! What the hell do you expect?

Everything was as it should be.

Above us a helicopter or a plane droned, maybe the traffic patrol from the highway; I couldn't be sure it didn't come from inside my head. The sound reached me, and I looked up, whirl and rumble, the outside world pressing down. And down here, the dry, chemically treated tobacco leaves and cigarette paper we oxidized into gas and ash floated up to meet it. What we couldn't draw into our lungs floated away, mixing with what we exhaled, the exhaust of our miserable existence raising up to join the layers of smog generated by our fellow man already weighing heavy on our heads, smoke in a smokestack blotting out what little light remained of the morning stars. I squinted and rubbed my head and eyes. *This shit has got to stop.*

Zack hissed the smoke from his cigarette through his teeth, as if he were smoking a joint. "God," he said, still holding his breath, "I'm glad that night-call is over."

"It's not over. You've got another eight hours to go, brother."

He was quite for a moment, long enough for me to realize I'd said the wrong thing. "You know what I mean." He exhaled explosively. "It's just my own work now, not everybody else's, too."

"I know." I felt sorry now that I had reminded him. "It's all downhill from here, my friend."

We sat without speaking for as long as I could stand it, then I said, "Was it a bad one?" Not because I cared, but because I needed to hear something other then the pounding in my head.

"Not so bad. I got to lie down for a couple of hours, but you know how that is. Sleeping like that, you know, in snatches? It's almost worse than staying up."

"Yep."

We loafed for another moment. "Are you on tonight?"

"No." I shook my head". "No, thank God."

❦　　　　　❦　　　　　❦

After rounds, I went back to the administrative office in the tower. Paper work and a weekly call schedule for the junior residents needed attention before I began my cases in the morning. My office door stood open when Vince arrived. (The door to my office was great, one of the few things about the old building I was glad they had not changed during the numerous renovations; it must have weighed a couple of hundred pounds. The dark, hardwood, walnut, or something stained even darker inlaid with fogged ornamental glass beveled on the edges, could have read "Private Eye" from the look of it. The word "Men," still legible from the inside, was covered over by a cardboard sign taped to the front of the glass that read "Chief Resident.")

I didn't hear him come in, but I saw him out of the corner of my eye. The pile of papers and unread journals strewn around in front of me obscured my view of him, but I could tell he was leaning one elbow on the bookcase, his backside wedged into a corner by the door. I ignored him. *Jesus*, I thought, *He'd look like Orson Wells if you gave him a fedora and cut his ass in half.*

A whiff of pungent odor emanated from the books, the old urology textbooks, or the manual on the interpretation of urinalysis that were on the bookshelf when I moved in. I couldn't quite tell. The books hadn't been opened in years. Green bathroom tile and part of a porcelain urinal stuck out below the bookcase. On occasion, a smell that I imagined being old, dry urine filled the office. By shuffling a few papers around, I tried to look busy. I picked up a pen, then put it down, but I couldn't bear stalling any longer. I figured Vince must have gotten the message: This *is my office you're in now, buster, and I'm not about to be pushed around, not here, not on my turf.* I looked up. "What the hell are you doing here?"

"You sure are busy for so early in the morning. It's not even seven yet."

"Attorney's work from sun to sun, but a doctor's work is never done." *I mean it, too, you lazy fucker.*

"Well." He cleared his throat and ignored my first question. "A man needs some relief from that kind of life. You know what they say, 'All work and no play makes Jack—'"

"Cut the shit. I'm no mood for your home-spun crap this morning."

"Now, what the hell's gotten into you?"

"I feel like shit, that's what."

"Now, don't go blaming me for—."

"Heaven forbid," I said, sarcastic.

He looked surprised. "You are feeling bad, aren't you?"

"Shitty. That stuff is awful."

He looked around, nervous, then hauled himself out of the corner and lumbered over to my desk. When all of him arrived, he hiked up his pants and straightened his suspenders like a Louisiana politician. Huey P. Long, about to climb upon the stump and deliver a speech.

My palms felt damp. I took them off the desk and tried to dry them on the thighs of my scrub pants.

He leaned on the desk, spoke in a whisper, low and breathy, "Well, I told you what the problem was."

"What's that?" I leaned forward, played dumb.

"You have to do it IV." He looked around again, over his shoulder, then back. "Dummy."

My throat tightened. My thigh ached from the first injection of Demerol the night before. My head ached from the Dilaudid. My stomach groaned from the sugary syrup. My mood changed, and in an instant, I was angry. "We shouldn't be doing it at all, God-damn it! It's dangerous, Vince."

"I guess you're right," he said, calmly, as if resigned. He straightened, "Right as rain." He fished around in his pants pockets, took out two pills and handed them to me.

"What the hell is this?"

"Percocet for your headache."

"Are you crazy?" I said, jumping out of my seat. I strained to keep my voice low, shoving his hand away. "I can't use anything while I'm on duty. Put that shit away before you get me fired!"

He laughed and dismissed my comment with a wave of his massive paw. "You are really something, you are. Do Demerol in the evening, then turn down Percocet in the morning." He shook his head. "But," he said after a long pause, "I guess you're right."

Through the window, the grayish-yellow dawn bloomed over the Philadelphia skyline, and a mixture of incandescent lamplight from my desk, and polluted morning pooled around my feet. The office expanded. Light is light, I guess, whatever the source; it all fills up the darkness and after a moment, I felt safer. Vince seemed smaller, more human. The smell of urine seeped from behind the bookcase again and made me look at the wall. For the first time, I wondered where the commodes had been. Thinking of the possibilities distracted me from the conversation. After a moment I looked back in Vince's direction. He had this expression on his face as if he were waiting for me to respond.

"Well? Did he?" he said after a moment

"Did who? What?"

"Did that guy die last night? Jesus, am I talking to the wall here or what?"

"Did who die?"

"The gunshot wound that Zack took care of in the unit. The one you mentioned last night."

"No, not yet."

"No? Amazing; Hmm. Well, it looks like your friend didn't get his hands on him anyway." He shook his head, baffled.

I shrugged at his small talk, waiting for him to get to the point.

He grinned.

"What?" I said, pretending I didn't know what was coming.

"Look," he leaned forward again, "How 'bout writing me for some more of that stuff? It's a damn shame; you having such a bad experience with it, and, well, I'm mad as hell at myself for not making you do it the way you should have in the first place. I'll save you some and we'll do it right this time. It's a damn shame, you feeling bad like this."

"No." I started around the desk, "I've got to get to the O.R."

He straightened up then, fast, as if I'd slapped him. "Okay, okay." He cleared his throat and put his hands up as if to stop me. "Look, don't get all in a huff. It was just a question, all right? Don't take this the wrong way, here." He pushed two pills into my hand. "You need these right now more then I do. Save them for later if you want."

Without looking I dropped them into my back pocket. "Thanks." The big, heavy door stood open before me. I felt grateful, but did not understand why. As I walked out I turned back toward him. He looked away, behind him, shuffled papers back and forth on my desk, and then he turned to me and smiled. I smiled, too. I thought I'd shake his hand, but then I took out the pen, wrote the 'script and handed it to him. I just handed it to him and walked out again.

Once down the hall I glanced at my watch: seven twenty. The crisp echo of my clogs on the polished back and green linoleum reminded me of church and how long it had been since I had been to confession. Confirmation, I guess it was, something like that, I thought, a long time ago.

CHAPTER 6

❁

"*The Adventures of Ozzie and Harriet!*"

The camera dollies up to a perfect White House. Ozzie's in the doorway

I squirm. "Mom, do we have to watch this? I hate this show!"

"Why?" She lowers the paper, "It's funny."

"I hate it."

"Oh, go on, watch it." She lifts the paper over her face again. "You know you'll like it once it gets started."

"No, I won't."

"Your dad likes it."

My father's sleepy lids float up for a moment, then back down. "Let him watch whatever he wants." He's been snoring on and off for the past twenty minutes.

"Do you want to watch it, Dad?"

"I don't care. It's funny."

"Go ahead," my mother says, "change it if you want. I don't think there's anything else on."

"No. That's okay, if Dad wants to watch it."

"If Dad wants to watch it. If Dad wants to watch it…" She mocks.

Harriet suggests that she join the volunteer fire department so that she can spend more time with Ozzie.

"Are you kidding?" Ozzie says, *"You gals take too long to dress!"*
"Oh, I don't know, we can be pretty quick."
"By the time you got your makeup on, the fire would be out!"
Laugh track.
I cannot stand this.

The kitchen beckons and I go, still looking back at the screen. The Nelsons' house is immaculate, not a thing out of place. As I turn away, I trip over a pile of my own books on the floor and land in a sprawl on my father's polished combat boots.

Laugh track.

"I told you to pick those books up hours ago, didn't I? Well? Didn't I tell you to pick up those books? See what you get? Are you hurt?" My mother asks, but she never looks up from the paper.
"No."

The blame follows me into the kitchen. The dinner dishes sit stacked on the counter. *Do the dishes,* I think. *The Nelson's don't have dirty dishes in their kitchen.*

"Hey," my mother barks and sits bolt upright in the chair. "What are you doing out there? Leave those alone; you'll break something. I'll get them later. Come in and watch your show."

The fresh milk I drink from the refrigerator makes me feel sick to my stomach. Why does my stomach hurt? It's my fault. But what? What's my fault? Is the house messier, or something, for my being here? That must be it. My parents work themselves to the bone. They are tired and worn out. They have to come home and take care of me. Because of me my parents drink to relax.

Back into the living room, my father sleeps in his chair, my mother sips her nightcap: a shot of whatever in coffee dregs. The Nelsons are all on the screen, Ozzie, Harriet, David, and Ricky. Very good. Very happy. They wave good-bye. I stumble.

"If you spill that milk in here," she says into her cup, "you're in trouble.

Laugh track.

❀   ❀   ❀

When I got home that night, the phone rang.

"Hello?"

"Hi."

Karla, shit. "Hey, what's up?"

"Oh, nothing. Just thought I'd call and let you know I thought about you all day." Pause. "I had fun last night." Low, sexy talk.

"Umm. Me too." Distracted. The bag of books and clothes that hung from my shoulder wrapped itself in the phone cord before I could put it down. I stopped flailing and stood in the middle of the floor, arms down, holding my things, getting angry.

The TV remote on the kitchen counter caught my eye. I grabbed it and flipped on the television, and quickly pressed the mute button.

"So, how was your day?"

"You know…" My words flipped like the channels: mechanical, recorded, bored. "Work is work. Are you at work?"

"Uh-huh," she giggled.

"What's so funny?"

"You said the word 'work' three time in a row,"

What's so funny about that? "Busy?"

"Not too. They got a liver for that kid I told you about, so it'll get busy around her later, when the transplant team gets rolling. They never get here until two in the morning."

"Where's the liver from?"

"Michigan."

I watched something in black and white. A WW II documentary. Shells exploded all around as men in steel helmets with rifles scrambled over mounds of dirt and crouched behind tanks.

"Michigan," she repeated.

"I'm sorry," I said, not meaning it. "I just walked in the door. Can I call you back?"

"Sure."

"Okay. Talk to you later. Don't work too hard."

"Okay. Bye."

In the bathroom, I stripped, and draped my rumpled scrub suit over the towel rack where I could grab it without groping in the dark of the morning. A fresh suit waited for me at the hospital. I could grab one and change when I had a little more rest. A good plan. I brushed my teeth because I noticed the toothbrush in its little rack. I dripped the minty blue foam into the hissing water. The toothbrush touched the back of my throat. I gagged, which made me think of the pills, the shots, the drinks, I shook my head, disgusted with myself.

Why can't I get this drug shit out of my head?

Because it's the only thing that makes you feel any better, you jerk.

Oh, yeah. I forgot for a second, there. But, I can't keep this up. I don't have the energy.

You get your energy from the pills.

If I don't get cleaned up, quit using, I'm going to be in deep shit. The drugs are making me sick.

So, quit.

I will. That's exactly what I'll do. I'll quit using the pills and the Demerol. I'll lose a few pounds, start running again, get myself in shape..."Now, I'm having conversations with myself. Jesus."

When I finished, I stood for a moment longer, making sure my stomach was settled. I splashed cool water on my face, went into the bedroom, rummaged around on the floor, netted a pair of sweat, pants, and put them on. It crossed my mind to crawl into bed, but I fought the urge.

I'm not giving up that easily.

The night would be over soon enough without me helping it along by closing my eyes. Back to the living room. As I passed the bathroom, I remembered and turned around. I bolted for the scrub pants that lay abandoned on the floor; I even ripped the pocket off, but only found one of the pills.

Fuck.

Even today, so many years later, I find it hard to distinguish between anger and panic, but I felt one of those feelings in that moment. The passion faded when, on my hands and knees, I found the pristine, white disk floating on the nap of bathroom carpet. The pressure of kneeling made the spot on my thigh ache, the spot where the Demerol soaked into the muscle after I pumped it in with the syringe, still hurt more then twenty four hours later.

The drone of the television, or the awkward back-flexed craning of my neck against the arm of the couch, woke me, uncomfortable, from a groggy slumber, thick like moss in my head. *Get up and turn off the television.* Through the dark I felt my way, hand over hand, into the bedroom and slipped in between the crumpled sheets. Then I started to dream: *Flying. An airplane losing power, losing altitude, no matter how I pulled back on the yoke. As the plane descends, low and slow, over a village of clay tile roofs and church steeples the silhouette of a woman, my mother, maybe, waving up at me comes into view. I want to wave back but I am occupied at the controls. Then, a sunburst, an explosion puts me somewhere else, and I am walking through a field of golden wheat as something mercuric moves toward me, through the field, coming up behind me fast.*

The voice of the nighttime FM radio announcer coaxed me awake in gentle, modulated tones, no clear words, yet. The clock on the radio flashed red: 5:00. 5:00. 5:01. Outside, I heard a car accelerate fast. Concerned, I pushed away the morning, pitched the covers off, the first thick layer of darkness. The dampness of the sheets under me, the fever-sweat, made me quiver. I left the top sheet off to dry. After a hot shower, I put my scrubs back on and went into the kitchen. No coffee. Too much trouble; not enough time. I couldn't remember the last time I had made any. A Saturday, maybe, some-time ago.

In the car I felt better.

Being up this early, once you get rolling, makes life tolerable. Nobody's around to fuck with you. The unmade mistakes of the day lay before me curled up and waiting like snakes yet to strike. *So, whom are you going to fuck-up today, smart guy? What important shit are you going to forget to do because you can't keep it all in your head, because, once again, you didn't get enough sleep?*

Possible scenarios passed before me like floats in some wretched parade. The themes of each included characters, such as irritable patients, ill-tempered surgeons, well-intentioned nurses, ill-informed residents, and poorly prepared medical students. The parade trailed on in my head until, at the far end, I saw a clown who resembled Vince and remembered the little bit of Demerol he said he would save for me.

So much for quitting.

This new thought gave me something, an expectation, to push through the day.

My life would not always be fucked up, I knew. After my residency, my life would be different. I could get through residency with the pills, maybe a shot here and there, some booze perhaps. You need something positive in your life when you practice medicine.

Fuck it. I'll quit later, when I have more money, more time, more rest.

A quick turn and the digital clock I kept propped on the dashboard skittered across the dash and fell to the floor on the passenger side. As I retrieved the clock from the floorboard, the time changed. Twelve hours fifty-two minutes and thirty-some seconds left to go. Smiling to myself I thought, No sweat. I can make this standing on my head. I reached for the silver knob on the radio, heard the metallic click, saw the greenish light behind the dial.

"You're listening to National Public Radio...."

As I pushed down on the gas pedal I heard the engine turn over, maybe too fast. *Twelve or thirteen more hours? Not including meals? Nothing to it.*

CHAPTER 7

Summertime: A hundred degrees in the Alabama shade. Or, is it Georgia? I can't quite recall. We move every year or so. It's hard to keep track of the moves. The weather, so hot and wet that breathing the air outside is like inhaling in the bathroom after one of my father's showers. The heat engulfs the county in a cloud of humidity, as if to smother the place in a steaming, wet blanket. I can't sleep with the swelter. When the phone rings, I pick up the receiver, but I don't say anything. I can't think fast enough; I just react.

"Hello? Honey?" It's my father. He sounds confused, excited. "Rocky? Rocky? Did you answer the telephone all by yourself, baby? Go get Mommy, okay?"

"Hey! What are you doing with that phone, you little son-of-a-bitch! Give me that," she screams.

I turn and stare straight into her nakedness. I look up, past the triangular patch of hair between her comely legs, past the sweat of her belly, past her breasts that hang off her like ripe melons as she reaches for the phone. When I reach up to touch them, she stands and puts an arm across her chest. She frowns at me.

"Hello? Hi!" Peaches and cream.

As I wander down the halls of our tiny barracks home, swiping my fingers over the walls as my path meanders side to side, I pass outside the doorway to my mother's bedroom. A man is in her bed. Naked he sits, his back resting against the headboard of my mother's bed, smoking a cigarette, rolling another one, pouring something dark from a clear bottle into an empty glass. I stare straight at him, not moving. He stops pouring and smiles.

I don't smile back. Maybe my eyes narrow.

I hear my mother behind me, still on the phone. "I know. I miss you. Call me back as soon as you can, will you? Oh, I love you too. This weekend? Oh, are you sure you should try to come all that way for just a forty-eight hour furlough? It will take you half that time to travel back and forth. Well, I know, but what about the money, and it's such a long way? No. No, your training will be over soon. I'd rather you wait and come when you can spend the whole week. I'd rather you rest up and not spend all your time traveling. Okay. I love you." She hangs up as she says, "Bye."

The man stares back at me, his skin glistening. He hasn't moved. "What's a matter, kid? You want some?" He holds out the bottle.

She moves past me like I'm not there. She leans on the door-frame and talks to him as if she doesn't see me standing there in the door-way. I smell something on her skin, something acrid, not sweat, as she passes, before she closes the door behind her. Her scent, or his.

Then, I hear them on the other side. "What's 'a matter with the kid? He just stares."

"Forget about the kid. Got any plans for the weekend, soldier?"

Daybreak and a whole hour passed before anyone in the city knew it. The elevated horizon of the skyline made it impossible for the earth to tilt far enough to let any sunlight creep over the buildings early in the day. A reddish orange hint of dawn managed to creep by, but only in patches. A poor excuse for a sunrise.

A strange refraction of the eerie half-light formed ghosts in my windshield that tried to blind me, vain apparitions of dubious pur-pose to accompany me as I drove to the hospital. A man walking from an alleyway looked up at me as I drove past. *Intruder*, his look said, *you had better just be passing through.* We exchanged glances as I passed. One down-shift and he disappeared.

My patients all stared like that; all over north Philly they loomed out of the darkness, out of nowhere, at odd times, on my way to work. I'd recognize a scar placed on a face just so, or a gait, unsteady and gimpy, that resulted from poor healing of a broken bone after aggressive treatment of a gunshot wound. Sometimes, as my former charges dragged themselves from dark corners, I shuddered with pride. *Here he comes*, I imagine them saying, *The one who saved my life.*

The sky went from dark to dawn and back again as I passed through various neighborhoods. Dilapidated buildings made valiant stabs at the sky. At that time of the morning, breathing shadows still shrouded the decay enough to convince one that the city was not dead, simply asleep. This morning, enough light seeped though for me to notice a young man. He looked out of place in his pressed military uniform standing on the street corner, home on pass, maybe, or returning to his post. Waiting for his bus, I wondered. For a second, a strange thought told me it might be my father, but of course, it was not. He'd been dead, by that time, for years. Slowing, I imagined myself asking if the boy needed a ride, but I pressed down on the gas-pedal, accelerated instead.

Three men in leather jackets stood around a place called The Crow Bar beside motorcycles bathed in neon. One of them stood, feet apart, a green bottle of beer shimmering in one fist, his dick in the other, and urinated into the street. He looked up as I drove by and our eyes met. He looked down again and gave his thing a shake. I looked away. Like most of the city, the buildings in Kensington are red brick row houses built more than a hundred years before. Whole neighborhoods of wood and brick stacked side by side. A neighborhood just like this burned to the ground when the police bombed it some years ago. Operation MOVE. Boom! Photographs on television and in the papers at the time, showed police dropping fire-bombs from a helicopter like the Keystone Cops, holding each other by the ankles, hanging upside down, dropping little round black bombs with sparkling fuses, or so it seemed on the video.

Life imitating art.

Boom. There goes the neighborhood.

The streets of the Kensington section smelled of death, not death so much as decay. There's a difference. Decay is life, a different kind of life, to be sure, but life nonetheless. The streets lived in the way a corpse lives, decomposing yet teeming with lower forms of life, abundant life, the life of vermin in a dump or maggots at home in a pile of rotting meat. Kensington lived the way a gangrenous limb lives on and on spurred by bacteria devouring it from the inside out.

No one in Kensington seemed to mind.

As long as a McDonald's or a Burger King turned up on a corner here and there, a place to get food in a hurry at the drive-thru, or, depending on your means, some place to find scraps of bread or beef on the ground or in a dumpster. Someplace to sleep when the weather turned ugly. Everybody seemed to accept the situation.

On my way through the neighborhood I ran a light here and there, three or four times a day. Giving the intersection the once-over before buzzing through was all that was expected if you were a white guy (safety first). My watch flashed the bad news. Fifteen min-utes, then I'm late. A taste, something metallic, rose up in the back of my throat. The pills did that. They left the taste of coins rubbed between the fingers, of gum wrapper foil touching a filling, hard to explain. I swallowed hard and shifted down. What do you expect from something manufacture by Dupont? The stuff is probably the end product of hydrocarbon cracking. You might as well be sucking on a piece of spare tire.

As I pulled into the parking garage of the hospital, my car sounded much louder, low and throaty, in the concrete echo than it did on the street. The '68 Chevy Impala had everything: great styling, lots of horsepower, without being flashy or expensive. When my father bought it he said he loved the car and had to have it. I have loved that car ever since. My ride was older then almost everyone else's on the road, so what? I was still quicker then most, and best of all, it was something of his that belonged to me. Sometimes, at a stoplight, idling next to a car driven by a car load of girls, or a woman I liked, I'd rev the engine, punch it and let four hundred cubic inches slam me back in the seat, like a jet on take-off. I'd look around for the other car, find it in my rear view mirror as it receded, growing smaller and smaller, then I'd laugh and turn up the radio.

❧   ❧   ❧

When I got to the hospital, I didn't page Zack right away. Instead, I went straight to the on-call room and put my stuff down. Once situated with coffee and aspirin, I went down to the O.R. to find clean scrubs.

"All quiet on the Western front?"

The male tech, a former soldier, was manning the desk. Once in a while, when we were alone, I made comments about the army to let him know I remembered enough to make him proud, but not enough to take him back. He'd been to Vietnam.

He smiled and nodded. "It's been quiet. There was a gunshot wound last night, but he never made it out of the ER."

Thumbs up and a smile. "Good work. Keep your head down."

"Locked and loaded, always. You know that, Doc."

The operator paged Zack for me. "Well, good morning, Dr. VanSlyke. I'll do it right away!"

Zack sat in the courtyard smoking a cigarette as usual and staring into the still dark morning like the biker I had seen pissing on the ground. Zack looked strange in the cafeteria glare, more like a scarecrow than a doctor.

"Did you get that trauma hit last night?" I asked, all business.

"That gunshot wound?" He shook his head no, slowly exhaling. "They called Tina, but he died by the time she got there."

"She opened his chest, I hope. Tell me she did that, at least."

He shook his head again. "Not as far as I know. They called the code and then ended it before she got there."

"God damn it! How many times do I have to tell those guys that trauma is a fucking surgical disease?"

He took another drag of his cigarette. "I don't think she minded much. It saved her all the paperwork. She wasn't up half the night trying to call the coroner, you know, all that shit. The ER doc took care of all of that."

"She's going to mind if she comes up short with trauma cases when she applies for her boards."

"I would have cracked his chest in the morgue if I had to. You know me."

I forced a laugh. "I wasn't yelling at you." I went over and sat on the picnic table.

"Sounded like it to me."

"I wasn't. Sorry. I've got a splitting headache this morning; just can't seem to shake it."

"Forget it. It's been a bad day. I don't need any more bullshit from anybody, especially you, the one reasonable person around here. It's not even about you, really, I just don't need to hear any shit right now, that's all."

My watch changes from 6:05 to 6:06. Not good. I looked back at Zack.

His thin face made his eyes swim in his head. "Dr. Barrister made rounds this morning for the first time in I don't know how long. He bitched me out about that guy dying last night. I wasn't even on."

"Did Tina call him?"

He shrugged. "Who the hell knows. It wouldn't have mattered anyway."

"It might have mattered if she had called me."

Zack sighed and took another drag of his cigarette. He glanced over my shoulder into the cafeteria and then back at me. "And, Rocky, some guy came snooping around here already this morning asking for you." He looked up in the air.

"Who?"

"That attorney that hangs around." Zack cleared his throat and started to cough. When he finished, he said, "He's been around here a lot lately. You know, the big guy." He made a circle in front of him and puffed out his cheeks.

The message sounded like a warning, like something suspicious, coming from Zack. I brushed it off; it didn't matter.

"I'll take care of it."

Zack nodded and looked at his watch. "I've got to get going. I've got a case at seven."

"Me too." I stood up.

❋   ❋   ❋

Tina sat at the third floor nurses station, making rounds, I supposed, writing in a patients chart, ragged and tired from her night on call. Even so, Tina looked attractive, petite with a head full of thick auburn hair. You could always read her handwriting, a trait that distinguished her from almost every other surgeon on the staff. Tina, a twenty-six year old, second-year surgical resident, always appeared unhappy. She forever looked terrified, and she muttered to herself in a way that disconcerted patients, nurses, and her fellow physicians. When a nurse or another doctor approached her, anyone with a stethoscope, anyone she perceived to be a threat, she looked up, open-mouthed, stunned, and froze.

That was the expression she held now as I approached her position.

"Good morning, Dr. Santos," I said, addressing her formally to put her at ease.

She looked up; no go. Deer in the headlights.

Too late, I thought. "What happened with that gunshot wound in the ER last night?"

"What gunshot wound?"

"Wasn't there some guy with a chest wound that came into the ER around midnight last night?"

"Oh, yes, but we were never consulted."

"You mean they never called a trauma code?"

"Oh, no, they called it, but it was all over before I even got down there."

"Did the ER doc end the code, or did you?"

"He did."

"Was there any chance you could have done a pericardiocentisis or a slash thorocotomy or something?"

She shook her head.

"Well, look, we've got to start pushing for these trauma cases, or you younger guys—I mean, well, you know what I mean—you guys are not going to have enough on your case list when it comes time for the residency review committee to certify us again. We are not a trauma center, Tina. Remember that. We've got to take advantage of these cases when they come along."

She watched me.

"Do me a favor. Get the record of that case, so we can present it at the M and M (mortality and morbidity) conference and light a fire under the ER director to get us involved with these cases earlier, okay?"

She nodded and frowned. I didn't blame her. She knew the ER doctor would tell a different story. He would say he was tired of waiting for her to answer his page and he ran the code himself. She would present the case to the medical staff at the M and M conference and then stand up at the podium and listen to the Director of Surgery and the Director of Emergency Medicine argue about the management of the case until they both stated, directly or implicitly, that she should have arrived on the scene in a timely manner; that it was her fault, no matter what the explanation.

Oh well. She should have responded to the code.

❦   ❦   ❦

On the way down to the O.R., I spotted Vince going through a door. I caught up with him. "You looking for me?"

He looked startled. "Howdy." He dressed the same every day, white shirt, loud tie. "I wasn't looking for you, but I asked your friend, Zack, if you were around."

"You probably wanted to give me my portion of that stuff, right?"

He cleared his throat and squirmed, then waved me into an empty room. "Look, when you didn't come over last night, I assumed you didn't want any, so I used it."

"You used it all?"

"Yes, but, it's no big deal. I'll fill another one for you today and have it for you when you get out tonight."

"I can't keep writing you Demerol prescriptions every fucking day. What the hell is this?" My voice rose and I could feel my face getting red.

Vince got nervous, acted funny, guilty like. "Look, I'm sorry, but you said you didn't even like the stuff, and you never answered when I said I'd save you some, and then when you didn't come over, I assumed that you weren't interested.

"I was fixing chest tubes in the unit at 10:30 last night."

"I was still up," Vince said, still defiant.

"Yeah, and I'll bet you sat there in bed just waiting for me to come over so that I could use the last little bit of Demerol, right?"

"Look, don't be an asshole. If you want me to fill another 'script, I will; if not, that's fine, too, but I don't need this shit."

"Neither do I."

We stared at each other for a moment. Neither one of us said anything or moved a muscle.

Anger scared me. I didn't feel it very often, but when I did it always sneaked up on me, like a passing freight train, catching me off guard, making me twitch with power I could never seem to control. It either exploded or dissipated too quickly.

Vince spoke first, inhaling then exhaling, backing down. "Well, I guess you're right. I did say I would save you some. What say you let me make it up to you? How 'bout writing me another one of those things, and I promise you that I'll save you some. Better yet, I won't even open it until I see you."

I relaxed. "Tell you what. I'll meet you after work, and we'll go pick it up together."

"Great." Vince put his hand on my shoulder and smiled. "That's just great."

CHAPTER 8

❀

*H*e drives a Volkswagen, I think. Something small. I sit in the back seat, too short to see out the windows. I can make out the tops of the trees passing by the side windows too quickly. The sensation of the motor turning behind my back makes me feel warm.

My mother sits in the front, on the passenger side, all made up. Her hair is long and shellacked with some kind of hair spray or gel. Dippity Doo. Her hair, a Barbie Doll coiffure with the edges curled up in a gravity-defying swerve, turns from side to side. I have a great view of the back of their heads. He looks at her and smiles.

Smiley passes her a bottle on the sly. She takes it, looks back at me, then out the window. I do not see her take a drink, but I know she does. She always does. He wears a cap that buttons down in the front. Something a cabby might wear. I think, *Dobie Gillis*, and giggle to myself.

"Oh no." I hear my mother's voice. "He's a good boy, aren't you, Rocky?" She turns back toward me. "He won't say a thing," Her smile tells me she's had that drink, "Will you sweetheart?" Her eyes are changing.

His eyes in the rearview mirror look right at me. Alone, isolated from the rest of his face, from the beamy smile, those eyes are angry and piercing, accusing, blaming, and they are staring at me. I try to look out the window, to avoid his stare, but I am not tall enough. I want to tell my mother, to warn her that the fellow is not who she thinks him to be and to make him stop staring at me, but she won't be interrupted, not now that the fascination of the alcohol has been cast. Forget it. She would respond, I know, but from somewhere else, some place in her mind that I would not recognize, someplace far away, unpredictable.

A gust of wind buffets the car, and I feel it shudder. The seat catches me, and I realize I've been falling asleep. No sleep, no matter how sleepy my eyes get, not with Smiley at the helm. That's the rule. I'm on guard duty. My father told me about guard duty. You can be shot for being asleep at your post. Nobody knows I'm on guard duty. It's a secret mission, an assignment between me, myself and I. But I know. I know.

The clouds peeking through the trees make little flashes of white, strobes of light that hypnotize me. A subliminal message, a bubbling glass of Coke between the frames of a movie sat, waiting, hidden behind all the repetition. The engine sound sings like a seventy-millimeter movie projector. My eyes close. The flashing sunlight through the windows turns the insides of my eyelids pink. My dreams are coming attractions.

My mother laughs. Then her sweet laugh dissolves into a scream of tearing and scraping, then I'm in bed. That's all there is.

I must be dreaming. I wake up. Guard duty.

When I open my eyes, bright lights fill the room. Men and woman in powder-blue masks and head-covers hover over me, snapping sheets like wet laundry on a line, in July. Metal jingles, like silverware being poured into a steel kitchen sink. I start to cry. "Mommy! Mommy! Mom?"

"That's good. That's a good boy. Call for your Mommy," the eyes behind the mask above me say as a rubber hand covers my face with a gas-mask. The directive confuses me, so I stop crying. I don't want to cooperate. The lights fade and the toy soldiers with red jackets and blue pants with yellow piping, black bonnets and stovepipe boots march in, arrest me, and lead me away to my execution. Gulliver's Travels. Babes in Toy land. The Sorcerer's Apprentice. Fantasia.

When I awaken, my bandaged head is propped on a pillow. My mother stands at the foot of the bed. I look at her a moment, but I can't decide my next move. "Don't just do something, stand there!" I settle on this phrase; it seems to say it all.

She laughs and cries as she turns from the window. She snuffs out her cigarette. She's dressed up. Dinner-dress and heels. She walks to the bedside to touch my head but stops when she sees the bandage that winds around it like a turbine. Her hand, suspended in mid-air, shakes and she cries harder. The black and blue under her make-up show through the tracks where the tears trickle down.

"What happened?"

"Nothing happened," she says. Then she buries her head in my stomach. "Nothing happened. It's all over now."

"Mommy, my head hurts."

I watch her press the buzzer. I remember the nurse at the bedside, the needle and the warm flush of the medicine that puts me back in the dream.

❧   ❧   ❧

6:30 P.M. I could have left the hospital sooner, but I stalled. Making a point. A late consult surfaced debridment of a bedsore or something. The on-call person could have covered that, but I took it, to kill the time, to stretch the anticipation.

The extra minutes ticked away to the rhythm of my tongue clicking against the roof of my mouth.

Make the bastard wait, I thought, *I'll show him.*

When I got out of my car at Vince's house I lost my mind and shut the door even as I saw the keys still in the ignition. Not even the buzzer and a red, flashing light on the dash stopped me. My keys flashed as the door slammed and the noise stopped.

Goddamn it all to hell! I locked the fucking keys in the car—again! You fucking idiot! (Once, when I was a kid, I lost my car keys after having made the mistake of carrying them in my non-dominant hand.) Situations like that occurred with enough frequency that I kept my personal items, my keys, my wallet, my pocket knife, and my money, in the same location each day, to avoid maddening searches. My preoccupation, I convinced myself, reflected my genius. Hell, Einstein once left the house without his pants.

Leaning heavily on the hood, I pondered the situation until a remembered the extra set of keys I kept taped under The wheel well for just such occasions. After I retrieved the keys and opened the door, I sat back and laughed at myself for being so absent-minded, then, I sat for a moment longer to let my heart and my breathing settle down before going inside.

Hell, I thought, *you've got lots of time.* I glanced up at the house. *Let's see how you like it, asshole Let's see how you like waiting for something you've been promised.*

❋   ❋   ❋

I didn't knock, just pushed the door open.

Vince leaned back on his bed. Still dressed in his shirt, tie, pants and suspenders, he lay there watching Money-line on the TV. Runs gathered on his silk socks where his unclipped toenails caught the shiny material. I looked away. "where's Karen?"

He said, "Well," but it came out, "W-h-a-l-e," with a long crescendo, decrescendo tones in his voice. His expression did not change. His hands rested behind his head, as if he had no intention at all of moving a muscle for some time to come. Hopes of my being smug when I entered the room dissipated into self-conscious amazement at Vince's lassitude, awe at his ability to swing from manipulator to sycophant, leaving me so easily disarmed.

He stayed lost in his television for another moment, ignoring me until I spoke. "Did you hear me?"

"What?"

"You know what!"

After what seemed to me to be another enormous delay, Vince motioned to his valet, across the room, beside the dresser. Irritated, I followed his command and fumbled around through his cufflinks and accessories until I found what he had sent me for. A bottle of Demerol sat there, obscured by his jewels along with a handful of Percocet; there must have been fifty.

"Get yourself fixed up." He smiled. "Then prop up here." He pointed at a chair opposite his bed. "And relax." He sat up, ignored the TV, and rolled up his sleeve. "Then when you're done, toss the bottle over here to me." I felt the shock settle in my face. He noticed it, I'm sure, and laughed. "Go on," he said, "Get to it."

When I got back to my condo, the air, smelled of the darkness, like an attic smells of mildew or a tool shed smells of rust. For a moment everything, the furnishings and appliances, looked out of place and I stared at my home from the doorway, as if I where a stranger to this place, the gray carpet, still new and chic, reminding me less of a domicile than a seedy motel.

Full tilt, so as to gain escape velocity, I crossed the hallway and I was in. My pack hit the floor as I reached for the phone. Reflex, Jesus. Conditioning. After I dialed the access number to my voice mail a woman's voice, pretty, if somewhat stilted and mechanical, informed me, "*One. New. Messages.*" and played it for me.

"*Where are you? I…*" Karla.

Click.

My scrub suit hung on the bathroom towel rack as I examined myself like a leper for areas of injury and decomposition. My scrub pants, where my arm had rested during the drive home, revealed bloody patches, a few drops of blood, not a lot, where my arm had rested on my thigh. After checking the bruise on my arm I pulled the pant leg around on the bar, twisted the material around into the light for a closer examination of the stain.

"Shit. God-damn it…"

I licked my finger and rubbed at the spot. *Fuck it. I'll get a fresh pair in the morning. Besides, what kind of surgeon doesn't have blood on his clothes? What's a little blood? No big deal.*

I turned back toward the mirror to check the injection site on my arm again. It looked red and puffy, but not bloody. The rug around my feet was clean. *Undress and brush your teeth; everything's okay.* The next thing I knew my teeth throbbed as if I'd been struck in the mouth and the sink was full of blood. I must have brushed them an extra long time. After I rinsed my mouth out in the sink I went to bed.

The first time Karla and I made it on the floor of my apartment, no fire burned in the fireplace. Burnt logs from the previous winter were the backdrops of our lovemaking, the remnants of a house fire: charcoal and stale smoke. She came three times, but her expression never changed once during the whole thing.

"Are you okay?" I asked, and she stared as if she had no idea what I might mean.

At the beach house, on our first date, after our first kiss, she stopped me from unhooking her bathing suit top, even as I felt her up. It was different at my place; at my place she walked in, turned off the light, and undressed. All business, no questions. Her tan, dark on her arms, legs, and back, contrasted with the translucent skin of her breasts and hips, where blue veins showed like vegetables through rice paper, outlining the contents of a steamed spring roll. The sight of her naked excited me, of course, (it was the first time,) and we made love in a hurry. She let me do anything to her I wanted. She never said a word. Afterward, in that guarded moment when two people reconstitute themselves after sexual dissolve, we stared at each other, her wanting to hear "I love you" and me wanting to apologize. Her expression never changed.

From then on she acted as if we were a couple, as if the sex changed something in our relationship. Her reaction seemed understandable. My reaction said, "I want no part of a relationship," but aloofness and neglect didn't seem to matter much to her. Our circumstances just sort of happened and they seemed to make her happy. Maybe I got uncomfortable after awhile, with her around me all the time, or when I got interested in other women, but most of the time nothing really changed. Maybe I said something. Maybe not. To be honest, I don't remember. The relationship just sort of happened, like a car accident with permanent repercussions.

❦　　　　　❦　　　　　❦

The phone rang, but in my dream, a buzzer blared, an emergency light ignited. *The fire, the loss of power made it clear we were crashing. The port side engine ran away, the airplane pitched forward over its own starboard wing. A spiral. The proper maneuver to control a spiral had something to do with the rudder and I worked the pedals and pulled on the yolk with everything I had.*

When I woke up, the phone was in my hand; I heard the rhythmic beeps of the message service.

My page gave the time: 5:01, but no pages had registered.

When I called the service, the mechanical female voice announced, *"You have one. New. Messages. To listen to your messages…"* I pressed "one" and cursed Karla, but Vince's voice was the one that talked back at me.

"Hey buddy, thought you'd still be around, especially after last night. Ah, ha, ha. You're probably already out there saving lives…Ha, ha, ha. Shout at me when you get a second. See you, Rock."

I hung up the phone and cursed again.

I've got to cut this shit out. Time to get up, anyway.

Twenty minutes is a lifetime when one is sleep deprived. And I saw my life pass before my eyes as I left my usual route to pass by Vince's house. Without knowing why, I drove there instead of going straight to work.

5:14 A.M. Still dark. Another hour before I'd see the light, but a light burned in his bedroom so I walked to the back door and found it standing open. *He forgot to lock up when I left last night. He must have passed out, too. I'm going to march right up there and tell him it's over. I'm through with this drug shit. I'm sick of waking up not knowing where I am or what I did the night before. That's why I drove over here: to let him know the score. I'm finished.*

Vince's bedroom door opened with a creak. Only the rumpled bed linen occupied his gigantic bed. Behind the bathroom door, I heard the water running. I sat down to wait in the chair, the same one he had pointed me to the previous evening, to tell him the fun was over. I sat in the corner of the room facing the bed, facing the bath, waiting.

A sound, like someone choking, or gagging, someone getting sick, came from the bath.

Brushing his yellow teeth. I thought

What seemed like a long time later he came out. The ribbon of light escaping under the door disappeared first. The door opened, flooding the dim room where I sat with even more darkness. "Well, Doctor," I heard Vince's disembodied voice say from behind the door, as if he knew I were there waiting. *How could he possibly know?* "Well, I see you got my message."

"What message?"

"I left you a message on your service this morning."

"H-m-m. I must have been in the shower."

"Um-hm. Switch on that light, will you?" He said as he exited the bathroom in stages. One body part followed the other out into the light, like a row of circus elephants, the trunk of one holding the tail of the other, belly, arms, legs, and backside, a human circus train, a steam engines pulling freight cars, freight cars dragging a caboose.

The scene was laughable, but I didn't laugh. "What'd you call about?"

"Oh, well," he said, sounding disinterested, "I wanted to know if you wanted some more of that stuff before I, you know, finished it off."

He was right, the Demerol had felt differently when I did it I.V., but I hadn't let on. After I slipped the needle into the large vein in the top of my forearm and experienced, for the first time, the beautiful sting that bloomed in my chest and flowered in my brain, my life changed, but I did not know that yet. Before too long, I would learn to love that pain all by itself, for what it meant: That I was not alone. For what came afterward: bliss. The burn crept up my arm, filled my lungs with hot steam, and just before my head exploded, left something metallic, (coins for Charon, maybe, the ferryman who conveys the dead to Hades over the river Styx,) in the back of my throat.

Zoom.

Vince didn't ask me about how shooting up felt, whether it was better, or if I liked it better that way. He ignored me. No chiding. He busied himself with his own preparations and left me alone.

"No thanks. I don't want to use that stuff ever again."

Okay."

"That's what I came over for, to tell you I don't think I can do this anymore."

"Do what?"

"Jesus, Vince, I told you, I can't keep writing…"

"I didn't say anything about you writing anything, did I? No, I didn't. I just asked you if you wanted some relief, some liquid sustenance." He held his towel around himself, like a Roman senator exiting a sunken bath, and tossed something shiny and hard to me with his free hand. "C. Calvin Waterman, the Director of Surgery," the label read on the half full vial of Demerol. My boss had written the prescription.

"Jesus Christ, how—" My face dropped. When I looked up again he laughed, an obnoxious sound that increased in volume until I feared it might wake the neighbors. The howl of the insane, a maniacal titter.

"Ha-ha-ha. Ah-ha-ha-ha. You want a needle?"

I got up from the chair and walked over to the window. "No. I'm going to break the bottle, then slit my wrist with the jagged end and pour it in."

"Oh, Jesus, don't do that! You might spill some!" he answered with another laugh. "Here…" He went back into the bathroom.

While he rummaged for a syringe, I looked out at the night. The sky was still dark. I looked across the street at an old Victorian mansion with a light burning in an upstairs window. Someone looked out from a split in the sash. A man, the fingers of his left hand curled around the curtain, squinted his eyes at me. I swear to God, he gaped at me. Then the guy turned off the light.

What could it hurt? I thought. *What could it hurt to get high this one last time?*

CHAPTER 9

❀

"**L**isten," my mother says to my father. "Listen," she says, but she means, "Look."

They stand across from each other at the kitchen table, like Rock'em Sock'em Robots, where my father has just slapped down the checkbook like a gauntlet thrown down before a duel. My mother points at the checkbook, her hands shaking, looking like she might say something, but that's as far as she goes. Her voice escapes her. My father stares at my mother as if he'll kill her, as if she should choose her next words carefully. But, he won't kill her. Not yet, anyway. Not his time.

She retreats to the sink, turns and shakes her fists at him. "Listen you son-of-a bitch!" He moves forward, one step, no more, makes a grab for her, but she pulls away. "Don't you touch me! It's not my fault if the army doesn't pay you enough to support a family."

My father picks up the checkbook ledger. "How are we going to make the car payment, Lou, huh?"

"It always about that fucking car, isn't it? That's all you care about is that God-damn car."

I walk to the window and stare out at the beautiful, metallic-blue Chevy that sits in the driveway. I feel proud every time I walk past the car, the first new thing I ever remember us having.

My father flips through the checkbook again as if he's lost something there, trying to create the illusion of making something out of nothing.

He swallows hard as he looks up and shakes the checkbook at her. He wants to throw it at her, I think. His face reddens, not the tight redness of anger, but the flushed, red, wonder of embarrassment, of fear.

"Where is it?"

"Where's what?"

"The money."

"I don't know what you're talking about. What money? There is no God-damned money."

"There was fifteen hundred dollars in the savings account last month. Where is it?"

"I have no idea! You've got some nerve coming in here and accusing me of spending our savings on...of spending our savings when you leave me alone for weeks at a time while you're out playing army man with all your buddies..."

"This isn't funny. Where is it, Lou? I mean it. You'd better tell me what happened to that money. I'm not fooling this time." He grabs her again, holding her a little too tightly.

She screams, "Let go of me you son-of-a-bitch! Don't you dare hit me!"

My father releases my mother like he's been scalded, a cup of liquid too hot to handle. He holds his hands up, palms out, a gesture of truce or surrender. "I won't hit you. What the hell are you talking about? I would never hit you!"

"You bastard," my mother says, as she wails into her tears and seizes the initiative to beat a hasty retreat into her room.

My father has long ago taken to sleeping in the extra bedroom.

He stares at the space where she stood. He stares a little too long, a moment beyond what might be explained by a startle, as if some poltergeist of her lingers and holds him captivated. He stands like that until its substance departs. With enough force to knock over the chair, my father picks up his field jacket and walks out the door.

❈   ❈   ❈

Later, my mother lights a cigarette. She wears a tight beige sweater and matching skirt. She sits cross-legged at the foot of the bed, dangling a matching beige stiletto pump from one of her feet. She leans forward on her knee to bring the cigarette and the lighter together without moving her hand or her elbow from its tender resting-place. The blue flame jumps to the beckoning of her breath drawn through the sweet tobacco. She takes a drag and removes the cigarette from her mouth with two fingers, all in one, elegant, motion, smooth, and sexy, and drops the lighter into her pocket book.

She'll say she's going somewhere respectable later, to church or the PTA, but when later comes, my father is not convinced. He calls around the post to ask where she's been. He will hear that no meetings were scheduled that evening. But, all that's for later interrogation. "Where did you go, mother?"

For now, my mother stands up, puts her cigarette in the ashtray on the top of the dresser and approaches the mirror. As I watch, unnoticed, she turns a small bottle of perfume over a couple of times, a slender finger covering the opening, a drop of essence landing on the tip, just below the long polished nail. She dabs the substance behind each ear and scent transforms the bedroom into a ballroom; that's Chanel # 5. She leans over the mirror like a model in an advertisement from *The New Yorker* or *The New York Times Magazine*.

No one else like my mother exists in rural Georgia. In that moment, I love her, not as a mother, but as a woman, as a captive of forbidden love. My mother is other fragrances, too. When a soldier speaks in a husky voice or strikes me in the face for interrupting a kiss he steals from her in the night, she is *Arpege*: my first hint of sex. When she receives a Christmas gift from my father, from an outpost overseas, a gift of animal musk doused in vanilla, she is *Shalimar*. When she drivers a red Buick 225, convertible, a car that neither of my parents ever owns, she is *Joy*.

My mother puts on a fur wrap and leaves. The click of her heels on the hardwood bedroom floor turns to clacks as her shoes travel out over the linoleum of the kitchen, and revolve to taps on the terrazzo of the foray. The concrete sidewalk and the blacktop driveway tap out their own refrain of Buddy Rich riffs. The car door slams behind her music. I'm already in bed and listening for the song of her return: tires squealing into the drive, doors slamming. Meeting her out myself, picking her up and taking her home, these fantasies fill my mind. I feel myself getting hard and think, *Chanel*. Tonight I'll dream of someone named *Chanel*.

Karla conceived. Considering the eventuality of a pregnancy after almost two years of unprotected sex shouldn't have been a surprise, but it was. A fourth year surgical resident with no money to speak of and a hefty pill habit. A nurse with no money to speak of, who drinks to get the taste of the puke out of her mouth, who just got knocked up by a broke surgical resident with a hefty pill habit. Now there's something to think about. She took her birth control pills except when she sensed she was retaining water. The dangers of not taking birth control pills consistently is taught by nurses to young girls every day, but, like me with my Percocet, she thought she knew better. "I'm a nurse, and besides a woman knows her cycle. It's an intuitive thing. Mind your own business. I know what I'm doing."

Okay.

Then one day she said "ouch" when I touched her breasts. She had begun to look even more round and doughy. She wanted me to guess what might be going on with her, but I refused to play doctor. When we were beyond guessing, she acted as if my suspicion made her think of the possibility she might be pregnant. We bought one of those stupid, over-the-counter pregnancy tests and managed to spill the thing all over the bathroom. We tore the directions in half fighting over the right way to perform the test, but, in the end, the little vial turned pink, or blue, or whatever the hell it was supposed to turn if the woman was pregnant.

Fuck.

Karla called the public clinic. The wait for her own gynecologist seemed too long. Fine with me. The sooner the better. We never talked about the process. No problem. Things got better for a short while after the plans were set. During the two-week delay before our appointment things went smoothly, all kindness and consideration.

"Can I get you something, hon?"

"No. I'm fine, but thanks for asking. How 'bout you? Do you need anything? Anything at all?"

"Not a thing, but thanks for asking. That was sweet of you."

And, vise-versa.

No rush. We began having sex again. One time, in bed, an attack of whimsy urged me to come inside her, something I had not done accept by accident in the past. As I was going down on her, before her juice filled my mouth, when I already tasted that she could orgasm at any moment, I pulled my head up from between her legs, mounted, and entered her in one thrust. Her head tilted back on the pillow, turned sideways, and locked. Her eyes narrowed, almost closed. Her back vaulted toward me, away from the bed, all shoulders and ass contorting. As her body twisted, the hollow between her tummy and the cleft of her hips cradled me as I pushed whatever lay inside her up even further, toward her ribs.

A more beautiful moment never passed between us.

On another occasion we both came at the same time.

The first enjoyable sex with her in quite some time took place as a result of a situation neither of us wanted. When I told her I wanted to be with her during the abortion. She said no. She appreciated the gesture, but I needn't bother. But I wouldn't have it any other way.

"Let's be practical. I'll drive."

The clinic's rules mandate the patient not drive; it's a liability thing.

✤   ✤   ✤

It astonished me how fast IV narcotics take effect. All at once I'd be warm and spent, yet awake at the same time. When Vince talked, it startled me a bit, because I forgot him. "God," he said. He sat up in the bed as if he had accidentally fallen back to sleep.

I looked at my watch.

Twenty minutes since the injection: Still plenty of time to get to work.

Vince, with the towel still wrapped around his corpulent middle, wiped blood from the back of his hand with his thumb. He swiped at the spot with the bedspread and the sheets. "Good God." He looked all around.

"Wash the stuff in cold water."

He looked up and laughed, "Where the hell did you learn that?"

"My mother."

"You are really something." He licked his fingers and wiped some more.

I noticed his mood change. His words slurred and floated, sparked, I assume, by my company or the blood or the Demerol.

"I'd better get going." I glanced at my watch again. "I've got to start making rounds."

He stopped wiping, leaned back and propped his arm on a couple of the pillows strewn about him.

"Don't go yet," he said with uncharacteristic softness, "You've still got plenty of time."

"Yeah, well, they've been on my ass lately…"

"Ah, hell, you can handle them. Sit with me for a minute."

I sat still as stone and let him talk.

"God, sometimes I can't believe…" His voice trailed off. "When I use this stuff, it's like I see the light at the end of the tunnel, you know, just over the mountain crest?" He made a hand over hand motion, "You know what I mean?" I nodded. "Like I'll be able to make it, like, like I'll make it to the top, and life will work out." I nodded again. I didn't say anything, just pretended to take it all in. "You understand, right? You're a doctor. You know how it is, the kind of pain people go through? You, of all people, should be sympathetic. You've got the power to make it better with powerful medicine dispensed at the stroke of a pen." The tears welled up in his eyes.

Jesus, God! He wasn't making sense. I looked hard at him as he went on. "Feeble. Goddamn feeble is what I was. Just a feeble little boy in a tough neighborhood. Did you ever play stickball, Rock? City kids play it. It's poor-man's baseball, and that's pretty damn poor. Well, I sucked at stickball, the only game in town. Jesus. I was a sissy, always getting chased down alleys and climbing fences to get away from the bigger boys who punched me and threw rocks at me." With tears in his eyes Vince held out his hands, turned them over and showed me his fat knuckles. "Those rocks stung my hands, Rock. Those rocks hurt when they hit me in the back and cracked against my head.

"Did you know I changed my name? That's right. I was Vicente Genivese Budilupo when I grew up, if you can believe that.

"I skipped high school one day in the spring semester of my senior year, took a bus from little Italy to a court house on the Lower East Side of Manhattan, and filled out all the paper work necessary to change my name. I got a forged New York State driver's license with a correct address to prove that I was eighteen for fifty bucks from a wise guy in the neighborhood, so I could file the papers. Vincent G. Buddy. No middle name, just an initial. Just like that. There was no way I'd put any Guinea names on my college applications."

He never told his father.

"Rocky, I got to tell you...have I ever told you about my father? What a son-of-a-bitch. Joined the fucking United States Army to get his citizenship. He beat the shit out of my mother when he came home on furlough, when he drank, of course. Only when he drank." He laughed and shook his head, "But shit, he always fuckin' drank."

He hung his head and sighed a heavy sigh. It turned to a rattle in his chest. The rattle turned to a cough, a gasp, then a choke. "Whiskey," he went on after a moment. "The fucking whiskey beat the shit out of my mother. That's what did it. He wasn't right with booze in him. Out of his mind is more like it. I tried to stop him once. He beat the shit out of me, too. Then, he hit her again to show me that I made matters worse. He knocked me across the room like a rag doll. He was one mean SOB when he drank. I remember her scream-ing..."

"I never knew any of that, Vince. I know what you mean." I said, but I didn't say a word about myself.

My eyes closed as he spoke and saw a bright flash, like stars, like a slap across the face. The flash faded in concentric circles of complimen-tary colors. My father's form emerged from that light, a silhouette, a mannequin, then a corpse, a soldier shot in the chest. Another flash and he disappeared, like magic.

My laugh betrayed my delight, my lack of understanding. Do it again, Dad, please. Dad? Mom?

As I opened my eyes, I noticed Vince eyeing me. He stood in the middle of the floor wrapping the towel tighter about his middle. "You'd better get going. You'll be late."

CHAPTER 10

*T*hey're at it again. The floor fails to filter out the voices.

"Where the hell were you?" There it is: the pregnant question. He's been out checking, making the rounds. He's had a few beers on the way. He's pissed. "Where the hell were you?"

No answer. My mother ignores him. She always does. She's lighting a cigarette, I'll bet, blowing smoke in his face. The smell of sulfur, the burn of the matchstick, seeps up through the cracks in my bedroom floor. It's a game: the sounds fill in the picture, scenes from a black-and-white movie, Janet Leigh in Psycho. The flint of a lighter sparks with two twists of the stone. Now my father's lighting up. Bogart. After a pause, I hear the metal cover close. My mother, still dressed to the nines, head tilted, becomes Lauren Becall in "To Have and Have Not." Still in her heels, tap, tap, tap, then, a little stutter step. He's grabbed her, or she staggers. A sound, more a gasp then a scream, comes next. My father means business.

"Let go! What? I went out for a drink. The NCO Club, where do you think. Now, let go of me you son-of-a-bitch, or I'll…"

His voice raises. "Or you'll what? Go on. Or you'll what? The NCO club, huh? That's rich! Guess where I've been? You want to know? I've been at the NCO club for about the last two hours. I got home ten minutes before you did."

I know where this is heading. She'd better lie. If she ever tells him the truth, he'll kill her. If she even hints it's all over…There's a long pause. I hold my breath. The silence is a vacuum into which my fear expands. The silence, white noise, rings in my ears, the sound of snow on a TV screen. The silence, so loud it drowns out everything but my heartbeat, the white noise of silence takes me away. Wherever that plane is going, the one over head right now, that's were I want to go, wherever cars go when they whiz by. The place where trains go when their whistles howl at the moon, that's where I'm headed.

She deserves a swat, but not a broken neck. I'm not sure he can pull his punch enough, not tonight. So, I worry. A while longer and my mind wanders again. The rhythm of my nervous legs as I rock back and forth puts me to sleep. No cracks or groans. They must be kissing. If it gets this far without a battle, they always kiss. The rustle of fabric and the muffle of voices tell me I am right. I'm relieved. I'm ashamed. I want to go to the bathroom, but I don't dare: it's across from their bedroom. Passion that intense can come out as love or hate. Best to stand clear. I pray instead, what little I remember from the TV:

> *Oh my God*
> *I am heartily sorry*
> *For having offended thee…*

The furnace kicks on. Under the covers I am safe; the warm billows of air from the overhead register burrow under the blankets. The warmth mingles with my own moist breath around my face. The furnace kicks off. Maybe I shiver.

I hear a plane pass over.

I hear a car pass by.

I hear a train whistle blow.

Peek through the blinds, I squint my eyes as I've done a thousand times, strain to see the lights of the train or a puff of smoke from a passing engine.

Tonight, I think, I see it.
It's my pillow, or my sleep, or a dream.

❦   ❦   ❦

This scrubby, male third-year medical resident and a female medical student waited for me in the unit. All medical residents look scrubby; that's part of the reason we surgeons call them fleas. The other part is because of their similarities of character: irritating but otherwise inconsequential. For this reason, their names don't matter. Most likely I never knew their names in the first place. Surgical residents don't waste memory on useless information.

They sat waiting at the nurses' station. The resident paged me then plopped in a chair to drum his fingers in anticipation of doing the one thing to his patient he could do well: transfer him or her to another service. The spot he chose to plant himself blocked the entrance to the nurses' station. "So what?" his posture said. A real prick. Dumb, too. The first thing anyone teaches you in residency is do not piss off the nurses. For a third year to still not have figured that out did not bode well. The poor, clueless, medical student hung out, wondering, no doubt, why she had chosen this god-forsaken profession.

They paged me and waited. I thought, *bad sign*.

The key was not to answer. Instead, I went straight to the intensive care unit when I arrived in the hospital, no stopping off at the on-call room. This tactic tended to unnerve the callers, the ones who stood and waited for the phone to ring hoping to be gone by the time you arrived after they had already made the dump, so the nurses could deliver the bad news: new patient to care for with nothing to operate on. Any medical resident worth his salt took a shower or ate breakfast by this time of the morning. Two things seemed clear to me as I arrived at the station: one, I dealt with an idiot, and two, he was a lazy idiot.

To dump a unit player, a really sick one, would make it worth his while to miss breakfast or delay a shower. A good dump, a high-maintenance patient from the ICU for example, lightened a workload a great deal. Getting rid of one such player meant the difference between a twelve-hour and a thirty six-hour shift at times. The problem he faced in dealing with me? Surgeons are inherently combative. There was no way I would take this patient without a fight, not unless it was clear I could operate on him or her. This was war.

"Morning." I said, faining a peaceful demeanor. "Did someone page surgery?"

"Yeah, fifteen minutes ago."

Too much sarcasm. He's scared.

You could smell it. He needed help. He was an idiot. This particular resident was a real asshole; I recognized him from codes, always barking orders and then disappearing before the work was done. *Lazy and dumb, bad combination in a doctor.* No good niche exists in the field for this particular sub-type. If you're lazy and smart, people leave you alone for fear of being annihilated in the argument that would ensue from a confrontation. If you're industrious and dumb, you're tolerated for the effort you demonstrated. If you were industrious and smart, you didn't work at All Saints.

At least you know what you're dealing with, I thought.

Dr. Asshole, here, I imagined, had been passed over as the chief resident of the medical service, probably more then once. Any medical resident who finished three years of training still breathing air could do the job of chief resident; to be passed over was pretty fucked up.

Corpulent, lazy, dumb, and already on my last nerve. "What can I do for you?" I said, playing friendly.

"I've got a lady here with a hot gallbladder. She needs it out right away." He looked at me as if to say, *This is a done deal. You might as well just sign her over.* He acted as if my fifteen-minute hiatus might have cost Mrs. Fat-fertile-and-forty her life, not to mention incalculable pain and suffering. He would make an excellent expert witness, some day. I saw this movie before.

The medical student with crossed arms punctuating her mentor's smug tone now frowned at me.

I smiled. "Mind if I glance at the chart?"

Dr. Asshole handed it to me. He began to look nervous; he figured, I guess, that I'd jump at anything that sounded like a surgical case. He wasn't happy; his demeanor indicated he wanted to throw the chart at me. Too late. The line in the linoleum had been drawn.

I smiled. "Thanks."

The patient, a fifty-one-year-old, white female, had never been pregnant. She had a long history of lung disease. This admission to the ICU resulted from a pneumonia that complicated her "diffuse pulmonary fibrosis;" in other words, her lungs were replaced by scar tissue. Her pneumonia occurred on the left side. It wouldn't explain "right upper quadrant abdominal tenderness," which, according to the chart, is why Dr. Asshole called the consult.

The last chest X-ray report indicated that Mrs. F-F -& -F had "diffuse pulmonary edema," her lungs were full of fluid. Gotcha! Clinically, the case wasn't adding up to a hot gallbladder.

"Mind if I examine the patient?" I said, walking away from the desk as the resident and his student froze in the midst of collecting their things.

"What-da-ya-mean? Aren't you gonna transfer her?"

I stopped after a few well-timed steps and turned. "Not until I determine whether or not she's suffering from surgical disease. You agree, don't you, doctor, that a medical patient is not safe on a surgical unit? This patient," I made a swishy hand-flourish in the direction of the patient, "for example, might end up with an operation she doesn't need; you wouldn't want that on your conscience, would you? Now, which one of you will hang out until I give you an opinion?"

They both looked at each other. He looked back down at his stuff. She knew. I smiled.

"I'll do it," the medical student said, her voice full of resignation.

"Great," the resident, said, "and don't forget to make rounds," Then he was gone.

Waving to the medical student to follow me I said, "So, what's the differential diagnosis of right upper quadrant abdominal pain?"

"I, ah, I haven't had surgery yet."

"I haven't asked you a surgical question yet."

She frowned and looked back to her resident once more, as she came around the desk. He was on his way to breakfast. She looked back at me. I smiled. Her smug tightness melted. "I, ah, I...gallbladder disease?" She sounded hopeful.

Giving her an, Oh, *brother* look, I said. "Good guess. That's one. What are the other five?"

We walked the rest of the way to the patient's bedside in silence. I watched her out of the corner of my eye as I continued to flip through the chart. She glanced about for someone to rescue her. She saw the flapping coat tails of the other students with smarter or more efficient residents scurrying down the hall to the cafeteria to gulp coffee and devour donuts before they all headed to morning lecture.

She wouldn't get any of those goodies today. It dawned on her. Lost cause. She looked up at me. Surrender.

I smiled. "Well?"

"I don't know." She exhaled capitulation. She took her hands out of her pockets and flopped her arms at her sides.

"Good. Now you can learn something. I'm going to teach you more medicine in six minutes then your lazy-ass resident's scut work," I pointed my thumb over my shoulder, "Will teach you in six weeks"

Her eyes got wide. Then, she smiled.

I smiled back. "Ready?"

She nodded.

"Okay. The differential diagnosis of right upper quadrant abdominal pain is—got a pencil or something?" She scrambled. "Ready?" She nodded. "The differential diagnosis of right, upper quadrant…" I pointed at the patient with my finger to demonstrate the exact location, to fix it in her mind. "…abdominal pain is as follows: hepatitis, cholicystitis, heart failure, pneumonia, appendicitis, and renal colic." I reached over and pulled the sheet down off of Mrs. F-F-&-F while my new protegee finished her feverish writing. My patient had tubes in and out of every orifice. Her eyes opened and she stared, unblinking, at the ceiling, no longer a sentient being, but rather a living textbook. At least, in a sense, her life still counted for something.

The cadence of her breathing told me she would be dead, were it not for the respirator: Ssssit, pooh-ah. Ssssit, pooh-ah. I listened to her lungs. No breath sounds. Her lungs were stiff, filled with fluid. I listened to her heart. It sounded like a stampede. I examined her abdomen pushing down, then releasing her left upper quadrant, opposite the area in question, moving down and clockwise until I finished in the right upper quadrant. When I arrived at the spot in question I pushed. She winced, and the veins in her neck bulged. I let go. The veins in her neck went down.

The bag at the side of the bed collecting urine from her bladder stood empty. The tube leading from the bag all the way to the urethra wasn't chinked. I looked at the student. "Do you know what hepato-jugular reflux is?"

"It's a sign of liver congestion. It's when the blood from the liver backs up into the jugular veins of the neck when you push on the liver."

"That's right. Watch this." I showed her again. "Now, why might this patient's liver be congested? Think about your differential diagnosis."

She crinkled her nose. "Heart failure?"

"Yes. Why?"

"Because the heart is not pumping blood like it's supposed to. The blood backs up into the liver?"

"Is that a question or a statement?"

"Backing up. The blood backs up."

"Into which part of the heart?"

"The right ventricle?"

"That's correct. Why?"

She thought about it for a moment. "Because the right ventricle pumps away from the liver and toward the lungs."

"That's correct, and what are the causes of right-sided heart failure?"

She screwed up her mouth, "Pulmonary valve stenosis, pulmonary artery hypertension, pulmonary fibrosis, and respiratory failure," she recited, and she was right.

"Does this patient have any of those?"

"Yes."

"Which ones"

"Pulmonary fibrosis, pneumonia complicated by respiratory failure."

"So what's the reason for the abdominal pain?"

"Pneumonia?"

"Could be, but if you look at the X-ray report, you'll see the pneumonia is on the wrong side. It's on the left."

She looked disappointed, as if she'd made a mistake.

"Don't worry about it. That's how you rule it out, by checking the X-ray. You learned something. Go on."

"Okay." The wrinkles formed on her forehead as she concentrated. She'd realized she could figure it out. "Right-sided congestive heart failure?"

"A question?"

"Right-sided heart failure. Her pain is from the congestion; from the blood backing up from the heart into the liver and stretching it."

"Bingo. Now, is right heart failure a medical or a surgical disease?"

"Medical.

"That's right. This was a bullshit consult. This patient didn't need a surgeon, she needed a doctor! Remember that. This lady almost got an unnecessary operation that probably would have killed her. I know surgical residents who would have taken her gallbladder out just for the experience. *Premium no nocari*. Know what that means?"

She shook her head. "No."

"First do no harm."

She stared at the patient with a look of amazement.

"That's all." I headed for the nurses' desk to write the consult.

"Want me to write it?" She followed me. "I'll write it for you if you want and you can come back and sign it later."

I smiled. "It'll take me two minutes. You go get some coffee."

She continued to linger until I finished.

I looked up at her for a moment. "So, you interested in surgery?"

Her look betrayed that she considered lying, but thought better of it. She shook her head, "Psych," she said with a little smile.

"Smart kid," I said, and meant it.

❧   ❧   ❧

To arrange the abortion took two phone calls, a preoperative visit for blood tests and the execution of a list of mindless questions designed for the victims of teenage pregnancy. The clinic staff never even asked my name. A tacit assumption implied that a male not be a part of the abortion process. Evidently my part in the process appeared nonessential to its pioneers.

Abortion, essentially matriarchal in character, assumes I planted a seed, period. No responsibility otherwise. Like a migrant worker toiling in a master's vineyard, I stood mute once the decision to uproot the seed I had sown in the owner's pasture became doomed and the owner was possessed with the idea of plowing it under. Seen as an enemy who sowed tares among the wheat, I had been a wild boar allowed to rut in the Lord's Vineyard. After the moment of conception I found myself out of the loop, an interloper who's celebration left destruction in its wake.

In medical school, I refused to learn how to perform abortions. "A matter of conscience," I told them; my prerogative, a conviction I felt good exercising. I did not tell them of the tip-off by a fellow student. Such a decision, it turns out, would lessen my workload and get me out of the hospital an hour earlier each day during my OB/GYN rotation. I thought about that decision now and, for some reason, felt ashamed.

The clinic staff warned Karla, "Just drive on through the pickets. If they touch the car, you can have them arrested."

In the waiting room I passed the time with a paperback. I hunkered down with something by Clancy, The *Hunt for Red October*. I sat in the front room reading the same page over and over again with all the mothers, sisters, and, to a lesser extent, brothers and friends staring at me. No fathers sat in this place. That designation got checked at the door.

The ambience haunted me.

After the procedure, Karla looked pale. Never had I seen pallor look so pale. She appeared the color of cobwebs and just as frail. It frightened me. What was I to do? For a moment, my medical training eluded me. What would I have done, anyway, given her a pill? So, I just smiled at her, like an idiot, but she didn't react. Her hair, slicked with perspiration, looked thinner then when she went in. She said the staff told her to drink something sweet, but she wasn't sure what they meant. Mixed drinks?

No alcohol, I told her, just reflex, something you say in post-op. I didn't know for sure. She hemmed and hawed and settled on one of those colorful slushy frozen things they sell in convenience stores. I stopped at the first neon sign I could find and got her the largest cup in the rack.

It cost only ten cents more to super-size it.

❧   ❧   ❧

After finishing the consult I closed the chart and stood up. I had in mind to get some coffee before heading to the O.R., but a rather imposing nurse blocked my exit.

"Excuse me," I said, as I attempted to make my way past her.

"You the surgical resident on the vascular service?"

"In a manner of speaking, yes."

"What's that supposed to mean?"

"I'm the surgical chief resident. I'm on everybody's service," I said, smiling trying to sound cute. A face likened to a Fiji stone carving took shape. She wasn't buying the "Mr. Nice Guy" routine. A stream of insults welled up in my head, resentments collected for all the nurses over the years who had bruised my ego and broken my sleep, but I managed to keep them out of my mouth. Instead, I swallowed the vitriol-like vomit. I was all business. Professional. "Why, is there a problem?"

"Well, if you guys would answer your pages once in a while, maybe we could learn who you are! I've been paging this, this..." She looked down at the chart, then yelled across the room, "Hey, Frank, who's that obnoxious surgical resident you've been dealing with?" Frank struck a pose like a dilettante and made a gesture that pushed his nose up in the air. "Oh, yeah, the woman, what's her name?" She turned to me, "What's her name?"

"Tina."

"Tina? I guess so. Tina."

"The one and only."

"Huh? Oh, yeah, well I've been paging this Tina all night long. It's about this triple lumen catheter, it's not functioning. We've been using to dialyze a patient over here all night." She pointed at the patient over there. "I've done everything I know how to do with the damn thing short of changing it over a wire myself." She hesitated. "Which we can do at University Hospital, but for some reason a doctor has to do it over here." She paused again for effect. When she realized I wasn't biting, she went on. "Anyway, I still can't get it to flow worth a shit. The pressures are through the roof."

"Tina's been tied up with a trauma all night," I lied, making a mental note to ream Tina a new asshole at the nearest opportunity. "How 'bout if I take a look at it?"

"You can look at it all you like, but it needs to be changed."

"Let's just have a look first, okay?" I smiled, knowing that the one thing I would never do, now, was change the damn catheter over-a-wire, a simple procedure designed to allow a change of the catheter without sticking the patient again. So firm was my resolve that I was bound and determined not to change the thing even if I had to blow the thing out with my own pursed lips. It was a matter of principle, really, or maybe spite. Like Zack used to say in the old days before his kinder, gentler self appeared, "Better to let a patient die the let a nurse think she's right."

She turned and walked back to my second Patient Battlefield of the morning.

Mr. Battlefield's chart or the history of his present illness did not interest me. He wasn't my patient. The triple lumen catheter, ten inches of stiff polyethylene three quarters of an inch wide, honed to a sharp point, placed under the collarbone through a small incision in the skin of the chest, provided access to the large blood vessel that plunged into Mr. Battlefield's heart. Access of this type would be very important to Mr. Battlefield, to get lots of blood into him, or to suck it out so it could be cleansed with dialysis. Placement of that catheter requires a basic knowledge of anatomy and some surgical skill, but mostly it requires the balls to jab a stiletto into someone's neck without injuring the lung, the heart or the great vessels. The catheter became my patient.

The four sutures that held the catheter to the skin of the chest were funky and told me the catheter had, indeed, been in for while. The removal of the sutures didn't bother the patient. His stare, his breathing, like the previous patient's, did not falter. When I freed the catheter, I moved it out of the skin about four millimeters. I watched the dialysis machine to see that the flow improved and the pressure dropped. They did. I sutured the catheter back in place. No injections to numb the skin. Injections were a waste of time and money in a case like this. Ignoring the uppity nurse in the process, I pulled off my gloves, picked up the chart from the foot of Mr. Battlefield's bed and wandered, triumphant, back to the nurses' station to write a procedure note.

Problem solved.

My mind was already gone from there and on my coffee. Then, the same irritating troll came back. "It's not working," she said, flat, smug.

"I'm sorry?"

"The catheter. It stopped working again."

Nurses could be unpleasant creatures. The note of satisfaction in her voice struck a sour chord in the victory march playing in my head. I knew I would say something nasty so I said nothing at all. I returned to the patient. The sutures I had placed were tight. The catheter hadn't moved. I cut the new sutures and moved the catheter another four millimeters. The pressures dropped and the flow improved. I was about to replace the sutures when the irritating nurse started again. "It's not working. Why don't you just replace it?"

In that moment, time froze.

Three impressions remain in my mind of that instant: The burning redness of my face, the frigid interval of my watch at the stroke of eight o'clock; and the sound of the nurse's voice, nagging, baiting. Almost two hours had past. The logistics weren't working out. Intern shtick slowed me down, zapped my energy. Hot lights and cold steel might keep me going. The O.R. was all that kept me going through crap like this, either that or some good drugs. It would take at least one half an hour to replace the catheter; another twenty minutes to get an X-ray to confirm the position before anyone could use the thing. Not good. My day circled the drain, in ever tightening spirls, as things stood. My mood was fast headed right down the shitter. "It doesn't need to be replaced," I said, short and sweet, then I reached down and shoved the catheter another three quarters of an inch into the patient's neck.

The pressures dropped, the flow improved.

Then, Mr. Battlefield turned blue and died.

They called a code. The "Do Not Resuscitate" paperwork still sat in the chart uncompleted. All the tubes and lines necessary to resuscitate were in place. All the medications ran in right up until the moment she died. I stepped back and watched. The medical people worked on him for ten minutes then called it quits. I went to finish my note. The nurse caught up with me.

"What happened?" she said. She looked concerned, in earnest.

"I don't know." I shrugged. I looked past her to the medical residents who huddled at the foot of the guy's bed formulating theories that would help me deny I killed him. "Why don't you go ask one of them? He wasn't a surgical patient."

She just glared at me, then turned and walked away.

She knew. It's hard to put anything over on a good nurse. A good nurse knows her patient. She gets the rhythm of the disease. Good nurses tune into the vibe. She knew the patient shouldn't have died. I could tell by the way she looked at me, back over her shoulder with her narrow eyes, that she knew I delivered the deathblow. I learned something as a student to help me deal with such situations: Better to let a patient die than to let a nurse think she's right. A surgeon taught me that. That mantra made everything all right for a while.

❧   ❧   ❧

Later, I visited the morgue.

The autopsy revealed that Mr. Battlefield's lungs were saturated with pretentious fluid. His kidneys stopped working, stopped filtering off the fluid some days ago. Fluid backed up into his lungs until there was no more room for oxygen. When the lungs could no longer supply oxygen to Mr. Battlefield's heart it stopped. That killed his brain.

Primary diagnosis:	*Renal failure.*
Secondary diagnosis:	*1. Pulmonary edema (severe)*
	2. Cardiac arrest
Cause of death:	*Respiratory arrest*

The pathologist let me examine the body. He just nodded, never asked, "Why?" He didn't say anything. Happy that anyone would take an interest in anything he did, he said, "Have at it." He moved his cigar from the edge of the autopsy table and clinched it between his teeth to make room for me. I examined the neck. The trachea, lungs, and heart had been removed. A bloodstain encircled the trachea. I noted it and set the lungs and trachea back in the tray. I returned to the body. I placed a probe in the hole where the catheter had been. It passed all the way through into the neck. There, between the muscles and soft tissue, I found a ring of clotted blood. I removed the probe, my diagnosis made: the patient had suffocated to death, a result of strangulation. When I pushed the catheter forward, it punctured the opposite side of the blood vessel. Blood from the ruptured vessel hemorrhaged into the neck, dropped his blood pressure and built up a blood clot in the neck that closed off the patient's airway. I killed her, strangled her as surely as if I had placed my hands around her neck and squeezed, but, from the inside out. The pathologist missed the diagnosis. No surprise when he didn't the correct mechanism of injury

"Thanks!" I said, with a little wave.

"Anytime, young man," The pathologist said with a smile. He picked up his cigar and clinched it between his teeth. "Anytime."

❊   ❊   ❊

"I'm telling you, I killed her!"

A large overstuffed red leather chair way too big for his office and way too expensive for the neighborhood cradled me as I sulked.

"Don't be so melodramatic, Ben Casey."

"Killed her as surely as if I had stabbed her in the neck."

"You're exaggerating."

"I saw the bruise on the trachea, Vince! The lady crashed the exact second I manipulated that catheter."

"Didn't you just get through telling me that the pathologist listed the cause of death as heart failure?"

"That's not the point."

Vince leaned over his desk and crushed his cigarette out in a black marble ashtray adorned with a gold faceplate with his name engraved on it above the word, President. He never explained where it came from. President of what? I thought, the first time I saw it.

He smoked Dunhill's. The little gold crest on the crushed edge, just below the filter, smolder in the ashtray. The scent surrounded Vince like the mysterious vale of his background. His smell darted about him like a recalcitrant puppy, in and out of my awareness, sometimes tolerable, sometimes distracting. The aroma followed in his wake like a barge behind a tugboat. He smelled like an attic after a house fire.

"That's exactly the point," He picked a bit of tobacco from his tongue, then he picked some more off with his thumb and forefinger. He lit another cigarette. "You listen here," he said pointing at me with the two fingers that held the cigarette, "You can sit there and feel sorry for yourself if you want, but the simple fact is the expert says she died of heart failure. Now, before your career is all over…" he hesitated long enough to light his cigarette again and take a long drag. "…You're going to have lots of attorneys like me trying to blame you for lots of things you didn't do, so…" He exhaled with a whoosh. "I would suggest you take your breaks where you can get them and button it. Know what I mean?" He took another drag. "Learn to live with it."

Squirming I scrunched up one eye and looked at him with the other. What he said made sense.

"Look," he said, softening, "You win some, you lose some. You tried to help the guy. Let it go. Here, have a couple of these." He handed me a couple of pills. "Oh, and we're just about ready for another script."

"I'm not sure these are going to be enough, today. This situation really has me screwed up."

"Well, well!" he sounded happier than I hoped he would, "This is a first! Why don't you write me for some of the other stuff and I'll get that 'script filled at the same time. We'll get out of here and go prop up somewhere for a few hours."

"Where?"

"I don't care. We can take the train down to D.C. and back, for all I care.

"Okay." *What the hell*, I thought, *It'll be good to get away*.

CHAPTER 11

❀

A scream fills my head, but I ignore it. Was that a scream? I've heard shrieks before, when my father was home, but this? Wait, my father's away, but, so what? The comings and goings of my mother's boyfriends no longer interest me. Still, this yell differs enough, lasts longer, maybe, or sounds more shrill, then what I am used to hearing that I sit up in bed, pull the curtains back, and stare out the window at the oak tree, or the pine, or the dogwood looking for the train, the car, or the airplane. With the drapes pulled back, I see a glimmer of moonlight peeking through the trees, or the flicker of a candle set in the mouth of a jack-o'-lantern, a flash of light in a window of the house across the way.

It is the fall of my ninth year.

Downstairs someone gets up to use the bathroom; I do not investigate the noise further. I fall back to sleep.

Soon, the screen door opens. Dad! I smile in my sleep. It must be a dream. My father, away on maneuvers, is not due in from the field until next week. Somehow I'm aware of this and use the information as an excuse to stay in my warm repose. Then, I hear his boots crossing the kitchen floor, making a beeline for my parent's bedroom. It's 3 o'clock in the morning.

Oh no! I think, *Oh my God, no!* Now I am awake, up and running across the floor. *Oh my God,* "Dad? Dad? Daddy?"

He'll kill her if he finds them, my mother and who ever she's with tonight. Down the stairs, through the living room, in the kitchen and out again, down the hall toward her bedroom I go. His boots catch my eye just before the flash. A bang fills my head and time slows down.

I close my eyes. He shot her. I smell something. I've smelled it before. What is it?

Duck blood soup.

I close my eyes, a slow-motion blink, and, in that instant, I again see ducks fly up in the air. Avery's sister and I watch as the ducks fly in slow motion, out and away from us. Then, we see the muzzle flashes and hear the guns crack. We cover our ears as the birds fall, tumble toward the water, once a mirror, now shattered. The dogs swim. Little wakes form behind them. The ripples on the surface of the crystal lake fan out from the dogs like radio waves with an urgent message. The birds float like discarded rag-dolls. Rings, concentric and perfect, converge on the waterfowl until the doggy-paddle disrupts them. The dogs pluck their prey from the water returning to shore with the clumps of limp feathers resting gently in their jaws.

We watch as they paddle out of sight.

Later, I sit with an old, polish woman, a friend of Avery's grandmother, as she cleans the birds. Avery's sister clutches my hand as we huddle together on a pair of stools, our fear mixing with excitement. The old women drains the blood from the bird's severed necks and collects the clots in a chipped, white porcelain basin with a blue strip around the edge. The chipped spot distracts me until everything becomes red and I can no longer look away. We watch as the old woman seasons the blood with suet, stirs and cooks it into broth. The steam rises from the curdled bowl until it fills our noses. It's *Czarnina,*" the old woman says, "*Stryb,* Duck blood soup. It's good."

Avery's sister's mouth waters; she's had this soup before.

I retch.

That's it. That's the smell

When I open my eyes, I see the flash again. The crack rings in my ears this time. The slap of the air and smell of the blood fills my senses. Soup? Nope. This time I know what it is. As the flash fades, circles of complimentary colors form an aura around my father. He backs into the hall (it's more like flying; his feet don't seem to touch the floor), a silhouette, a mannequin, then a body. Another flash and he disappears. I know, now, he's been shot.

Time moves so slowly.

My arms and legs are leaden, like I'm running in a dream. The atmosphere is crystal clear, but as thick as Kayo Syrup. The harder I try, the slower I move. When I arrive at the door to my mother's bedroom, I stand stock-still in the middle of the doorway, too young to protect myself from the monstrosity on the other side.

The man who just shot my father sits, propped up in bed, naked to the waist, smoking. As my eyes adjust to the dark, I see that he wears fatigue pants and holds an automatic weapon across his lap. He points it at me. "Eat this," he says. My mother's head is in his lap. She has no ears. Then, I see that he wears them on a string around his neck. "Eat this, you little Gook bastard! Me number one GI! You number ten Gook bastard!" He pulls the trigger. *Click.* Misfire. The M-16 is notorious for jamming; the barrels warp during rapid automatic firing. I've heard my father complain about that. My father thought the M-1 Garand was a much better weapon.

Crazy sounds behind me, in the room where my father fell.

"Rock, get down! Get down, baby! He's killed your mother…"

My father crawls, just like I imagine he would do in battle. My father, the hero, drags himself along the floor, ignoring the blood in his mouth, his heaving breath, the pain and the numbness in his legs. That's the kind of man he is: A real soldier. He keeps fighting as long as he can, as long as there's blood in his veins. He dials some number, maybe the MP's.

The soldier in my mother's bed tries the weapon again. Same thing—jam. The fucking thing's jammed, and right in the middle of a firefight. He sits up and starts to break the weapon down. It discharges a burst, maybe four rounds, loud cracks, and strobes of light. He looks startled. He throws the rifle against the bedroom wall. When the rifle lands it comes to rest alongside something, all that s visible of the rest of my mother's body, her beautiful legs.

As I watch, the soldier covers his ears with his hands and mimes a scream. He presses the sides of his head so hard his arms shake. His jaw is locked open, his skin sweats. He turns toward me. He cannot believe his eyes. His senses have deceived him. Flabbergasted, he leans forward, takes a moment, and gets me in focus. The "little Gook bastard" transforms into a little boy who looks like the kid whose mother he's been fucking. He looks a lot like me. He throws his head back, laughs so hard, without making a sound, that it leaves him breathless. He reaches for an ashtray and tries to retrieve something from the bottom of it. He gets a hold of it, whatever it is, a cigarette I guess, and strikes a match. He inhales hard. I can hear the sound, raspy, and I see a spot glowing brighter and brighter in the dark, on his lips. A firefly in the night.

"Hey kid," he squeaks, suppressing a laugh, "you want a hit?"

He holds the joint out to me.

He'd been to Vietnam.

CHAPTER 12

*E*ddie Haskel, my hero.

Eddie, alone, seems real to me; not Wally, not Beaver, not Ward or June. Eddie tells it like it is. All the parents buy it, too. One minute he's hassling the Beave, tough guy, and the next, "Oh, good evening, Mrs. Cleaver! How are you today?" He's an angel. I love it.

"Just fine, Eddie, would you like a cookie? Can you stay for supper?" Quick cut to Wally rolling his eyes.

One can learn a lot from Eddie Haskel.

When I get Mrs. Boil to take me into her home I'm thinking of Eddie.

What would Eddie do?

Mrs. Boil, young and pretty, lives next door. Her husband is away in Vietnam. They got married just before he deployed. My parents talked about their situation all the time: "What a shame. They never had a chance."

Now she lives alone. On Saturdays I pretended to rake the leaves or pick up trash around her house, just to get a glimpse of her, an Eddie Haskel thing. One spot on her lawn is almost barren where I rake, over and over, then spread the leaves around again, where I pick up the same piece of paper and throw it down over and over, again and again, for hours, until my twiddling fidgets catch her attention. When she notices me I squeeze out a blush and act surprised. On occasion she waves me to the door, gives me a quarter, or a dime and a smile.

Sometimes she gives me a cookie.

Mrs. Boil's body, small and pretty, I behold as perfection. Her skin smells like coconuts, her perfume smells like love. She seems about thirty years old, but who knows? Everybody seems about thirty years old to me. Her hair straight, stylish, and long, never goes above her shoulders, except when she runs her hands through it, holds it up to fan her neck, or shake it out.

A flower child.

Sometimes while my parents fight or after they disappear into a bottle somewhere, I sneak out and walk around Mrs. Boil's house until I find an open window, one with a short shade. Like I imagine Eddie would do, I position myself not too far away, off in the shadows, out of sight. I pulled my thing out through my zipper, getting hard just thinking about seeing her. If I wait around long enough, I almost always catch a glimpse of her, in her nighty, combing her hair. A few times, an MP shining his spotlight in the yard almost catches me, or, a neighbor walking the dog gets suspicious and stops for a look. The danger makes the whole thing even better, more exciting. I play with myself until I see her for real, then I jerk it fast a few times, until I get the feeling, right there and then, right in her yard. The process doesn't take long once I see her. After I finish, I tuck myself away and creep back to my room. Right into bed I go, without even brushing my teeth, and drift off, on the wings of my release, to sleep.

Eddie Haskel, my hero.

❦   ❦   ❦

The living room sweltered with all the cops and emergency crews in and out mixing with the heat dissipating from my mother's corpse, the moisture from all of her spilt blood. A fat cop sat on the arm of my father's chair, his fat legs crossed despite their girth, the back of his shirt pulled out and hiked up over his hairy back just enough for me to see the crack of his ass. He sweated, breathed hard, and smoothed down his oily hair each time he looked up from his pad. He tapped the pencil against the side of his head with his chubby fingers like a drummer taping on a cymbal and asked me lots of questions that I did not answer.

"Now (puff) can you tell me what you remember, son? Tell me what you saw (wheeze). How long had your mama been, er, seeing this fella? The shooter?"

Instead of speaking, I stared at the badge that dangled from his coat pocket; I watched it swing, back and forth, back and forth, with the heaving of an organ bellows, to the rhythm of his metronome puffing and wheezing: Ssssit, pooh-ah. Ssssit, pooh-ah.

Where is my father? Where are the MP's?

It troubled me that I saw no MP's, just local cops, though I'm sure they were there. I found out later that the Army let the local cops take the lead in murder investigation. It was a political thing designed to avoid turf battles.

The only question I heard was, "Anybody we can call?"

"Yes," I said without the least hesitation, "Mrs. Boil, "She lives next door."

Eddie would have like that. Quick thinking.

Mrs. Boil came right over. "It's absolutely no problem. Rocky can stay with me until this whole horrible mess gets straightened out. Okay, Rocky?" I nodded and smiled. She smiled, too, but with a strange expression on her face. How horrible for her. Her eyes appeared focused, but on something far, far away. She stayed that way for a moment, and then she came back from wherever her mind had taken her. She looked down at me with much compassion and gently took my hand. "Ready?" she said and smiled. I turned red, nodded, and bent over a little to try to hide my erection.

Later, she spoke quietly to me. "You understand that this will all be okay, don't you? That it will all work out?"

I nodded.

She said the same thing again that night, when I crept to her room after she had gone to bed. She was not yet asleep and she heard me enter. "What's wrong?"

She put me up on the couch before retiring herself, but I couldn't sleep, thinking of her lying there, almost naked, in the next room. It took no convincing for her to let me into her bed. "I can't sleep."

Before I knew it, I laid down beside her. She just hauled me into bed with her like our sleeping together made perfect sense. She turned me on my side, faced me away from her, and then draped her arm over me like we were two lovers in repose. The looseness of her nightgown, the freedom of her breasts against my back filled my chest to bursting. Her legs against my bottom felt so hot I thought they might burn me. "You're trembling." she said, "Poor baby; you must be terrified." My trembling had little to do with terror. She couldn't feel my hard-on, not with me facing away from her like that.

"Isn't this fun?" I heard her say, "Isn't this fun, Rocky? Our little slumber party?" I heard her say these things but I couldn't speak. My breath came in waves, short and choppy, gasps that barely reached from my mouth to my lungs. Blood pounded like a tom-tom in my ears as the captured bird that was my heart battered its wings against the cage that was my chest. When the cadence of her breathing changed I mustered the courage to jack off. In two seconds, it seemed, my hand was full and wet. Gently I massaged the juice into the cool, starched sheet in front of me wishing it were her skin stretched, tight and cool, under my hand. Thanking God that it wasn't.

❧   ❧   ❧

The monumental Philadelphia train station stands, like the Parthenon, at the corner of Thirtieth and Market Streets, providing easy access to Drexel University, the University of Pennsylvania, and the rest of South Philly. Coming east on Market, into the city, the modern architecture makes way for the monolithic, neoclassical grandeur of the station, once you hit Thirtieth. Vince and I didn't come that way, though. We came from the North, down I 295, the highway leading from the Mainline. We followed the Schuykill River past the perpetually decorated boat houses of the university crew teams, past the Museum of Modern Art where Rocky Balboa ran, triumphant, up the steps. As we exited into the city at Thirtieth I did a little dance: life imitating art.

"Good God almighty," Vince said, "What a piece of work."

The marble columns of the Thirtieth Street Station, wider then a man, stand at least two or three stories high around the outside of the building. "Jesus," I said, looking up. Inside, the space above the stairs that descend to the trains appear like the descent to Hades. Small, dingy signs dangle from long, black chains strung from the colossal, dungeon-like ceiling warning, like the sign to the entrance of Dante's Inferno: Track # 12, and by inference—Abandon hope, all ye who enter here. Wide and steep, the stairs go on, forever down, taking forever to move from the station to the tracks, like a soliloquy in an Ayn Rand novel, a brooding atmosphere of pure noir. As we entered, you could almost feel Atlas shrug.

The cast in our living novel hustled back and fourth, dressed in back and white, from shadow to shadow. My mind entered a universe with a god named Raymond Chandler, where sixteen-year-old hookers waited around the next corner for me, Philip Marlowe, to save them. I looked up at Vince. Vince looked enough like Orson Wells to be my Citizen Kane sidekick who would bankroll the whole thing, as long as I provided the drugs. Hell, the trip was about the Demerol, and Demerol was pure fantasy, everything, all the time. I was high before we even bought the tickets. I was rolling before we ever made the train, before the gold was anywhere near my veins.

"Two round trip tickets on the through train to D.C." Vince chicaned and fobbed.

"That will be eighty-two dollars. How will you be paying?" The man in the booth, looked as though he should be wearing some kind of hat.

"Credit card" Vince said turning to me, patting his pockets, reaching inside his coat. "You do have a card with you, don't you? You could take this off your taxes, you know."

What? Are you fucking kidding me? I thought, *You're the fucking moneybags.*

He saw my blank stare, read my hesitation more than my thoughts. "Oh, never mind," then, "Shit, here you go."

After he signed the slip he stopped grousing, and smiled. "Lets get something to read."

We walked to the center of the great hall where news stands and fast food counters squat like Bedouin encampments on the vastness of a marble desert. I picked out a *Scientific American*; he picked up copies of the *Wall Street Journal* and *USA Today*. Props for the Passion play. He took the magazine out of my hand and laid it on the counter along with his papers. "Want anything else?" I looked at him. "Go on," he said, smiling, "Get something." I picked up a package of wintergreen Tic Tacs and a pack of Bemen's chewing gum and set them down alongside the periodicals.

"Remember this stuff?" I said tapping the gum, "They used to sell this stuff in the fifties. My dad used to chew it all the time." Vince ignored me. "A Franklin! Jesus, got anything smaller than a hundred dollar bill?"

"Remember Clove and Blackjack?" He said pointing at the Clove and Blackjack under the glass.

"Yeah, my father used to chew all that stuff. He'd buy handfuls of it before he went out to the field."

Vince stuffed the change in his pocket and handed me a twenty.

"What's that for?"

"You need it?"

"Nah, why?"

He shrugged, "Oh, I don't know, I just thought you might need a couple of bucks in your pocket."

"No, I'm cool."

"You sure?"

"Yeah, why?"

"Because if you need any, you know, all you have to do is ask."

"I will. Thanks," I said, feeling like an asshole for what I had been thinking moments before: that he was a cheapskate at heart.

"I'm going to go into the bedroom and lie down."

Funny, I though. *Unusual.*

In all the time I knew Karla, I never knew her to take naps. She returned from her Officer Basic Course a changed woman. Karla the air force reserve flight nurse, Jesus. She joined the air force, decided to give the service a try, after an argument we had about me being away so much. "What a scam," she said, "You get all that money from the reserves just for having your name on some stupid list." Bullshit jealousy, pure and simple.

"I'm sorry. I don't like the idea of the army calling you up, sending you anywhere, placing your life in danger anytime they feel like it. Why do you do it anyway?"

"Why do I do what?"

"Belong to the Reserves; God damn it don't you ever listen to me?"

"I'm listening. Jesus, keep your shirt on, will you? First of all, I'm an American citizen. Second of all, it's a family legacy. Third, the pay is great, and fourth, because I WANT TO, THAT'S WHY!"

"So it is about the money! I knew it!"

"That's what I just said. And, if you're so worried about it, why don't you join? Nobody's saying you can't join and get your slice of the pie, too."

So, Karla joined the service, just for spite. Six weeks later she left, off to San Antonio, to her officer basic course, and now she'd come back.

Her first affair I discovered by the pictures she brought back. She went out of her way to show them to me. In each one, she stood behind the same guy; the same fucking guy. In one, she adjusted his hat. In another, she buttoned his shirt. Always in a group. Always explainable. Innocent. Plausible deniablity. The scenario made sense.

"Who's the dork?" I pointed to the dork.

"Who? Oh, him?"

"Yeah, him. The guy you just happen to have your hands all over in every one of these pictures."

"Oh, I don't know. Just a guy I knew in training."

"Just a guy?"

"Yeah, Just a guy."

"Just a guy in your unit."

"Yeah."

"So, did you fuck him, or what?"

"You're a pig!"

Right; I'm the pig.

Back two weeks and still taking naps in the middle of the afternoon. Well, fine. So, I knew she wouldn't mind if I used the phone. Why would she mind? So, I just picked up the receiver, that's all, an innocent mistake. When I kicked in the door to her bedroom, the length of her face and the width of her eyes grew, as if her face were melting. She stopped talking, and I heard him say, "What's the matter?" One sharp movement downward of my index finger and it was all over. "Hang the fuck up." I mouthed the words. She didn't move.

"Karla? Honey?" He said, confused at her silence.

"Hang the fuck up."

"Karla?"

"Say good-bye, Goddamn it."

"I've got to go," she said in a weak and pale tone.

The whole thing seems so foolish now. I didn't hit her, but I thought about it. I did shake her once or twice, though, and said, "Why?"

She didn't answer. Just stared at me.

Our sex was great that night.

❧   ❧   ❧

Vince and I walked in the general direction of the track and I felt fine, together, important. With that magazine under my arm, my tie smoothed down and my sport coat buttoned I felt fine. We stopped home just long enough to make me into a businessman and Vince into a senator. These were the parts we played. With the collar of my overcoat pulled tight, I waited for something to happen. The other people crisscrossing the station wore serious expressions. They had someplace important to go. What the hell am I doing here? I thought after a while. Now I felt out of place. Being a traveler, yet going nowhere.

"*Dixie Limited, now boarding, track twelve, Dixie Limited to Wilmington; Baltimore; Washington, D.C.; and Richmond, now boarding, track twelve.*"

"*Abandon hope all yea who enter in.*"

"What did he say?"

Vince looked at me. "Who?"

"The guy on the loud speaker."

"I think he said 'All aboard, please', why?"

"Nothing. I thought he said something else. Never mind. Let's go."

"I'm waiting for you."

Vince leapt down the stairs to the platform like a man half his size before I even got the words out of my mouth. The silver Dixie Limited took on passengers like the silver tube of an Electrolux vacuum cleaner absorbing carpet lint. People pushed and shoved their way toward the cars as if it were beyond their power to be left behind. Vince faked left, then cut right with gridiron precision that led us toward the back of the train. He moved so quickly for such a big man that, for half a second, I mistook him for a poltergeist.

"All aboard, please."

To follow him I changed direction, and followed near the back of the flow of travelers until it slowed to a trickle. We boarded one of the last cars and found seats away from the other passengers.

"It won't be long now," Vince said, and I knew what he meant.

"Abandon hope all ye that enter in."

"All aboard, please."

We were golden.

CHAPTER 13

$\mathcal{E}$ very night for over a month it goes on like this with her molesting me. Creeping to Mrs. Boil's bedside every night, my heart pounding so loud I fear it will burst, is all I think about. *Her husband's away at the war*, I think, *She needs this*. Every night she pulls me into her bed and wraps her arms around me, just like the first time, her front to my back, but then it changes, a philandering interlude develops. Now she moves a little, a rhythmic motion of her hips, not rocking, more like squeezing, tension and release of her thighs, every night now, always the same. It goes on like this for weeks, too long for her not to be aware of what's happening. But I pretend not to know, and so does she.

With each progressive molestation I feel her hips move as she mashes her legs together against my bottom. Her breasts push hard against me now. Her nipples harden under her satin nightgown. Her arm drifts down over me. Her fingers brush against my thing. She fumbles so I help her take it out. She plays with me until I come in her hand. Seized with terror, I pretend to be sleep, but I let her finish. After I come I am so sensitive that it starts to hurt, but she doesn't stop until she rubs me dry again. She must be asleep, I think, convinced her behavior is automatic for a married woman. I think about the way she touches me, how her limp hand and soft fingers brush against me so slow after I take myself out of my pajamas. Sometimes

I drift off to sleep like melting, sometimes I do it again myself, sometimes my stomach roils and I feel like I will be sick. When I hear her breathing slowly, I know she's finished.

In the morning, when she moves back and forth in her nightgown preparing my breakfast, it's as if nothing has happened between us and I can think of nothing else but the next time. The thought of that simple touch makes me hard and I am embarrassed to get up from the table. "Drink your juice, now, like a good boy. Hurry, or you'll be late for school. Hurry, now. Shoo! See you when you get home."

In school, too, it's as if nothing has happened, as if my mother had not been murdered, as if my father were not lying crippled in the hospital, as if I was not being molested every night. Maybe the teachers call on me less and less; maybe nobody seems to check my homework. I miss getting shit for not doing my homework, but otherwise it's okay. What I miss is washing the blackboard or cleaning out the cloakroom at least once a week for not doing one assignment or another. I haven't washed a blackboard in weeks. And now it seems I have won a gold star. In the top left hand corner of my most recent paper sits a gold star. I'd forgotten about the English composition I turned in some weeks before the murder. Quickly, I read it over to see what I might have done to make this particular paper stand out. Nothing. It's a mystery.

At first I am happy to win the star. To win anything at all is major. The more I think about it, though, the less sense it makes. I never earned a gold star before. Why now? What did I do differently to deserve this one?

My teachers say I have, "good ideas," but my handwriting's poor and my spelling's worse. "Try printing," they say. "Print instead of writing cursive."

I try, but my papers still come back marked, "Sloppy." Red pencil marks my "Frequent spelling and grammatical errors." These marks are so frequent that, now omitted, I almost miss them. Then it dawns on me: the teacher hasn't even read this paper, not with all those circles, lines, arrows, and notes in the margin missing.

Don't get me wrong: I want the gold star. Who wouldn't? But now that it sits there and begs for an explanation, it's more of a let down than I would have expected. When my name is announced for earning a gold star, applause erupts from my classmates. Applause and funny looks. The looks pass like vapor from one student to another, then back to me. These looks travel across space and seep through the cracks in my face left by the force it takes for me to maintain my smile. The applause gets harder, more pressured, the longer it goes on, but I'm not sure what to do. I keep my seat, pretending not to understand. Miss Goodheart insists I stand, waves her hands and makes a big fuss. At last I stand, surrender really, and walk, defeated, to the front of the class.

My fingers tremble, the paper crinkles like dried leaves. My hand holds the paper up tightly to keep it from falling. My voice cracks, like potter's clay and almost shatters against the stone faces of my classmates, along with my composure. Miss Goodheart's face is stone, too, but her's is chiseled into a smile. "What do you say, Rocky?"

"Thank you."

The class is still and quiet when I sit down. Everybody knows my circumstances, I'm convinced. Miss Goodheart's smile tells me that nothing has really changed, I am really no better of a student then I was before my family was destroyed, a gold star replaced some red pencil marks on a page, is all. I've earned nothing. Some pity, maybe, from Miss Goodheart, but not much else. "Well, shall we move on?"

For the first time since my mother's death, I feel like I am going to cry. I sit stock-still and pray for the class to get moving. I want to disappear again behind the wooden desk. My mother, dead more than a month, is not much more than a memory to me already. Her death makes me feel like a baby, like something fragile. Until I go home to Mrs. Boil and she lets me crawl into bed with her, lets me curl up in her lap with my cheek pressed against her breasts, and my back pressed against her fresh hair, her supple body, I am a stranger in a strange land. My whole body forgets, then, the reason I am there, the reason I have gained the privilege to receive this special touch from her hand.

My mother, in the ground while my father is still in the hospital, never crosses my mind, as crazy as that sounds, as long as Mrs. Boil is humping me. My preoccupation with the frotage of my lovely neighbor is so complete that to ask her, or anyone else, about my mother's funeral plans never occurs to me. Strange. Maybe the coroner's office makes the arrangements, or the army. Maybe my father handles things from his sick bed. No one mentions anything to me and I don't think to ask. I do not attend my mother's funeral, to the best of my recollection. I'm sure all concerned thought it would be better that way.

※   ※   ※

The train rolled out, and Vince and I settled in. We removed our jackets and situated our periodicals. Vince sent me on a run to the club car for a couple of drinks: two beers, a Bloody Mary and a Manhattan in a plastic cocktail glass (they were on special). By the time I returned, he was already high. His head lay back on the seat and with his cuffs undone and his sleeve rolled up.

"Good God, Almighty," I swore as I sat down the drinks and covered him up as best I could with his jacket. He looked like he was near death; his mouth was dry and his breathing wasn't normal. His chest heaved for breath; snored as if it were his last breath, the agonal respirations we in the business of death and dying call Chain-Stokes breathing, the death rattle. Not to worry. I'd seen him like this before. He'd come around, and if he didn't, well, fuck him. I drank the highball. *Fuck him.* I thought; then I remembered who had written the prescription for the drugs that were killing him and, for the first time, thought, *What if he does die? I'll be guilty of murder.* Panicked, I felt in his pockets for the Demerol and the syringes.

"Looks like your friend's already konked out."

The conductor. Jesus.

"Oh, he gets like this sometimes. He's a diabetic, and we just ate a big meal before getting on the train. I'm looking for his syringes so I can..."

"Does he need help, a doctor or something?"

"No, no. He'll be fine. Actually, I'm a doctor and..."

"Then, I just need to punch the tickets." He smiled, but his eyes said, *You're giving me way too much information.*

"Tickets. Right. The tickets. Hold on, Oh, here they are." I pulled my hand out of Vince's pocket as I heard the vial of Demerol fall to the floor of the car. I froze. A cold, paralyzing fear like a spinal anesthetic crept over me. Time slowed down. The conductor reached down and seemed to take forever to pick up the vial. The light flickering through the window gave him the cogwheel motion of a silent movie. He pulled his glasses to the edge of his nose, turned the bottle around in his hand, and read the label. My heart stopped. The conductor pushed his glasses back up and looked at me for a moment, then back at the vial. "Here's your friend's insulin." He said, "You must a dropped it."

"Oh, ah, thanks. And, here's the tickets." He took them, punched them and moved on. He tipped his hat as he left. "Have a nice trip! Let me know if I can be of any help."

I just smiled. After he had left the car I collapsed in my seat and exhaled. *I've got to cut this shit out.* After a moment I found the syringes, fixed myself a shot and rolled up my sleeve. I drank the Manhattan then mainlined the Demerol. Vince was still out, the son-of-a bitch, and I used as much of the stuff as I could. I wanted it gone before he woke up. He already had used one-quarter of it. He would have used it all, if he could have. Now it's my turn.

❧   ❧   ❧

"Hey, come on. Get your sorry ass up," Vince said, shaking me. "It's ten-thirty already and we just got into Baltimore, for fuck's sake! Let's get off here and catch an earlier train, or we'll never get back in time. We'll be good for shit in the morning."

His voice sounded like the histrionic blare of a train whistle. His lips moved with the motion of a fish mouth. I couldn't understand a word he said, but I followed anyway; I caught his drift. When I stood up the train lurched into the station. The motion of the train threw me off balance; the motion of my stomach threw my head into a spin and I almost threw up. It took a moment for me to get my bearings, but the delay gave me a chance to notice the unopened beers still lying on the seat. I stashed them in the pockets of my overcoat and headed for the door.

My stay in Baltimore was a blur. The station, a shrunken, truncated version of the station in Philly, made me feel even more disoriented. The place expanded around me like a bubble of yellowed marble, rippled blacks and browns, and twisting columns the color of taffy that stretched into the heavens like pillars to the dome on the Temple of Aesculapius. Vague recollections of a syringe and a bathroom stall blurred with washed-out snapshots of the station, empty and quiet at that time of the night. We were there less than an hour. God only knows, or cares, what took place.

The train pushing north arrived. We boarded. Little about the trip back impressed me, I remember nothing of the ride, nor do I remember what happened to the balance of the Demerol. My first seizure occurred during that trip. A seizure might explain the poor condition of my memory, the loss of time, and the dishevelment of my clothing.

"Get yourself cleaned up. You're a fucking mess. Jesus," Vince commanded upon our arrival back in Philly. The drool on my shirt matched the bloodstain my sleeve. My tie lay on the floor, knotted in such a way as to suggest that it doubled as a tourniquet. My coat and jacket that had been laid across my lap hid the fact that my seat was wet.

"Shit, what the hell did I spill, the beer?" I said out loud, but then I noticed the beer still in my pockets. It would be clear to me later that I had pissed myself. Passengers simply went on about their business attending to the disembarkation. Vince flew out of there. My long coat hid the wet spot in the crotch of my pants as I slugged along up the escalator and out of the terminal. I cursed.

CHAPTER 14

One day I come home from school to find Ms. Boil standing at the door wearing a big smile, as stony as Miss Goodheart's, plastered on her face. An expression I haven't seen her wear since the night of the shooting and, all at once, I know what she is about to say.

"Your daddy's came home from the hospital today! Isn't that wonderful? Now you'll get to go home and sleep in your own bed and everything. Isn't that nice? You tell your daddy that you were no trouble at all and that you're welcome over here anytime. You tell him that if he needs anything, any little thing at all, all he needs to do is ask, Okay?"

These things she says block me from the entrance of her home more surely then the parcel of my clothes that stands already packed at her feet. I can't take my eyes off of her feet.

"Here," she says, lifting my chin, "This is for you," It's a religious medal. A Saint Jude medal. You wear it around your neck. It will protect you." After she helps me fasten it around my neck, she tucks it inside my shirt, kisses me on the forehead, then turns me around, and, with the tiniest shove, sends me stumbling on my way, across the lawn with my little bag, to finger my medal under my shirt. I guess she was Catholic.

My mother was Catholic. I know this because my first cousin on my mother's side, my mother's brother's son, Christopher—the name means "Christ barer"—known to me through his infrequent visits to our home, becomes my confirmation sponsor not long before my mother dies.

"Why don't you ask your cousin, Christopher? You like Christopher, don't you? I'll bet he'd say yes if you ask him."

So I ask Christopher to be the guardian of my soul, and he agrees. Christopher, I learn in confirmation class, had been the patron saint of travelers, but is no longer. He had been purged. The church that canonized my sponsor's namesake then purged him makes no difference to me at all. My mother made me send Christopher a few birthday cards, but that is about the end of his sponsorship of me. Christopher becomes a schoolteacher, I hear in whispers and hushed tones, and molests one of his students. The parents of the victim, a little boy, purge Christopher from my life like the church purged his patron from sainthood.

My Saint Jude's medal is different; it will always have meaning. Saint Jude: the patron saint of lost causes.

🍁   🍁   🍁

My father's new chair, with all the shiny chrome holding it together, makes me ill when I see it, as if the shine is too intense, like I've been out in the sun too long. The shin of the snaps on the blue vinyl seat back match the gleaming hollow tubes that support my father's dead legs, keeps them from splaying out too far. Three tries and he manages to get the thing turned around. When he pivots the chair to get a look at me I hardly recognized him. He forces a smile, tries to sound enthusiastic. "Hiya, Rock! How's my boy? Let me get a look at you" He's lost a lot of weight. His face is so gaunt. His eyes are sunken ships, his cheeks collapsed sails. I recognize him, but just barely.

He's only half alive, I see now. Not just his legs. Everything, his body, his personality, has changed, diminished, become less than, the way a shadow is less than a person. "It's good to see you, son. Did you miss your old pop? Huh? Come here and give your daddy a hug." Once his arms are around me, I cry again, only the second time since the shooting. I can't help it. "It'll be okay, son, don't worry. All this will work out."

What does he mean, 'Will work out?' I can't imagine what he means.

He never breathes another word to me about the whole affair; my mother's murder, anything. He never tries to explain. I wonder if his legs will get better, or if we're still in the army. If he mentions my mother it is in passing. Forget the guy who killed her, who put him in the chair. He is never mentioned. He doesn't even mention the chair, so I don't, either.

"Come on now, stop crying and get your old man a beer, goddamn it. I've been dying for a beer the whole time I was in the hospital. Go on now. Grab me a beer and get my medicine; it's in the bathroom on the counter. Get yourself one, too, if you want. A beer, I mean. You stay away from that medicine now, hear?"

Later, I watch him sit in front of the television, in that chair, and drink his beer. I wonder, *what are we going to do now?* I think of Mrs. Boil right next door. Just about now she'd be getting ready for bed. "You'll have to do a little more around the house from now on, cleaning up and so on, until I learn to navigate a little," he says, laughing a little, twisting the wheels on either side of him. He's feeling better, relaxing. That beer's kicking-in, I think, kicking in big-time. I don't know yet about how the pills affect him.

"But you can handle it, right little man? So your old man doesn't have to stay in the hospital? Sure you can; I knew I could count on you. If any body asks you just tell 'em we're doing just fine."

❦   ❦   ❦

The transition from a life with an alcoholic, promiscuous mother to a life with an invalid, bitter father happens—bang!—Like a slap in the head. It's not too meaningful, but memorable none-the-less. Some old soul, older and harder, more capable and controlled than mine, possesses my child's body, begins to live my retched life for me. My father's hospitalization, his surgery, his recuperation, changes my life as much as if I had been the one shot in the chest. Learning to take care of him, learning all of those things, seems to take place in that instant when I cross the lawn from Mrs. Boil's front door to the crime scene.

If her husband returned from his tour of duty I never saw him. Coming home from school one day, passing their house, I notice it is empty. I never see Mrs. Boil again. Who knows if her husband died overseas? Who knows if she finds someone else, has children, or dies of breast cancer? Seeing the empty house makes me feel sad, but not unhappy; I know, all at once, that I can give her something now, something special now that I will never see her again, a gift in return for all she's given me. You see, for Mrs. Boil, in my mind, anyway, she is forever young.

Soon after, we move to Savannah so my father can be closer to the VA hospital. After that, I take care of my father, I become his wife, his nurse, his only companion. I take care of him like this. Everything. Everyday. For years.

My father's catheter empties urine from his spastic bladder into a collection bag. I empty the bag. When he's constipated, I dig stool out of him with a gloved finger. The smell makes me gag; I vomit almost every day. The enemas should keep him regular, but they never work; he never seems able to hold them in. His bedsores, painted with a paste of talcum powder mixed with Milk of Magnesia, never heal. Some nurse suggests plastic surgery when I find part of the right buttocks eaten away to the bone, but my father refuses any surgery. He hates going back into the hospital. My small interventions help to keep him free. By watching the VA clinic nurses on our rare visits I learn their tricks, all of their invasive techniques.

❧   ❧   ❧

From time to time, I catch myself looking. The scene: a nurse cares for a wasted old male patient, one who sacrifices his need for dignity in favor of a bowel evacuation or a voided bladder; one who forfeits his need for modesty but gains a tube or line, something handy for him to receive morselized food or medication, when the more natural orifice stops accepting such necessities. When the nurses notice me watching, I smile. They think they've caught me flirting. That's not it. I let them believe it is, but it's not. They are used to that kind of behavior, all the whistles and stares in the night, in the middle of a long call. That they understand. They come to expect the harassment. Sometimes, if you treat them right, with courtesy and respect, they might even encourage you. "Hey Rocky, as long as you're here, why don't you come down to Three West and watch me change Mr. Gorky's Nasogastric tube. He's in Trindelenburg, the head of his bed is almost touching the floor, and I have to bend way over to do it."

"Now, why would a tired old surgical resident like me, with something like twenty hours left to go in his shift, spend what little free time he has doing something like that?"

"Oh, well, didn't you notice? You were standing there, I thought you might have noticed. Well, maybe because I'm not wearing any underwear? Maybe something like that?"

They would never understand me standing there to catch a glimpse of a man who might remind me of my poor father.

✤   ✤   ✤

As I left the train, on the way to the car, something happened. The last thing I remembered was bending down to pick something up off the ground, my tie or something and shazaam! I woke up in the emergency room of a hospital. The talking heads stared down at me. They spoke in low voices, muted tones, murmurs, sounds one hear's when coming from a confessional. They looked down at me all at once. "You've had a seizure," someone said, a conclusion I would not have come to on my own; I wouldn't have grasped the concept.

I've had a seizure.

"Try and rest."

He must be a doctor, only a doctor could say something that stupid.

He was a doctor, an intern who had yet to learn that to tell someone who's just had a seizure "try and rest" is like telling a brown bear in winter, "try and hibernate." There is nothing to do but rest after the uncoordinated electrical discharges spread over the brain causing every muscle in the body to twitch like a marionette. Tonic clonic it's called, grand mal. The force is so great that, at times, it can break bones. Rest? You bet I did. My eyes closed and I went right off to sleep. Peaceful. Sometime later, after they explained everything to me, an intern showed up and asked me the usual questions. Vince taught me the best way to deal with such situations. "Tell the truth." The concept goes something like this: There exists elements of truth, you see, in every lie, and lies in every truth. It's all in how you look at it. In attorney thing, he said.

I answered. I told the truth.

Yes, I was a doctor. No, I was not working (not at the moment of my seizure, anyway); I was on a research sabbatical (for about two hours) during my surgical training at All Saints. No, there was no need to call them. Yes, I took drugs, narcotics, for a back injury I sustained lifting a patient (true for every surgeon). No, I don't have a prescription; I used samples from the clinic. Yes, I had a family history of seizures (I guess, if you went back far enough). Yes, this was my first seizure (unless you count what had happened on the train).

The doctors gave me a good going over. The staff knew I'd be expecting certain tests, checking them off in my head: EKG, CT Scan, MRI, sleep EEG, blood work. Doctors are notorious problem patients, but I was on my best behavior. I didn't raise any eyebrows when they suggested the medical student do a rectal exam. They didn't ask any questions that were too embarrassing, like, for instance, what are those marks on your arm. Even-Steven. Don't ask-don't tell. My doctor and I didn't quite wink at one another, not exactly, more like professional courtesy, like he understood and decided to let it slide. "You've had a reactive seizure." The stupid one again, the one who liked to state the obvious? "As you know, doctor, an exposure to some kind of, oh, toxic agent, shall we say lowered your seizure threshold. If you have any idea…" (At this point he stopped, covered his mouth, and coughed into his fist a time or two to clear his throat,) "…what that substance might be. I suggest you rid yourself of it."

I looked at him as he turned from the window and headed out the door. We were co-conspirators in a plot called silence. We never saw each other again.

Vince covered for me at work: personal business to attend to; something to do with the military. Who lied about the military? Administration knew I joined the army reserve, a direct commission, captain in the medical corps, in a surgeon's slot, no less. Surgeon, right; a warm body on a list of names in a paper army was more like it. Picking up the baton for my old man and getting a check for it in the process seemed a pretty good deal. Vince told them I had ticket stubs and orders to prove I'd been activated for something secret, no way I could call, very hush-hush. I could tell them but I'd have to kill them, the whole lot-of-em. He told me this, as I lay there in my hospital bed and I stared at him, the cheap detergent and extra Clorox from the over-laundered sheets soaking into the rind that was fast replacing my skin and making it crawl.

"Are you fucking crazy?"

He laughed and laughed.

When he told me he knew where he could get a set of orders cut, I flipped.

"Jesus Christ, Vince!"

"Just for a couple of days, of course." He knew a general and a couple of colonels, friends of his father's. "Don't sweat it," he told me, "it's no big deal.

Vince had balls as big as pineapples

"Look, you stupid prick, it's my little ass that gets dropped from the residency and packed off to Fort Leavenworth, my epaulets in one hand and my gold braids in the other, if things go sour. No fucking way. I won't do it."

"Okay."

"I mean it, Vince."

"All right."

"How the hell could you pull something like that off, anyway?"

"You just let me worry about that."

❧   ❧   ❧

After twenty-four terrifying hours, I hobbled, still light-headed, out of the Our Sister's of Saint Nicholas Hospital, on Broad Street, downtown. The move from the wheelchair to the car about killed me I was so weak. After, leaning on the door handle for a few moments, the feeling of nausea lifted. I rolled down the window and restrained my urge to puke. "I'm not sure I can work today. I feel like shit."

Vince laughed, "You ain't going to work today. You ain't going to work until next Monday."

I looked at him.

"And," he went on, "you'll probably get the Community Support Award from the hospital this year for your service to God and country."

"Jesus, what the hell are you talking about? I don't feel like playing guessing games here, Vince. If you've got something to say, say it. Otherwise, take me to the hospital, and I'll tell them I just got done with my Agent Orange training, or something."

He just guffawed and chortled. Then, he handed me the letter.

Addressed to Capt. Rocky VanSlyke, USAR-MC. The envelope looked authentic, official, from the government.

I opened it and read:

TO:

    Capt. Rocky VanSlyke

    USAR-MC

FROM:

    HQ 1st Army

    MRRAB (Medical Ready Reserve Augmentation Battalion)

    Ft. George G. Mead, Md.

Sir:

You are ordered to report to Active Duty at the above station no later then 1200 hrs. on (blank). Your duty will continue until (blank), where upon you will return to your point of departure, and be relieved from such duty.

    Brigadier General Walter J. Puppnick

    HQ 1st Army

    79th ARCOM

    Commanding

"What the hell is this?"

"Your orders. What does it look like?"

I read the paper again and looked up. "What the hell for?"

"Uniforms."

"Uniforms?"

"Yep. The Army's changing the Class B uniform, and you're going down to the Ft. Mead PX to get you a couple."

"You're kidding."

"You've been ordered to active duty, and you're drawing captain's pay the whole time."

"Jesus, Vince, how the hell did you arrange all this?"

"I have my ways. That's how I sold the hospital on the idea; they're not paying you for the time you've been out, but you don't give a shit about that."

"You put this together in twenty-four hours?"

"A couple of phone calls." He snapped his fingers.

"So who's…" I looked down at the letter, "General Puppnick?"

"Well," he smiled, "he's my stepfather."

"Your stepfather?"

"He's an old army buddy of my father's, like I said. He knew my mother for years. He was after her the whole time, but she would never put out until after she and my father were divorced. All that Catholic shit, you know. She wouldn't marry him until my old man was dead and buried.

"Anyway, I told him you've been in the reserves for over a year and that those sons-of-bitches at the hospital have been fucking with you about your, ah hem, participation. You haven't even been able to get down and buy your damn uniforms, you poor bastard, you. I didn't even have to ask him. He just called some corporal or something and said, 'Cut this doc some fucking orders!'" I didn't even have to ask! Jesus, I amaze myself sometimes," he laughed.

"What the hell am I going to tell the hospital when I get back? I sure as hell can't tell them I got ordered to active duty to buy uniforms. Can I?"

"Who cares! Don't tell them anything. You can tell them to suck your dick, for all I care. Tell 'em it's classified and if you tell them, you'll have to kill every last one of the sons-of-bitches. You just flash those orders if they give you any shit. Have 'em put a copy in your personal file, though. Be sure you do that."

I could not believe my ears.

"And if I were you, I'd offer to make up your time on the call schedule," he said. "It's just a suggestion. Then they won't have a damn thing to bitch about, not if you make up the call."

"I always make up my call, Vince. You know me. I take more goddamn call then anybody else in the whole God-forsaken place and you and everybody else knows it!"

"I know. I know, but I'm just saying."

"Okay. Fuck." I shook my head.

We both sat there in the car for a while to let that little bit of bluster hanging in the air dissipate, then I said, "So, what do we do now? I feel like shit. I'm not sure I can travel."

"Well, you probably feel like shit because you're in withdrawal. You came off that stuff too fast." He reached in his pocket and pulled out a 2 x 4 inch vial with a purple label, "Go on, fix yourself up. You just leave the driving to ol' Vince."

"Where the hell did you get that? Never mind." I put my hands up. "I don't even want to know."

"Don't worry about it. I took care of it."

"Fuck it. Give it here."

I sat back and looked at him as I rolled the vial around in my hand. We were already heading for the freeway, 95 South toward Wilmington. I held the vial up, tapped the windshield and said, "Vince, isn't that the place where they put that bronze statue of Stallone? The Spectrum?"

He just snickered.

       ❧   ❧   ❧

The Post-Exchange (PX) at Fort George G. Mead sold more then uniforms. It wasn't just a clothing store, not by a long shot; they sold everything. The place looked like a Walmart: rows upon rows of dry goods, many of which are just as over priced as one would find in any discount store. With the U.S. Army Battle Dress Uniform pants and blouse under one arm, a pair of Corcoran jump boots under the other, and a hand full of subdued insignias that needed to be sewn on the sleeves and pockets, I made my way to the checkout line as Vince perused the aisles. For some reason the thought of him wandering, unable to buy a damn thing, made me feel most excellent. *I'm the one with the commission; I'm the one with the I.D.; I'm the one who can buy things around here, not you.*

With my head still spinning from all the activity at the checkout I stopped at customer service, stapled the receipts for the uniforms to a copy of my orders, hailed Vince, then headed over to check in at the Medical Ready Reserve Augmentation Battalion Headquarters (MRRAB-HQ). After locating it among one of the many nondescript buildings that dotted my photocopied map, we hopped in the car and headed across the post. A soldier sat at the door of what looked to be a simple office, modest for the headquarters of the MRRAB.

"Captain…?" The Specialist 4 at the reception desk said as he scanned the orders I handed him. "I'm sorry, can you pronounce your name for me, sir?"

"VanSlyke. Captain Rocky VanSlyke."

"Yes, sir, of course. Sorry, sir."

"My mission? Why, the uniforms," I said, holing up the bags that held my purchases.

"If you say so, sir." Spec. 4 Reynolds said waving a hand at me, "What ever you say, we believe you." Reynolds set the orders on the typewriter.

"Where do I sign in?"

"Sign in? Oh, you don't need to sign in or anything. We're a little bit, um, looser with you doctors." He looked up and smiled. "You all have such busy schedules and all. We understand all that. I'll just type in the dates," He rolled the orders into his typewriter, "And put a copy of your orders in your 201 file; it will look good when they review your file for your next promotion. You should be up for major in six months or so. How long you planning to be with us?"

"Just over the weekend."

"No problem, sir." After he finished typing he copied my orders and handed them back to me. "You're good to go, sir. Enjoy your weekend. Stop by again and see us. We don't get a chance to meet our doctors too often, you being so busy and all."

Vince and I drove to Annapolis and checked out the Naval Academy the following day. At Vince's suggestion, I took the opportunity to try on my new uniform (sans the proper pins, patches and insignias).

"The uniform's the important part, who needs all that other junk."

"That other junk *is* the uniform, Vince. I look like a jerk."

Vince just laughed.

"Ha, ha; big joke, right? It's my ass that gets court-martialed."

Vince grinned. "There's a pharmacy I know of in the area. My guess is they'll fill one for us."

"Let's go. Am I stopping you? No. So, what are you waiting on…"

We drove sixty-four miles out of our way, but he guessed right. The pharmacy filled the prescriptions, even on my out-of-state pads. Later that day, we pulled up in front of the Baltimore train station. Vince stopped the car in a zone marked, "No parking. Loading and Unloading of Passengers Only." I looked over at him. A lizard smile looked back.

"What?"

"You need a return ticket."

"For what?"

"Think. If you were supposed to be on duty in Maryland you're going to heed a return train ticket dated today to match the one from two days ago, right?"

"If you say so."

"Go on, take the train back, and I'll meet you at the station in Philly. You'll have all the loose ends tied up."

I got out of the car.

"Oh, you'd better leave your stuff. You don't want those pads and stuff on you. Somebody might grab them."

"Oh, okay." I handed him my bag.

"Here," he said, handing me twenty dollars and a few pills, "Get yourself something to read. Prop up and relax. I'll see you in a few hours."

As he drove away the wind blew me inside the terminal trailing rain or snow, my hands jammed in my pockets, full of pills, my shoulders jammed against the revolving door. The Baltimore station troubled me. My uniform, new, not tailored, and lacking proper insignia, hung on me like new clothes on an old scarecrow. My skin slithered under the unlaundered uniform shirt. The whole-unmatched ensemble felt stiff, scratchy, and ill-fitting. Standing in line to buy a ticket on the next train back to Philadelphia made me squirm. A frantic, terror-filled moment, helped me locate my wallet. With the ticket in hand and a copy of the *Sunday New York Times*, I found a corner and hid. A hard bench and forty-five minutes kept me company until my departure.

My head ached.

My stomach churned.

My skin oscillated cold to hot.

The pills!

The beer washed the pills down but didn't stop my gags.

❦   ❦   ❦

The ride back, a parade of smokestacks, abandoned buildings, and the rocking rhythm of passing train trestles, took forever. The pieces fell together. Vince left with the Demerol. The excursion back took a long time.

CHAPTER 15

❀

*M*y father dies slowly, in degrees, like a corpse cooling, from the time of his shooting. He drinks a lot and takes pain pills by the handful. Most days I give him all the booze and drugs he asks for. When his bowels get too bound up I hold off on the narcotics for a day, two if I can coax him through with alcohol. The constipation caused by the medicine makes his digging his stool out of him by hand, more difficult. If I don't do the manual disempaction his belly gets distended and he begins to vomit, then he'll have to go to the hospital.

Sooner or later, he begs. "Son," he says with tears in his voice, "Son, don't leave me this way. You can't leave me this way, Son. Your daddy can't take the pain. Be a good boy and give daddy his medicine. Be a good boy, now." So, I give in and give him the morphine.

When I talk with the doctors at the VA hospital about how much pain medicine he uses, they just nod their heads, listen attentively, then ruffle my hair. "Your poor daddy has a bad injury, there son. There's not much more we can do for him."

They keep writing the junk for him; my father the junkie. Who am I to tell him he can't have his drugs? At least he quiets down, somewhat, when he's high. At least he's not so angry.

Sometimes he has a far off look in his glassy eyes and smiles to himself. I watch him sit in his chair in front of the television with a beer. The bottle hangs there in his hand, its amber contents almost as flat as his expression. If I ask him what he thinks about, his expression changes, his smile becomes a scowl as murky as a thunderhead. His moods, then, are dark enough to blot out the sun. Sometimes he screams at me, sometimes he hits me, then, he cries.

❧   ❧   ❧

Even in college, with a few dollars in my pocket from flipping pizzas and a chest full of muscles from swimming every free moment, I was a loner. Women terrified me. The finesse of courtship and lure bewildered me. The women in my classes ignored me. At work, if I spied any telltale signs of interest from my female patrons, it was directed at the kneaded dough I sent spinning into the air. If I tossed the pizzas way in the air and caught them behind my back before the dough fell to the floor, I might get an appreciative glance. That trick always drew a laugh and a little applause. Once inside the store, though, the women got all chatty and lingered at the counter with their friends until the pie arrived, piping-hot, in the box, then they just left. If it were not for the dawdling conversation and occasional furtive glance, I might have thought myself invisible. Maybe later, I thought.

Oh, I got razzed all right.

"VanSlyke, you fag, you're never going to get any pussy with your nose stuck in that book all the time."

"Fuck you, Avery. I'm saving myself for marriage."

Some customer's daughter or co-worker's sister always lived in my head, but the social complexities of the whole dating thing, out in the real world, bewildered me. Long, involved fantasy relationships sufficed for me, (that, and a little soap in the palm of my hand). Pinning my ass against inside of a shower stall and dry humping my hand took care of it; dry humping and binge drinking. Nothing relieves sexual tension better then a good bender, if you're willing to put up with the hangovers (and boy was I willing).

❦   ❦   ❦

Avery, my boyhood friend, and I met up again in.

Avery's father finished his army career in Vietnam with a bullet in the head, a victim of friendly fire, but his family finished up in Georgia, like mine. It's like that with folks in the army. They all seem to end up living wherever they were living when their soldier musters out. You run into them in cities nearest the army post where they finished their last assignment.

Walking across the campus one day I heard my name.

"Hey, VanSlyke, you honky mother-fucker, why you be messin' up the bucolic surroundin's of this fine institution of higher learnin' with them baggy-ass pants hanging off yo skinny white booty-ass? And what's with that long greasy flaxen you call a doo?"

"Avery!"

"In the flesh, my brother. Where the hell you been all these years?"

Avery became a black man. None of that "Afro-American" shit for Avery. He was black. Avery's father got promoted to colonel at just about the time my old man got popped in my mother's bedroom when she got herself dismembered. When Avery told me his father had been killed during his tour of duty in Vietnam, I said that my father died in the war, also. He knew I lied. He told me so one night when we drank enough. He said everybody in the fucking army knew my parents, knew who my father was. Sargent Slaughter, they called him, and my mother was the headless whore. Avery kept quiet about the names; he kept it to himself for my sake, but then, one day, it just came out. "I'm sorry, brother," he said when he told me the story, and hung his head.

"No biggy," I said. "I figured it would be something like that, bro."

He put his hand on my shoulder. "That's cool, man, that's cool, my Army brother."

Avery grew up around white people in the army and we both grew up around the army, so we kind of hit it off again right away when we met up at Georgia Tech. Blacks and whites did not hang out together, not in the south, not at the time. Avery didn't care. We found each other again, two misfits, though for different reasons.

"The army gives us a bond, you know? Fuck this racial bullshit. Let's go smoke some grass."

We smoked dope in my dorm room late at night and talked about how Avery should become a 'walk on' for the football team.

"Fuck that noise."

"No shit, Avery. You remember how you used to outrun the MPs after we stole the candy and cigarettes from old man Dilbert's place? You're like the wind, my man."

"Fuck that. I want to go to medical school."

Avery was quite smart.

"What does playing football have to do with medical school?"

Avery rolled his eyes. "I'm not gonna bust my hump so the white man can get some laughs. Medical school, man. That's what's happenin'. Boy, sometimes you are the stupidest, fucking, honky. God, nigger. Lord-have-mercy."

We laughed and laughed, drank beer and whiskey on the weekends. Talked about getting me laid. Avery had a lot of girlfriends, but I never did.

"Fuck that. I want to go to medical school."

"Fuck what, Rocky? What on God's-green-Earth could fucking have to do with going to medical school?"

I rolled my eyes. "Sometimes you are the stupidest, fucking nigger-man…"

We laughed and laughed.

We were going to go to medical school together, but it just didn't work out.

Avery and I free based cocaine once or twice, just before Richard Pryor lit himself up and made freebasing so popular. Avery told me he didn't like it very much but smoking was cheap and helped him stay awake. When he smoked cocaine, he could study longer or drink more, so he planned to keep smoking it. I told him I didn't like the stuff for the same reasons and that he could have the shit. I needed sleep.

Avery skipped too many classes in our junior year, got some girl pregnant, a pretty little Asian thing, and dropped out of school a semester before graduation. He took a semester off, until the baby was delivered. He seemed happy and excited, but for some reason, he never went back to school. I saw him once that last semester. He looked skinny. When I asked him how he liked being a father, he said he'd been working a lot.

"She lost the baby, man, then blew out to California to finish school."

The last I saw of him, he stopped to ask if I could spare ten bucks. "Sure. Of course, man. Here."

He'd get it back to me.

"Forget about it."

I didn't ask him what he wanted it for. I never saw him again after that.

The bang, bang, bang momentum of the train cars colliding as the train pulled into the thirtieth street station in Philadelphia woke me. The cars wrenched back and forth against the couplings as they adjusted to the engine's flux in speed. My previous arrival a few days prior bubbled into my memory like froth growing on draft beer flowing from a tapped keg. My unfinished, disheveled uniform hung about me like a collapsed tent. After hauling myself up and stumbling out of the train, I ascended the long stairway from the hellish track with as much military bearing as I could muster. Upon arriving at the top of the crowd of passengers I rode crested and broke on the expansive, metamorphic rock desert of the main floor, its great alterations of limestone and dolomite, desiccating my senses as I scanned for Vince's moon pie face. *Lawrence of Arabia,* I thought, *Gunga Din.*

Once out in the open, all the headlights of all the cars in all the streets surrounding the station diverged, white and yellow beams crossing one against the other in all directions, heading away from me. The colors of the night all melted into gray. A moanful horn beeped twice. Vince eased the Caddy up beside me. The passenger door popped open, and I sat down hard.

"Doctor," he said, "how was your trip?"

Sometime later—God only knows how long—Vince dropped me off at home. Before morning, the phone rang, but, as I picked up the receiver I heard Karla banging on the door. How could this be? I thought, staring at the black plastic object in my hand, I was just speaking with her a moment ago. Then, the door opened. I could not see her in the dark apartment, but I heard her heels, tap, tap, tap across the floor, and felt her anger in every step. Then, a blinding flash and searing pain stabbed my eyes.

"Jesus, turn that thing off, will you!"

"Rocky?" Her face was a star burst, shining white, a featureless outline, a fallen angel in the too-bright artificial light, "Rocky, are you having an affair?"

"Turn it off, goddamn it!"

"What?"

"The goddamned light! Turn it off."

"Okay, okay, Jesus…" She flipped the switch back down.

"God Almighty."

"Are you?"

"Am I what?" I struggled out of my pants; I must have gone to bed fully dressed. "Ouch, goddamn it!"

"Having an affair."

"Jesus, Karla, I'm too damned tired for this shit."

"It isn't shit! It's a legitimate question. I have a right to know."

"Isn't that your trick? Having affairs?

She stared back at me.

"Well, isn't it?"

She didn't look angry or afraid, just tired, the way my mother had looked after a few bad days, when a drink or a pill were all she wanted in this world, but a few hours of sleep was what she really needed.

She never answered, just exhaled and took a step back.

"I'm sorry."

"What's wrong with you, Rocky?"

"I don't know," I said, and I didn't.

CHAPTER 16

✿

$\mathcal{M}$y father says something to me when I get home from school, but I don't understand him. Another hospital visit has left him dazed with grief or pain, or both. I know he's not right. He never mumbles unless he's fucked up badly.

"Come here and give your old man a kiss."

Dull-eyed and groggy like this, I do not know him. Moving to his side, I clutch the cold metal arm of his chair, pull myself up on my tiptoes and do as he says, but it's like kissing a stranger. If any part of him still exists, I can't imagine where it might be. I live with a stranger.

At night, after he's ready for bed, we watch television. It's a ritual. Most of the time it's okay, except for Thursday nights when we watch *Ironside*.

"*Perry Mason* with training wheels," He says, and laughs.

I think, *He'll enjoy the show. It's something we can watch together.*

He appreciates it, at first, the irony. My father gets the message: You can still be whole, but then the comments start, bitter ones. "Ha! Maybe I should do that for a living. Shit, I liked this guy better when he could walk." Then he sniggers a laugh full of venom and pain. If he's really hopped up or drunk, he starts in with, "Oh, yeah, right! Like anybody could do that kind of shit from a fucking wheelchair!"

Then the empty cans start to fly. "Who thinks this shit up, anyway? I hate this fucking show. It's total bullshit!"

Every week he insists on watching the show. His rants scare me, but I never say anything to him about it. I just sit there and make sure he doesn't hurt himself. I decide we will watch something else the next week. We never do. If I pick a different station, he always changes it back. It's the only time he mentions a wheelchair.

One time he throws a full beer can the TV tube and it explodes. At first, I think the whole thing is pretty funny, the idea that he had broken the picture tube, the splash of the beer and the spewing foam. After the initial shock we both laugh. *Elvis*, I think, *I live with Elvis, fucking, Presley*. Then, I think of how he will react in the morning, how I'm going to have to clean things up after I get him to bed, how he will blame me tomorrow

Now, I've got to figure a way to get another TV.

          ❈   ❈   ❈

"Where the fuck have you been?" Zack asked.

"I can't talk about it."

"Not that, I know about that. I'm talking about this morning. I've been paging you for an hour."

"You know about it?"

"What, that army bullshit? Hell yes! Everybody knows about it. I want to know about this morning. I've been on for three days straight, man. I need some relief!"

"I'm sorry, Zack, I just got in this morning. I haven't even slept yet. I just dropped my stuff and changed. I came right over."

Zack softened, "Well, can I get out of here an hour or so early today?"

"Absolutely. You can leave now if you want to. I'll cover your cases. Go and get some rest."

His eyes got big and then narrowed. "I better not. Schwartz gives me a case every now and then, and I need vascular cases. I may cut out when the OR's done, though."

"Fine. Just let me know before you do."

"Okay, well…" He nodded as he turned. Over his shoulder he mumbled, "Welcome back." Then he stopped and turned back again. He looked broader, stronger, and taller, like pictures I had seen of my father when he was a boy. He hadn't changed his hairstyle; he still wasn't wearing socks. I even wondered if maybe he quit smoking cigarettes, but I saw the familiar bulge of the pack at his left breast. He took a step closer, close enough for me to hear him without raising his voice, for me to smell burnt tobacco on his breath. It was obvious he had something to say but changed his mind.

"What?"

"Forget it," he said as he pulled back. "I'll talk to you later."

"About what?"

"Forget it, I said. It can wait."

His eyes focused on my pupils, examining them. "Look, Rock," he went on, "I don't want to get involved with your personal life, but people around here are…"

"Are what?"

"Starting to talk."

"Listen, I can't help it if the fucking army…"

"Oh, cut out the army crap, will you? I'm not talking about that and you know it!"

I thought, *If he wants the truth, I just might give it to him.* I was just about ready to talk, but, then he looked away. "I don't know what you mean."

He looked relieved, then angry again, then resigned. "Yes, you do. And so does everybody else around here with his eyes open. You're never dressed right. You're either not here or you're here for days on end. You're either nowhere or you're everywhere. Either way, people are noticing."

We looked at each other for a moment. "When the hell do I have time to put on street clothes?"

"You've stopped answering your pages. You're hanging around with your attorney friend, what's his name, Fatso? Look, it's none of my business, okay? I just hope you don't get hurt."

"Listen, I don't know what the hell you're talking about." I glanced at my watch. Want to go burn one real quick?"

Zack stepped back, tense. "Yes, you do." After a moment's hesitation he brightened. "And no I can't. Got to go. My public awaits." He smiled at me for the first time, clasped my shoulder, and waved as he departed. "Look, if you ever need anything, you know, you want to talk or something, just let me know, okay?"

"Sure," I said.

❦　　　　　❦　　　　　❦

Later that day, in the O.R., I asked the scrub nurse for some "0" silk suture. When I had trouble grasping the needle driver Dr. Waterman, the attending surgeon, scolded me yet again. "Hey, Rock, Goddamn it, look at your hands! How many times have I told you about that shaking? Jesus."

"I know," taking a moment to rub my hands together and smooth the latex gloves across each finger, "I had a little too much coffee this morning—Knife—I took care of this guy in the unit last night—Snap, please. Thank you. I drank coffee—Cut, please. Thank you—about 2 A.M. I'm going to have to cut down on that stuff—Another '0' Proline on a cutting needle, please. Okay lets run this closure—sorry."

"Then you'd better stop drinking coffee altogether, if it makes you shake that much. You've got a hell of an intention tremor there. This is the last time I'm going to tell you. Fix it, or I'm pulling you out, understand?"

"Okay, I will, Doctor Waterman. Sorry. It's just that—"

"You better stop whatever it is you are doing. If you're going to work on my patients, you better damn-well stop."

"Yes, sir. I understand. I will. Thank you for pointing it out to me. It will never happen again."

❧   ❧   ❧

"This is Dr. VanSlyke." I groaned, "Let me speak to Mr. Buddy. I wasn't merely shaking. I was sick.

"One moment please," the voice said, "I can transfer you now…"

"Hello?"

"Vince?"

"At your service. With whom am I speaking?"

"Vince, it's me. I didn't know who else to call."

"Rock? Jesus, are you Okay? I didn't recognize your voice! You sound like shit."

"I feel really bad."

"You got anything?"

"Not a thing."

"Where are you?"

"My on-call room."

"You need something to take the edge off?"

"Either that, or I'm going to end up in the ER"

"What ER? Where?"

"Where? What da ya mean where? Here, that's where, at our place. I can't even move!"

"Good God Almighty, don't do that."

"Can you come down and get a script?"

"Don't worry about it. You want pills or what?"

"Not pills. They won't work fast enough. I've got to get on my feet quick, before something pops over here and I'm up all night operating…"

"On my way," he said. "Don't move."

"Thanks, pal."

"Anytime. Anytime."

CHAPTER 17

❀

*I*n the evening, after the dishes are done, before the television shows begin, I can sneak out for a few minutes and wander by the Port of Savannah. I am thirteen or fourteen, not much older, still thin and molting. Fear, is my escort, my constant companion, my playmate. For a while I am not sequestered in the house. Out in the evening world I pass by like time, walking.

It's like a morgue, that house. Something I hear my parents say in my present memory. "This place is a morgue. Let's get out of here."

The real morgue is coming; the real morgue is here; I live in it.

With a pack of my father's cigarettes rolled up in one sleeve I head out to wander. First I pass by the Old Guy, the one next door in the wide-brimmed Panama hat who always beckons.

"Hey Kid!" he says, waving his arms, and I just know he wants something from me, so I pretend he's just waving and return the salute.

"Hey yourself, Old Guy!"

I end up down by the water smoking the cigarettes in small puffs. The white-blue smoke of the North Carolina broad leaf moves in and out of me, across my pearly, baby-white teeth, but I don't inhale, I don't know how, this is just experimentation. The gas in my mouth presses against my pink cheeks, but I don't breathe in. The smoke just rolls around on my tongue, bitter and burning, biting and smooth. The fumes sting like a mouth full of bees until I learn to take a real drag. Smoking and drinking takes some getting used to.

To see me walk down the sidewalk, scuff at the gravel, look up at the sky, you might mistake me for a street urchin, some missing person, a face from a milk carton, a hustler, maybe, or someone who might turn up on a tabloid talk show years later to tell how, as a child, he sold himself for money. But I am not so lost or misplaced as that. I am not homeless. I am not for sale. Still, the cars slow to take a peek at me, to look me over. I roll my shoulders forward, scowl, and walk faster. In the drivers' expressions I can read their thoughts. Right neighborhood, the men think, riding in their fancy cars. Right neighborhood, so what's wrong? These men glance in their rear view mirrors. Then I see the paranoia creep over them seeing a cop car waiting down a side street. Their expressions grow pallid. They glance again, then, speed away. Too bad. Nice looking kid.

Assholes, I think, then I wonder why they pick on me.

❦   ❦   ❦

"The phone's been ringing," I said, because nothing else came to mind.

"Oh." Vince smiled. He sat on the edge of the bed in my call room like a priest hearing a confession. He even folded his hands in his lap. The room seemed warm enough, but I felt cold. The window, opaque with frost, appeared black except for a ghost-like reflection of myself. Vince crossed one leg over the other, as did the cop who interviewed at my parents house after the shooting, an ankle over his knee. The sight of him sitting like struck me funny and I snickered. His expression, a little faraway, or hopeless, seemed odd. I slid down in the chair next to the window.

"What's so funny?"

"Nothing," I said waving a hand at him, "Never mind."

"Look, uh…" He leaned forward, closer to my desk lamp. When he did, I saw his moon face shining. He leaned back, abruptly then, as if the luminescence burned him. As I watched him, tried to listen, his words seemed garbled; he rambled. ("Blah, blah, blah…").

"Look," I said, getting frustrated, "Get to the point."

"Do you really need to stay here tonight?" he said at last.

"Jesus, Vince, I'm on call."

"So what?"

I couldn't believe my ears.

"What do you think this is?" I looked around. "What does this look like to you, the fucking Hilton? Vince, I'm cracking up in here, okay? I need a fucking fix."

"That's what I'm saying. That's it exactly!" He leaned forward again. "You can handle things by phone, can't you?"

"Sure I can handle things by phone, UNLESS I HAVE TO FUCK-ING OPERATE ON SOMEBODY! You know, I'm on call, right Vince? You know what 'on-call' means, don't you? It means I have to be here if there's an emergency."

The shiver in my voice communicated my fear better then the words. "Haven't you got the stuff?"

"Look, you don't need to be around here all night. Why don't we just slide out and come prop up with me somewhere comfortable?'

"What about the stuff? Where's the stuff?"

"I thought I'd come over and get you first. You know, see if you wanted to get the hell out of here." He stopped again and looked around. "This is a dammed awful place for you to be holed up, feel-ing the way you do."

"I called you four hours ago, Vince! Four fucking hours!"

"I know. I got tied up. I'm sorry, but let's get outta here."

"Tied up? Tied up with what?"

"Listen. Listen," he said again. "Look. Here." He handed me two white pills. "This should tide you over until we get that script filled."

I got up and downed the pills with a hand-full of water.

"Now call the operator. Tell her you're going to run out to your car to get some books or something. Tell her if she doesn't get you in the room, that she can page you, but that it might take you a moment to call her back."

I hadn't thought of that, so I picked up the phone and called. "No problem," said the operator, "No problem, Dr. VanSlyke, and good to have you back. We're all very proud of you, you know for your, uh, pardon me, you know, for your service. I hope I'm not giving away any secrets, or..."

"Thank you," I smiled. Big joke. Then I didn't feel so good again.

"That's better," Vince said when he saw the new look on my face. "Now come on. We don't have all night."

CHAPTER 18

❀

"Where have you been? Where have you been, Goddamn it? Rocky? Answer me!" The front door and the screen stands open. The foyer is cluttered with wood chips and street debris. He sits in his wheel chair, all silver hoops and tight spokes, now tarnished and broken, the blue vinyl almost black, stained and torn. My father sits in the doorway blocking my passage, trapping me between his anger and the danger outside, trapping me between a sinking derelict of a man and the river rat johns.

"I was talking to the Old Guy next door, you know, the one with the wide-brim Panama hat?"

"Liar. Your're a God-damned liar just like your mother!"

"I was siting in the Chevy—" I said, then, changing the subject, "I saw a rat, out by the ships, it was huge! It ran across my feet. It scared me." I point out into the street in the direction of the ship even though he can't see past me, out in the night. "Right over there."

"Serves you right, you little shit!" He spits. "Serves you right for sneaking out of here without doing your chores."

"I didn't sneak."

"Shut up." He wheels at me and I feel the sting of his hand across my face before I can move to get out of the way. "Shut up, you lying little son-of-a-bitch! You're just like your mother! I've been trying to find my medicine the whole time you've been out gallivanting." My face turns hot and tight where the slap lands. The pain sets my eye to watering. "Oh, you going to cry now, are you? You big baby. Get in here and find that medicine before I give you something to cry about. You make me sick. Look at ya…"

He rolls back into the gloom, the big silver wheels glinting in fading twilight as the chair wobbles from side to side. I don't hate him. How can I hate him after what he's been through? He can't help that he's sick. Later, he won't remember any of this, anyway. He'd deny it if I brought it up.

"Okay, Dad. Okay, I'll get it."

    🍁   🍁   🍁

As the big Cadillac pulled into the parking lot of Dom's Downtown Druggist, my hands sweated. The moisture in my palms matched the dewdrops on the inside of the windshield. "It's about time. Why we drove forty-five minutes to Wilmington, Delaware, escapes me." I had no idea what we were doing way the hell out here.

"I take it you have your pad with you?"

I held up the pad and shook it, then I peeled the top sheet off and handed it to him.

Vincent G. Buddy
Demerol 100 mg/cc
Sig. 150 mg/IM Q 4 h PRN pain
Disp. I multi dose vial (refill: none)

He chuckled, looked at it, and shook his head. "Doctor, this is a thing of beauty! You are something else. A real piece of work." He took the prescription and got out of the car. As an afterthought, he pointed at the telephone as if to say, *You know the drill.* I nodded. He glanced at the script one more time and mouthed, "This will only take an minute, then we'll go get ourselves fixed up." He gave me a thumbs up as he walked toward the store.

I waved, closed my eyes, and hoped that the phone wouldn't ring.

Festered questions floated past my soul like dead rats, bloated and rotting, drifting by in a canal. What the hell am I doing all the way out here? Why did I have to come with him at all? Why am I not back at the hospital where I'm supposed to be in case the shit hits the fan with a trauma or something? I let these thoughts float by undisturbed until they passed out of sight. My body pitched on what felt like waves of seasickness. I heard the car door open, and Vince crawled inside.

"Back so soon?" I said without even opening my eyes.

"Let's get out of here."

CHAPTER 19

"*H*ey, kid, isn't it past your bed time?"

The boy who says this knows my father is an invalid. "Shot by a wacko," he says. He knows about my father's wheelchair, and about my mother the whore. He knows my father never leaves the house. I am the only kid I know who comes home right after school every day to care for a parent. But, not today. Today I pretend I am free. I stay after school for a basketball game. Once in awhile, when I prepare his dinner before-hand and leave a note on the refrigerator or the oven for him to feed himself, I hang out. My father doesn't like it, but he doesn't grouse if I leave him enough medicine and come back late enough for him to have passed out.

Seasons are just a date on the calendar when you live in Savannah. Nothing changes. The weather's hot and it rains once in a while, then it cools off a little and the rain stops. That's about it (except for an occasional hurricane). Savannah in the fall can still swelter. On my walk home, the boy catches up to me. I am 15-years-old. This guy must be older. Seventeen maybe. I have never seen him before.

"Hey?"

I stop.

"Hey, what's your hurry, fag boy?" Another boy grabs my arms as the first one steps around blocking my way. The second one grabs me at the elbows and yanks my arms back before I can wriggle away.

"What the—" The first guy lets me have it, punches me hard in the stomach. My knees buckle. The cheap shot knocks the wind out of me and I just hang there as they finish roughing me up. When they let me go, I crumple into a pile. More tired out then hurt, I lay there catching my breath, feeling ashamed.

"Fag boy," the one who landed the punch says and the other one laughs.

My lower lip swells, and I taste blood in my mouth. My teeth hurt. When I don't get up, they leave. When I can breathe I get up and go home. It never occurs to me to ask myself why they beat me; it almost makes sense. But I've learned a lesson, too: stay *on your toes; never let down your guard.*

Months after they've forgotten all about me, that same boy asks me to do his homework for him. I am a good student; I work hard. Everybody knows that.

"Come on, be a pal, would'ya? If ya do good, you can hang out with us!" he says to his pals who all mug their agreement with him. "We'll all be buds. You can do my homework and we'll all look out for you, me and my other buds here." He elbows his buddies, who snicker into their hands, as if I won't notice.

"Sure!" I say, "Sure I will. Who wouldn't?" I play it up real big. "Just meet me in the empty garage on Channel Drive after school tomorrow. You know the one, across from the bridge, the concrete block one with the metal roof. I'll give it to you there. It's on the way home, and I don't want anyone else to see me do it. Know what I mean?"

"Oh, I know."

"You don't even have to pay me."

"Pay you?" He rolls his eyes at his pals and they all laugh. "Fuck, if you say so. Okay. Why not? Big secret." He turns away. "All hush

hush and everything, woo…" He wiggles his fingers back and forth between us. Big joke. Big laugh. "Sure, why not. But you better be there," he says, turning and threatening, "Be there or else, understand?"

"I'll be there. Don't you worry about that."

"You're the one who'd better worry, pal, if you don't show up, see? Just be there or else." Everybody gets a big laugh as they turn to go.

I smile, too. *Meet you? Sure I will. I remember you. Just you wait.*

The garage where I meet the boy smells of old tar and turpentine. There will be rats the size of ally cats in there. But I don't mind, not today, not with a couple of beers under my belt. (Stashing one or two, now and then, when the old man wasn't looking was a breeze). The place has been abandoned as long as I've lived here in Savannah. As my eyes adjust to the dark, I see rat droppings the size of cat turds scattered about. I kill the last of the beer. Rats lie atop the abandoned fifty-gallon oil drums, on the broken wooden pallets and in the cracks of the broken concrete floor. Their shifty eyes stare out at me from the long shadows, but I hold my ground. They scatter when the bottle I hurl at them shatters nearby, and then I am free. My eyes take a moment to adjust. A short piece of pipe laying on the ground among the droppings catches my attention. I pick it up

Today I am at home among the rats.

The long, rusty hinges creek as the boy opens the door. I see his silhouette, flat, and two dimensional, more like a shadow then a person. He stands for a moment framed by the white light of the open doorway, checking everything out.

"Hey kid!" He doesn't even know my name, "Hey kid, you in here? You'd better be here, no kidding, or I'll…"

"I'm here."

"Where?"

"Over here," I say, loud enough to activate his sonar. He walks in my general direction, unhurried, with one hand covering his eyes, blocking the glare through the tiny window a top the cement block walls.

"Where are you?"

"Over here."

When he can see better, he spots me, drops his hand and starts to walk faster. He walks right up to me, and I let him come. When he is almost on top of me, I take one step toward him, out into the broken light, one step to slow his momentum. We stand face to face for the briefest of moments. I want to be sure his eyes adjust. I want to be sure he can see me. We consider each other for another moment.

"So, you got it ready? You got my homework ready, fag boy?"

Oh, so you do remember. Even better. "Nope"

"Hey, you'd better be kidding or I'll…"

"Or you'll what?"

He doesn't answer.

"Or you'll what?"

"Why you little…" He takes a step toward me—I step a side and raise the pipe. He turns toward me, looks me right in the eye, just before I bean him. The sound of the pipe hitting his skull makes me wince, makes my stomach flip. His legs buckle; he collapses like a puppet cut from its strings, lands on his side, and moans. His legs curl until he's in the fetal position. He lies there, holding the front of his head, rocking back and forth. He doesn't say another word, just groans and whimpers. After I am sure he's not playing possum, I take a step toward him and lean down so I can whisper right in his ear.

"Do your own fucking homework."

A moment passes and I toss the pipe into a pile of rags in the corner. I don't stop to check if there is blood on it or anything, I just throw it aside. I'm done. As I step over him, I can see two other boys watching us through the garage window; they must have climbed up to get a better look, too frightened to follow him in. I stare right through them.

"You want some, too? Huh?"

They duck below the sill, out of sight. I wonder if one of them might be the one who held me down when I got jumped and I take off running, but by the time I get outside, they're gone. The exhilaration of the moment is too much for me and I collapse, giddy and a little drunk—a little sick.

At home, my father shouts, "Hi, son. How was school?" He hollers from the living room. The television blares. I can tell he's high and I am glad.

"Swell, Dad. Just fine."

"Anything exciting?"

"Not much. I met some guys after school. That's all."

I see the boy again; I see his friends, too, but they never acknowledge me. *Maybe I dreamt the whole thing*, I think, *Maybe I just got loaded*; or, maybe I only recognize them through the eyes of fear. From time to time, I get the feeling that the other kids give me strange looks. They stand around in small groups and whisper as I pass, as if they've heard something about me, *He stood up for himself*, I imagine them saying. I hear the whispers and they seem different to me, more positive somehow. It makes me feel good and self-conscious all at the same time.

❦   ❦   ❦

"Rocky. Are you asleep?"

My eyes felt like they held down with lead sinkers.

"We're here," Vince said, the smoke from his big cigar filling his words.

"Where the hell are we?"

"Around the corner from the hospital. You ready to get yourself fixed up again before you go back?"

Again?

I looked at my arms, and sure enough, bloody track marks on the back of my left hand indicated that I had, indeed, been shooting up.

"Shit." I pressed down hard on the bloody spot. "Yeah, sure. What the hell." While he fumbled to fix up the syringe for me, I asked him the question. "So, why did you want me to go with you tonight?"

"Oh, Jesus, do we have to go over this again?"

Again?

"Well—ahem—pardon me, I just want to be sure I understand," I said, attempting to cover my failing memory.

He aspirated the drug out of the vial and into the syringe, then, handed me the syringe and exhaled. "Okay, look, this is what happened: I got hassled earlier this evening when I tried to fill the script you told me to write…"

"What script? I didn't tell you to write any script."

"You don't remember calling me and asking me to get you something?"

"Yeah, but I didn't tell you to write any script. I told you I would write it and you could come and pick it up. "

"What's the difference? I just saved you a little time; I mean it wasn't like you were going to say "no" or something, anyway…"

"Jesus, Vince!"

"Look, it doesn't matter. As long as you approve it and your numbers are on the thing, it doesn't matter…"

"FOR CHRIST SAKE!"

"Just listen to me for a second, will you? Let me tell you what happened, at least." He waited until I quieted down, then he went on, "So, I went in and the pharmacist questioned the signature, but instead of calling you as I suggested, he called someone else, and."

"Who?"

"I didn't wait around to find out."

"Well, who would it have been?"

"I don't know."

"Who, Vince!?"

"I don't know. The police maybe, or the D.E.A."

"Oh, Jesus Christ Almighty! You got the script back, didn't you? Please tell me you got that script back."

"There wasn't time."

I sat for a moment absorbing what Vince told me and tried to figure it out. "So what do we do now? Do I say it's a forgery, or what? I just deny knowing anything about it, right?"

"Well, no, I don't think we can do that. I think it's better if you say that I had your permission to write it."

"What? Why? Why should I have anything to do with it at all? Why not just pretend that some lunatic stole one of my pads and tried to pass one?"

"Well, because..." he hesitated, weighed his options. "...Because I think the authorities will be able to identify me. If they get me on something, I could go back to prison."

"Back to prison?"

"And it might even bounce back on you."

"What are you saying?"

"I spent a year in the federal prison camp at Elgin Air Force Base for prescription fraud five or six years ago."

I stared at him.

"It was a fucked up thing. I picked up a prescription for a friend. The doctor knew. It never should have gone to court. I tried to do somebody a favor. You know how that goes. Some of my political enemies got their teeth into the thing. The governor was all set to pardon me. The deal was in, but an emergency came up the day of my sentencing. He couldn't do anything once the paperwork was signed."

My beeper went off.

"That's why I work in this fucking shit-hole of a hospital. You can't get a real job, once you're a convicted felon, no matter how fucked up the thing was, you can't get a license to practice law."

As he rambled on I picked up the car phone. "This is Doctor VanSlyke."

"Doctor, this is the hospital operator. I'm sorry, I can hardly hear you. Are you in the hospital?"

"I'm getting something out of my car. What's up?"

"Oh, I'm sorry, of course, well, there is a…a Detective Degrasse from the Sheriff's Department calling for you. He says it's important."

"Okay. I'll call him back as soon as I get inside, when I've got a better connection. Get a number for me, okay? I'll call you right back." I hung up the phone. "Jesus, Vince. Jesus, what do we do now? It's the cops. They want to talk to me."

"Talk to 'em. Tell the truth."

CHAPTER 20

*D*uring senior high school calculus the door to my room opens and two people, a man and a woman, step in. The whole class turns its collective head to follow them in, like the crowd in some slow motion tennis match. They walk up to the blackboard. The teacher, dressed in blue slacks and a beige cardigan, stops writing formulae, brushes chalk dust from her hands and greets our guest with quiet gestures. The man stops at the front of the room, by the first row of desks, and crosses his arms in front of himself like some secret service security man, but does not speak. Security people all look the same like the guys left jumping on the bumpers behind presidential limousines, when Presidents like Kennedy are shot.

Will he touch his ear? I wonder.

The woman whispers something to the teacher. She nods over her shoulder in my direction, and then the woman takes two steps forward, says my name. "Rocky VanSlyke?"

I stand up by the side of my desk as is the custom in school. "Yes, ma'am?"

"Rocky, would you gather your books and come with me, please?"

"Yes, ma'am."

Once outside the room, the woman turns to me, "Rocky, I am Mrs. Cole from the principle's office; there's been an accident. Your father's been taken to the hospital. Mr. Simmons from security is going to drive you there to make sure you get there all right."

Mr. Simmons. Security. Um.

I nod. "Yes, ma'am." I look at the big guy. He does not touch his ear.

Mrs. Cole does not know what happened, does not know the details, only that some repairman or other found the door of our house agape and my father unconscious inside. "Don't worry about coming back to school. You're excused for the day."

I nod and hang my head, though not because I'm sad.

"Please let me know if there's anything I can do."

"Yes, ma'am." Who knows what she means?

❦   ❦   ❦

"Detective Degrasse, please."

"Speaking."

"This is Dr. VanSlyke. You left a message for me?"

"Yes, Doctor. Thank you for returning my call. I apologize for bothering you so late, but we had a situation come up that we need your help with."

"Whatever I can do."

"This shouldn't take long. Doctor, earlier this evening a pharmacist in Philadelphia intercepted a prescription for injectable Demerol.

"Intercepted? I don't understand. How do you mean, intercepted?"

"Well, this particular pharmacist filled prescriptions for your patients in the past at other pharmacies around the city. He happened to be moonlighting at the pharmacy where the prescription passed this evening, a real break for us. You've heard of our special task force? It's been in the papers."

"Um."

"Yes, well anyway, this pharmacist states that a tall, middle-aged, obese man entered the store around seven this evening, presented the prescription in question, represented himself as the person named on the prescription blank, and asked the pharmacist to call you to confirm its legitimacy. The pharmacist recognized a forged signature on the 'script, not yours, as I'm sure you've guessed, and he called us."

"Yes?"

"Well, we wondered if you might be able to come down to the station, say, tomorrow around noon, and confirm whether or not this signature is a forgery."

"Certainly."

"Fine, fine. Well, then, I won't keep you. Thanks for your cooperation."

"Anytime, good-bye."

"Oh, uh, Doctor? While I've got you on the line, do you have a patient named Vincent G. Buddy?"

"Ah, yes, I do. Why? Does this have something to do with Mr. Buddy?"

"Well, we're not sure yet. Have you ever prescribed I.V. Demerol for him?"

"Ah, I can't answer that. Medical records are confidential. I would have to get a release of information from Mr. Buddy to discuss that."

"You do have medical records for Mr. Buddy, then?"

"Of course."

"So, when he signs a release, or if we get a subpoena you can produce them?"

"I'm sorry, what?"

"The records?

"Oh, yes, right. No, that won't be a problem."

"How long would it take you to do that?"

"Uh…I'm not quite sure. I'd have to contact Mr. Buddy and see if he would be agreeable to that arrangement, um, and then have him come in and sign a consent. Probably a day or two."

"You'll still come in and look at the prescription, though, the one that passed tonight?"

"Absolutely"

"Good. Well, we'll see you tomorrow then."

"Good night…"

"Oh, Doctor?"

"Yes."

"One more thing, if you don't mind."

"Yes."

"May I have your home phone number?"

"555-0641."

"Thank you."

"Is that it?"

"Yes, that'll do it, thank you."

"Good night."

"Yes, good night."

I hung up the phone and looked at Vince, who had followed me into the hospital and was sitting beside me, as stiff as a board, monitoring the call on an extension. He hung up the other receiver. He didn't look worried or nervous, but serious, attorney-like. He'd never looked look like an attorney before. Sales representative? Yes. Preacher? Yes. But, attorney, never.

"So, what do you think?"

He shrugged. "Maybe they've got something, maybe they don't."

"So, uh, do I need to bring a lawyer with me?"

"Naw." He waved his hands. "They're just going to take a statement from you tomorrow. I'll act as your legal counsel for now, on the QT from the hospital. Then we'll see what happens."

"We'll see what happens?"

"We'll just have to see."

"Okay. Okay, all right."

CHAPTER 21

❀

When my father dies, it's as if he's already been dead and gone for quite some time. As if what was left of him after the shooting was simply catching up. The closed casket holds my attention as I shake the hands that float by. The people attached to those hands, I do not know. I hear voices, like vapor, "We're so sorry." "Such a shame." "So young...So young." The words sound complimentary, almost congratulatory.

The uniforms catch my eye. These soldiers served with my father, I guess, but so long ago, now, that I have no hope of recognizing them. These men must have heard about his death through the Veteran's Administration. Men in dress uniforms, jungle fatigues, and Class A's sit in wheelchairs or stand on crutches.

Armless sleeves pinned up at the elbow, legless pants pinned up at the knee, drape over the casket and touch the flag that covers my father's body with whatever is left of them.

Murmurs sound like "Peas and broth," but must be, "Peace, brother." These strangers, with tears in their eyes, mumble phrases like, "That lousy, fucking war..." and "He died for his country, just the same." The troops mention "friendly fire," "fratricide," but I don't know what they mean.

My father's death, the exact moment of his demise, determined "accidental" by the VA medical examiner, is anything but. When I'm in school, he takes his own medicine. He's done it for years without a problem. All of a sudden he takes too many of his pills?

That's it? That's the explanation?

Accident, they say, not a suicide. The decision is designed to save the VA from the blame, from an explanation of all my pleading that they do something about his pain, about how he eats the pills like candy. I read the burble between the words and see the looks above the smiles. It's not your fault, the report says, it's better for you this way, better for the insurance. But somehow I think, No fucking way. But that's not what these men are talking about.

Peas and broth; peas and broth.

As I pick out my father's casket I wonder about my mother's funeral, maybe for the first time. "The silver gray one is one of our best sellers," the undertaker says, "Simple, yet durable. It's a little more expensive than the standard, but your dad was a soldier, you say? Well, we give a ten percent discount to the family of soldiers, and we'll file the burial insurance for you with the VA."

"Okay."

"What would you like us to bury him in?"

I looked at the casket again then back at him.

The undertaker smiles at me, "I'm sorry, you misunderstood. I mean, what kind of clothes?"

"I want him buried in his uniform."

"Of course," the undertaker says. "

We should have one here by four or five o'clock tonight at the latest. Keep in mind that it may have to be laundered or need a button fixed."

"Okay," I say. "Okay, thanks."

After I find my father's uniform, I run all the way to the dry cleaner. "Extra heavy starch." I say. I wait there for it. The cleaning takes an hour. Then I run back to the funeral home with the coat hanger, stiff as cardboard, flapping behind me.

"What's this?

"His uniform."

"There must be some mistake? We can't bury him in this!"

"Why not?"

"Because it's just not right, that's why! I know you're upset, son, but—"

The starched fatigues, shiny olive drab and black, hang on the hanger like the cardboard cutout of a man.

"I thought you said he could be buried in his uniform?"

"His dress uniform, son, not his field fatigues."

"This the only uniform I've ever seen him in, and they've been starched!" I protest. "This is what I want him buried in." I am getting upset. "You said it would be okay! I just did what you said."

"It's just not done, son, unless…"

Later that day, I see my dad in his field uniform again. I think of how strong and peaceful he looks dressed for battle. The blouse in his fatigue pants at the throat of the Corican jump boots is perfect. The boots look new because that half of him that wears boots died a few years before the rest of him. An afterlife for a man like my father, where he must ford the banks of the river Styx in black and green war paint, a bayonet clinched between his teeth, scale the cliffs of Mount Olympus, and mount an attack, with courage and stealth, to storm the gates of heaven, to gain entry to any kind of afterlife worth living, demands the clothes he wears today; they give him an edge, I know.

In heaven, he is a soldier again.

He wears an expression both proud and brave as they close the lid of the coffin, displays the proper bearing for a military funeral. For the first time in years, he looks happy. He lies in his casket with his arms at his side, waxy fingers curled at attention, not hands crossed in front of him like the mortician wants. Alive, he might look intimidating; a tall man and broad. In death, he appears long and deflated, ready to slip through the crack into eternity. No matter, today, if eternity arrived a few years too late.

The two memories, the one of him in the coffin and the one of him at the shooting, merge at this funeral, allowing him to die only once, way back then, and avoid all the mundane suffering. "No one will even care, son. Closed caskets don't have the same stigma they used to, not with all the boys coming home from the war they way they do," the undertaker says. Then he smiles and closes the cover. So, my father is buried in a closed casket, but not until I am sure he is wearing that uniform, a soldier going into his final battle.

In the last few years of his life, he lost it. But it wasn't his fault. His quiet resolve turned to anger, pain, coming at different times, from unpredictable directions, as he watched the body count rise on television. His fellow soldiers coming home from the war broken like him. He disappeared into his anger, punctuated by brief moments of brilliant sanity marked by a certain look or comment, a certain turn of phrase, as when he commented on McNamara's ego and the psychology of sending men to die to save face. That sanity is stabled now, the untamed horses of his anger are undisturbed in death, now in repose allowing his demeanor to soften and grant him serenity.

Gone is the paraplegic alcoholic who, like a coward, took his own life.

I am happy for him.

I wish he had died in the war.

      ❀   ❀   ❀

"Thank you for coming, doctor, won't you sit down?"

"Why thank you, detective." I patronize.

"Would you like some coffee or something?"

"No, thank you, I'm fine."

"Mind if I have some? It's been a long night, and it isn't over yet.

"Not at all, please, go ahead." Mr. Congeniality.

He was already up and standing over the coffee maker. He raised the pot as he would in a salute of some kind, a toast, the way he might have raised a beer. Detective Frank Degrasse did not look anything like he sounded, which is to say, he did not look at all professional. He wore long, tangled hair that hung down the middle of his back. He sported a goatee. A plaid flannel shirt protruded from a leather vest, blue jeans and cowboy boots finished off the ensemble. He displayed his badge on a chain around his neck, and as he turned to pour in way too much sugar for one cup of coffee, I saw the empty holster for a small caliber handgun, a .38 Special, stuck in the back of his belt. He looked like he should carry a nine-millimeter Glock like all the other drug guys carry.

I liked him.

"Now, let me get some vital statistics down here." He rolled a triplicate form with wide margins and ruled lines into the typewriter. He went through the whole Miranda thing, "You have the right to an attorney…" I wondered, as I watched him, what a guy like this was doing in the Philadelphia County Sheriff's Department; he looked like a hick lawyer.

"I'm going to the FBI Academy as soon as I finish law school. This shit is for the birds." Banter, I could tell. Rhetorical. He had no interest in getting familiar with me. This was business, pure and simple. He did not ask or expect me to respond to his comments, and I didn't. "And, the fucking DEA? Jesus. Those guys are worse then the goddamned drug dealers half the time. Social Security Number?"

Everything went all right for about the first half an hour until he asked, "What is your relationship to Mr. Buddy?"

"Pardon me?"

"Mr. Buddy, the guy the prescription was written to? What's your relationship to him?"

"Are you asking if I'm related to him?"

"No, I'm asking if he's a friend, or if you work with him, or if he's a client, you know, like that."

"Well, humm," I cleared my throat, "Well, I guess it's a little…" I made a circle in the air with my hand, "You know, complicated."

"Complicated?"

"Well, I work with him at the hospital and he is my patient."

"You mean also your patient."

"Pardon me?"

"Well, he sees other doctors besides you, correct?"

"He may. I don't know for sure."

"I see, and in what capacity do you work with him at the hospital?"

"He's the corporate attorney for the hospital."

"So, you work with him like, what, like on malpractice cases? "

"Well, no. Not exactly."

"What then?"

"Um, well, kind of as a consultant, like if he needs something medical explained to him."

"You're still a resident, is that correct, doctor?"

"Yes, that's correct."

"So, why wouldn't the attorney who represents the whole hospital go to someone in authority, like say, the director of surgery to get his questions answered?"

I didn't answer, but I could feel my cheeks getting red.

"Doctor?" He said after a minute.

"I, uh, I don't know Detective Degrasse, I guess you'd have to ask him that."

He sat for a moment looking at me, like there should have been something more to my response.

"It may be because the chairman is busy most of the time, and as the chief resident I'm sort of his aide-de-camp."

"I see." He turned back to the typewriter, but he didn't type anything. "So, how is it that he comes to be your patient? Is the chairman too busy to see Mr. Buddy for that, too?"

"Jeez, I don't know." I got angry for the first time, more at his tone than the question itself. "I guess that's another one of those questions you'll have to ask Mr. Buddy."

"I intend to…" he said with an even tone, and then trailed off again.

"And," I said, starting to feel self-conscious, "he'll probably tell you that it has something to do with the fact that I still practice emergency medicine when I moonlight. Unlike my mentor, the chief of surgery, I still have some expertise in primary care."

"I'm sure that's exactly what he'll say. Now, did you write that prescription for Mr. Buddy?"

"What prescription?"

"The prescription I mentioned last night."

"How would I know? I haven't seen it yet."

"You haven't?"

"No, I haven't. I thought that's what I came up here for."

"Of course." he said, sounding sheepish for the first time, "Here it is." He opened the top drawer and took out a plastic bag containing a crumpled piece of white paper the size of a single sheet of toilet paper, only thicker. He passed it to me. I noticed the 'script was printed with my name and DEA number. The handwriting was Vince's.

I glanced over it, to make it look good, then I said, "Well, it's certainly my prescription pad, but I didn't write it."

"You didn't? Are you sure?"

"Yes, I'm sure."

"You are absolutely sure?"

"Absolutely."

"Well, I guess that settles that," he said looking over the paper work, "Thank you for taking the time to come down."

"Anytime," I said as I rose from my seat and turned from the desk.

"Oh, doctor…I'm sorry, one more thing."

"Yes?"

"As Mr. Buddy's physician, do you have to write reports to his parole officer if you prescribe a narcotic for him?"

My jaw slackened, my face reddened and, without meaning to, I slide back into the chair. "Parole officer?"

"Why yes, surely he told you about the fourteen months he spent in federal prison for prescription fraud and diversion..."

"I—" I caught myself. "Like I told you last evening, Detective Degrasse, I have to have a release from Mr. Buddy before I can speak with you about his case. I have not had a chance to contact him."

"I understand."

"Is that all?"

"Yes, thank you again."

"Of course." I rose again and turned to leave.

"Oh, uh, doctor?" He said again as I reached the door.

I turned once more and faced him again, but this time I didn't say anything.

"If you plan to contact Mr. Buddy, I suggest you do it soon. I'm having this script sent for handwriting analysis today. If it shows what I think it's going to show, Mr. Buddy may not be available to you for very much longer."

I left.

CHAPTER 22

※

A few days after the funeral the Old Guy grabs me. It is morning, and I am carrying boxes and pails of garbage across the front lawn to the curb with all the enthusiasm of a man bailing water from a swamped skiff. He catches me flat-footed. I am too distracted to make a polite getaway.

"Hey, there, young fella! Doing a little spring cleaning are ya?"

He must have planned his approach for an hour to be sure I wouldn't scurry away. "Yes, sir," I say, well mannered, self-conscious.

He moves closer. This is the first time I have seen him walk and I realize that this trek across the grass has cost him: He winces with every step. "I'm so sorry about your Pappy, son. You've got to start thinking about where you're going to live now that your Pappy's gone." He reads the surprise on my face, and chuckles. "I'm retired Army myself, you know. Yes sir. I was a chaplain in the 101st Airborne Infantry. That's how I broke this here hip," He says, shifting his hand from the wooden cane supporting him so he can use it to bang on the offending hip. "Pure al-u-min—um. Marvalous. Anyway, shattered it jumpin' into the Ia Drang Valley." He chuckles for a second or two, shakes his head as if remembering, then looks up at me. "I known about you and your Pappy for quite some time. I been keeping an eye on you," He says, and winks. "Your lease runs out at the end of this month, and the landlord—same as mine, you

- 219 -

see—won't rent to single teenagers. No way." He shakes his head, takes off his wide-brimmed Panama and wipes his brow with a red handkerchief he fishes from his back pocket. "Never has." He replaces the hat. "I've lived in this neighborhood twenty years and I've never seen it; not once."

"I know," I say, but I don't know, not really, not until this moment. Then I think, *What do I do now?* And this kindly person reads my mind and answers my question for me.

"Young fella like you should be in school. You can live in the dorm, and the army will pay you." He reads the shock on my face with delight. "That's right, the G.I. Bill—that's how I became a chaplain. You can live on the money. Use it for anything you want. With a little job on the side, you'll do just fine." He leaned a little closer. "A young fella like you, you don't want to just lie around all day and try to live off your old man's pension benefits, do ya?"

"Hell, no. What do I do? I mean, how—what do I do?"

Well, now," he says reaching into the breast pocket of his tropical shirt, "you just call the man on this card." He pulls the business card out and hands it to me. He watches me for a moment, standing there, leaning on his cane. With hands still full of garbage, I shift my weight and strike a pose that lets me take the card. "I guess if it were me I'd move to Atlanta, go to Georgia, maybe Georgia Tech, become a bulldog," he clicks his tongue twice and winks, "The girls are prettier up there," he says with conspiracy in his voice." Then he turns, heading back across the grass, back toward his porch. "Let me know if there's anything I can do," he shouts over his shoulder.

"Hey, thanks, Mister. Thanks a lot," I shout back, in response to which he rises his cane.

Now the pails of junk don't seem quite so heavy. I carry on with a bit more bounce in my step. I make a few more trips to the curb. Everything goes that won't fit in a dorm room. No nest of evil memories for me. Not anymore. I am going to school and I am going with a vengeance. With a last glance at the Old Guy's porch I spy an empty wicker rocking chair teetering as if it has only just been vacated. I never see him again and it occurs to me that he might have been an Angel.

❦   ❦   ❦

"Are you fucking kidding me? You're a convicted felon?" I heard myself say as if in a dream.

"I told you that the other night."

"No, you did not. I never heard that before, not until this cop brought it up."

"Oh, Jesus. All right. It's not the kind of thing you spread around."

"Spread around! I've practically lived in your house for the past four years! I've been your doctor, or your Doctor Feelgood, for Christ's sake, for almost as long. You could have warned me. We could have been a little smarter about the way we passed those scripts."

"Look, after I got out of prison, my wife left me, I got stuck with the kid and no job. I moved up here and found work. That cost me some, ya know? Now I'm an elder of my church. I carved a niche for myself when nobody in my profession would help me. I made a place for myself in this city. It's just not the kind of thing you talk about."

"Well, Detective Degrasse was sure talking about it. And because of that, I'm sure I sounded like an ass and probably incriminated both of us in the process! Have you read the newspapers lately?"

"I've read'em"

"This guys gunning for guys like you and me."

I expected this to ruffle him, but it didn't.

"I thought it would be better if you didn't know," he said, his voice quiet, even. "I wanted you to be able to deny anything honestly. Plausible deniability, ya know? I did it for your own protection." His voice sounded flat, hallow, but with a bit of tension around the edges where the truth seeped out, like water flowing from a bath tub onto a floor. His voice, rising and falling like a windstorm, blew all the meaning out of his words. "Look, why don't you write me, you know, a real one," Vince said in a way that made it sound like a great idea. "Enough for both of us, and maybe some Motrin to go with it. We'll go to a motel somewhere close by, prop up and figure this thing out."

"What? Write another script? Are you kidding me?"

He shushed me with his finger, pointed at the phone, and then at his ear. He mouthed the word "bugged."

"Are you sure?" I whisper. "I mean, don't you think that's kind of risky right now? Are we being watched?"

"So what if we are?" He shrugged. "What looks more suspicious, continuing the treatment or stopping it all of a sudden? It's a legitimate prescription. What the hell are they going to do about it?"

"Yeah, I guess you're right. I guess it would look kind of fishy to just stop. Let me go get my pad out of the car." I got up, happy to have a reason to do something other then wonder if I were about to be arrested. Then I stopped and looked at him for a long moment. "I hope you know what you're doing."

"Trust me. They've got nothing."

CHAPTER 23

*M*y father's papers are kept in a metal ammo box. Painted army green, the box is stenciled with the words, "Shells—4.2 Mortar." One of the last things I do when closing up the house is pull the big clasp that fixes the lid tight on that box and go through my father's papers. There, among the old bills and military forms, is an envelope, addressed to him. The return address is Fort Leavenworth, Kansas. I have no idea why this particular document catches my attention. The letter, old and rumpled, rests on top of the pile of other old and rumpled papers. Nothing strikes me about this envelope, except, maybe, that it is handwritten. Once I spot the letter I am compelled to read it, I am as entranced as a child voyeur, drawn to the bedroom window of the woman next door is. The letter, yellow and cracked, breaks as it unfolds.

August 10th, 1968

Dear Sgt. VanSlyke,

This is a hard letter to write, but not, I guess, as hard as it will be to read. I have no idea of your condition, or even if you be able to read this. I only know that I have to write it and so here goes. My name is Gary Kupeck. I am the man who shot you and killed your wife. I do not remember any of this, but I believe what I have been told. I am a murderer.

At the time, I was a soldier just a few weeks stateside after a one-year tour in the land of Vietnam. You may be thinking that I am going to say how war is hell and that I was out of my mind when I did all of those horrible things to you and your family, but I am not going to say that. My mind was not right, that much is true, but what I did had nothing to do with the war. My life was destined to go wrong. You see, I am a drug addict and alcoholic, and did not even know it at the time, although I had all the danger signs my whole life, just like my daddy did when he beat my momma. I was powerless over them drugs and the alcohol that twisted my mind and twisted your-alls lives too, and the life of your wife and, was there a child?

It may ease your mind somewhat to know that justice was served in my case and that I shall never see anything but the inside of these prison walls and the rock pile again. I want you to know that I am a changed person. I am recovered from the addiction. I accept my life as it is now. I take responsibility for my actions and accept my punishment. I will spend the rest of my pitiful life breaking rocks in this jail which, I know, is nothing to you but it is something.

Understand that this letter is my humble attempt at amends and comes to you with no hope or expectation. No one is to blame if you should hate me forever, but it is my hope that the knowledge of my miserable life will lessen your suffering and help you escape and evade the enemy 'hate' that destroyed my life.

You are in my prayers.

Sincerely,

Gary P. Kupeck
Former soldier, U.S. Army

I fold the letter and put it in the front pocket of my shirt.

❦   ❦   ❦

"I'd better go get this one filled myself," Vince said," Just in case; you know what I mean?" I wasn't sure what he meant but I nodded. "Just drive around the block a few times and answer the phone if it rings, to confirm the script, you know the routine." He motioned to me to move into the driver seat. Without considering where I might be going, I put the big Caddy into drive and headed out into the streamers of red and white lights as the night filled up with rain.

My lack of familiarity with this part of the city forced me to search between the headlights and taillights for the route. When the cell phone rang it startled me. My heart jumped into my throat, but I answered it pronto and got my voice under control. My voice, trained after years of practiced control truncated the fear until it came out sounding like anger. "Dr. VanSlyke," I said, short and punchy.

This better be good.

For a moment, silence, the delay of wireless technology. Then I said, "Is anyone there?"

"Well, Dr. VanSlyke! What a surprise. Fancy getting you on Mr. Buddy's cell phone."

A voice inside my head sounded like panic as it grabbed me around the throat.

"Speaking of Mr. Buddy, I hoped to get in touch with him. This is Detective Degrasse. Is he there?"

"Uh, I'm sorry, Detective, but he's not," I heard the same voice in my brain saying, Oh shit, oh shit, oh shit!

"Um, I see. Well, if you happen to run into him, that is, when you return his cell phone—this is his cell phone, isn't it? I mean, this is his number I dialed? Dr. VanSlyke?"

"Yes?"

"This is Mr. Buddy's cell phone, isn't it?"

"Ah, yes."

"That's what I thought. Well, anyway, would you tell him to give me a call?"

"Uh, I sure will, yes."

"Would you give him my number? I believe you have one of my cards?"

"Yes."

"And, I assume that this means you've had a chance to speak with him about the release of information you mentioned?"

"He's considering it, detective."

"I see, well, thank you, doctor. Good night."

"Good night."

"Oh, ah, doctor?"

"Yes?"

"You boys stay outta trouble now, ya hear?"

I hung up.

❋   ❋   ❋

Vince stood waiting in front of the drug store when I pulled up. He motioned me into the passenger seat so I slid over to let him back in. I asked him if he filled the prescriptions, and he said no.

"What happened?"

"Nothing. Nothing at all happened. That's the fucking problem. I know another place right up the street. We'll get it filled there."

When I told him about Detective Degrasse's call, he did not seem at all surprised. His reaction or lack of one calmed me.

"What'd Degrasse say?" When I told him he said, "They've got nothing."

He's an old hand at this, I thought. He knows what it all means. He's got it all under control, thank God. When we got to the other drug store, he asked me to write another prescription.

"What for? What happened to the other one?"

"Shit, I must've left it at the other place. Just write another one." When I suggested we go back and get the first prescription, he said, "Just write the goddamned thing, and let's get on with it."

I did.

He'd dug us a bigger hole, I knew, but, by now, I didn't care. Still, I didn't want him angry with me, not until I got a fix and had some relief. The last person I needed to have angry with me was Vince, not with Detective Degrasse lurking about.

Before long, we arrived at some cheap motel. I ducked inside and drew-up the Demerol under the thin light filtered through a shabby lamp, unwrapping the syringes like a gay hustler tending to his condoms, Vince undressed (his cloths landed in a sloppy pile like mud sloughing off a pachyderm,) and flopped onto the bed like a john waiting to get fucked.

Doing drugs with this pig is like fucking him: it feels pretty good until someone you know sees you doing it. The first fix made every fucked-up thing seem right again, for a while. My brain knew, as I pushed the plunger and felt my heart light up like a Japanese lantern, that all this shit would work out.

CHAPTER 24

The dorm resonates with laughter every night, fading in and out like AM radio static: CKLW, fifty thousand watts, fading in and out. In the evenings, the sound rises out of each room like scratchy songs from so many blown and twittering stereo speakers. The noisy voices, like bees buzzing, drift from each window and into the street. Certain dorm windows, illuminated here and there, contrast with the unlighted ones, drawing attention to the seductive shadow dance of thick jocks and delicate coeds.

One of Avery's girlfriends always hangs out in my room even when he's not around. She plops on my couch with her feet up on my desk making it hard for me to study. I look at those sneakers, sandals, or painted toes from time to time, and try to decide whether I love them there on my desk or resent them. She kicks me in the ribs and I squirm, loving it, hating it. Thoughts of Avery's sister flutter into my awareness like geese from a pond, but Avery shoots each downy fantasy from the sky with bullets of information, "She's pregnant," he says, "Has been a few times. She's married now and putting on weight."

Later, when Avery comes by, he laughs and his girlfriend giggles. I can hear them there behind me. I have no idea why they are there or what they talk about. When it gets quiet, I glance around to catch a glimpse of them making out. They stare at me as if I am an idiot, then laugh and laugh. I ignore them and go back to my studies.

We hear a crash, like a cymbal, or church bells, a refugee from the marching band clutching his instrument, struck by a car. Avery gets up from the couch and opens the door to my room. He peers out. The harsh light from the hallway cuts him in two at the waist, hot and cold.

"What is it?"

"Huh?"

"What is it? What's up?"

"Don't know yet. I'll go check. Something's going on at the other end of the hall."

He leaves, and when he returns he shuts the door and sits down. No comment.

"So, what was it?"

"No savvy, yet, my big white brother. Looks like that Asian brotha at the end of the hall might've took a header out his dorm window. He got a B in organic chemistry or something." Avery shrugged. "Guess he wanted to do the medical school thing. That's what everybody's saying."

"Jesus, Avery? What should we do? Should we do anything?"

"Naw." he waves me back to my books. He is all ready engrossed again in the television. "Somebody called the cops. There are already forty people out there and they'll all be up all fucking night making statements. I been there." He shakes his head. "Shit, he's dead for sure. Not a damn thing we can do for him now. Did you know him?"

"Naw."

"Me neither. He was probably a physics geek, or something like that. All those Asian guys are physics geeks. I'm going to hit the sack in about fifteen minutes. When those cops come knocking, I'm out."

Avery never makes it to his room. He fall asleep in my ratty armchair after his girl leaves. "Don't want to miss the action," she says.

Later I stand on the arm of one of the chairs, the one I found abandoned in one of the storage bins, waiting. After a time I peek out the window and see only some red flashing lights, everything else is too far out of sight. I'd have to go downstairs to check it out. Instead, I sit back down and study.

❋   ❋   ❋

"You've got a problem!"

These words accosted me like a band of muggers as I left the bath. Halfway across the living room on my way to, God knows where, I realized the voice did not come from inside my own head.

"You've got a serious problem!"

My eyes fluttered and crack as I tracked the sound. Karla. "Hi!" I said with as much enthusiasm and I could summon, and moved on toward the kitchen.

"Did you hear me?"

"How could I not hear you? You're screaming."

"I'm not even talking loud, Rocky. What the hell's wrong with you? I've been here half an hour, and this is the first time you've spoken to me. I've been half out of my mind with worry. I feel like I'm going crazy." She grabbed her head on either side. "I thought you were having an affair. I haven't seen or heard from you in over five days! I've called the hospital. I've called Vince. I've called the police, for Christ sake, and nobody has any idea where you are half the time."

"I thought I'd give you and your boyfriend, there—what's his name?—A chance to be alone."

"Oh, don't give me that shit again! This doesn't have anything to do with me, and you know it! I think you've got a problem with drugs. That's what I think. I'm not fooling anymore, Rock," she stood up. "And, I'm not just going to sit around and watch you kill yourself."

"So, what's that supposed to mean?"

"You know what it means." She picked up her purse. I noticed, for the first time, that she was nicely dressed, like she was on her way to a business meeting, or a date.

"Looks like you made up your mind about this before you got here." She didn't look at me, just straightened her skirt and acted aloof, turning her nose up and adjusting her pearls. "Okay, so let's assume, for the sake of argument, that I do have a drug problem, which I don't, but let's say that I do. Your answer to that is to just walk out?"

"It's your problem."

"After all of two years together, you're just going to walk out because you think I've got a drug problem, is that right?"

She acted careworn again. "I've done some checking, Rocky. There is nothing I can do to help you until you figure out that you need help."

"Checking?"

"I've been a member of Alanon for three month's now."

"Good god in heaven—"

"Don't patronize me, Rocky, or I'll walk out of her right now."

"All right, all right, don't get you panties in a wad." After considering her for a moment I decided she was serious. "So, this is not just about you fucking some other guy? Is that right?"

"Look, I can't put up with this anymore!" she screamed, losing her cool for the first time. "I can't concentrate on my job. I can't sleep. I'm starting to purge again when I eat. People at work are starting to ask questions."

"About what?"

"About the way I'm acting, that's what! They're starting to think that *I'm* on drugs for Christ sake! It's difficult to explain with all the investigators calling day and night."

"What investigators? What are you talking about? Did someone call you trying to start trouble?"

She quieted down.

"Well?"

"Some detective called the floor asking for me. He left a number, but I haven't called him back."

"Well, don't! Was it Degrasse? Was his name Degrasse?"

"I think so. Something like that. I don't know."

"Well, just forget about him. That guy's trouble. Is that what all this is about?"

"No, it's not. It's about you disappearing for days at a time, not calling, taking showers with the door to your apartment wide open."

"The door was open?"

"And you having empty vials of Demerol in your gym bag."

"What the hell were you doing in my gym bag?"

"Oh, for God's sake! You have got to be kidding me! You haven't heard a word I've said, have you? I can't take this anymore," she said as she move toward the door.

"No wait, don't go, listen, honey, there is something I've been meaning to tell you about, something I need to talk about."

Her pace slowed and she turned, her arms tight across her chest as though she was clasping a child to her breast, her lips tight.

"It's Vince."

"Pardon me?"

"Vince is the one with the problem, not me. He's been stealing my prescription pads and writing for Percocet, but he keeps the pills for himself. I just found out about it. I'm cooperating with the police, that's why I asked you about the cop."

"And what about the Demerol?"

"That's his too. He leaves the bottles everywhere."

"You're telling me that you're not using drugs?"

"No."

"You're not taking any Percocet or shooting any Demerol?"

"No."

"All of this craziness is you running around cleaning up after Vince and cooperating with the police because *he's* the one with the drug problem?" I nodded. "You're lying."

She turned on her heels, "Goodbye."

"Wait, you've got to help me!"

"You want help? Get honest with yourself. Go to Dr. Waterman, tell him what's going on, and ask him to get you into a program."

"Are you crazy! I am the Chief surgical resident for Christ's sake! I'll lose everything, five years of training."

"So, you admit you have a problem?'

"I—I mean the scandal, with Vince and everything."

"What scandal. What's the scandal if he's been stealing from you?"

"You don't understand."

"Goodbye, Rocky."

"If you leave, don't come back."

"I won't."

"That's it. I'm not kidding. I don't have the time or energy to have people walking in and out of my life any time they feel like it, not with the job I've got."

"Yeah? Well, from what I hear, you aren't going to have to worry about that much longer, either."

"And just what the hell is that supposed to mean?"

"Get some help, Rocky." Karla wondered at me for a long instant. "That's what it means."

When she left, I felt relieved.

❧   ❧   ❧

I saw Karla once more, after the arrest.

"Can I stop over?" I asked

"Uh, okay, but you'd better be alone."

I hung up the cell phone and asked Vince to wait in the car.

She met me at the door of her condo, across the river in Jersey. I knocked, although I still had a key. It did not seem right to walk in, anymore. Some of my things still resided there, clothes and some papers. That was my excuse. I hoped she might fill a prescription for me, one last time, now that things were hot.

Vince's idea.

"No." She looked at me, her face expressionless, eyes empty. "No, honey, no." She tilted her head and touched my face once before withdrawing behind the door, like a nurse touching a sick patient, one not likely to survive the night.

Then she shut the door.

CHAPTER 25

"**W**hat happened?"

My own voice.

"What happened?"

The Medical College of Georgia, steeped in tradition as it is, counts Friday evening as hallowed. For generations, Fridays form the veritable hub of the students week, that time when the student body gathers at a dump call "The Cave", a local gin mill, for drinks and dinner and more drinks. Nice, healthy, stress management. Work hard, play hard. Every Friday. Casual. No problems.

Except for tonight.

"What happened?"

"You had too much to drink," Mike says. My roommate's voice. I can't see him yet. I'm having trouble focusing. My roommate and I are in my room when I realize that I do not remember how I got here.

"How—? How—?"

"How, yourself, big injin chief! Well, ol' buddy, you had a couple more than you usually do, and I think you were mixing pretty heavily there for a while, you know, beer and hard liquor, and those shitty liqueurs and all that sugary stuff." Mike's voice trails off. "Hell, you had a little too much, that's all, just a little too much to drink."

His voice is light and bouncy again. "You've been working too hard my friend! That's what medical school is all about!"

"Oh. Oh, yeah, that must be it."

"You'll be okay after a good night's sleep."

"Good night's sleep," I say, but it comes out like, "Gooneighsleap"

My sleep is fitful. Trails of shadowy impressions connect my last memory with my hangover. I hear voices. My parents?

Let go of me, goddamn it.

How much did you have, huh? And whom did you fuck in the process?

Let go of me you son-of-a-bitch.

My head, filled with the racket of such echoes, inside, pounding their way out, is, in actuality, filled with the sound of my roommate, up, moving around, making coffee, and talking to himself. We share an apartment. I get up, shuffle about, peek through the door to my room, then go to the bathroom and vomit.

Down the hall in the bathroom, I see myself for the first time since the blackout. A dying ghost; it's a wonder I made it down the hall. The mirrored door of the medicine cabinet stands open, looted in some predawn raid. As I rut around for some pills or elixir, anything to take away the pain, I catch a glimpse of myself again, a blurry, distorted taffy of flesh, pulled and stretched, looking like an image in a carnival fun house mirror. I lean into the reflection, pull the door closer on its hinges and examine the pasty flesh to be sure its me. Then I vomit again.

The voice of my roommate drifts in the hall. An auditory hallucination.

"How's your head?"

An involuntary jerk lofts my scalp into the open door of the medicine cabinet. "Jesus,"

"Wow, easy there, champ. You might hurt somebody."

The side of my face feels like sandpaper. "Oow, Jesus, Mike, you just scared the shit out of me."

"Yep. All alone on Planet Hangover, huh? How is it?"

"Like Pink Floyd says, 'When…

…I was a child…

…I had…

…a fever. My head…

…felt…

…just like…

…a big…

…balloon…" I sing the syllable, "loon" for a long time.

He clears his throat. "Ahem. Oh, I've been there."

He looks wide-awake.

"Yeah, and I've got a biochemistry test and an anatomy lab practical on Monday. I'm fucked. Got any Motrin?"

"Motrin? You are fucked up. Didn't you study your pharmacology on the non-steroidal anti-inflammatory? Motrin will burn a hole in your stomach when you gastric mucosa is normal and you, judging from the blood in your vomit over there, have a roaring alcoholic gastritis. No Motrin. Take about eight of those Tylenol you've got in your hand."

"Is that what these are, Tylenol?"

"Right, and a few cups of coffee. And a couple of these." He held out his hand.

Cradled on his palm I see two yellow triangular tablets. "What the hell are they?" I pick up the pills and fondle them.

"Dexedrine. You'll be able to study for the next three days straight."

"Dexedrine, huh? Speed?"

"Well, I see you studied some pharmacology anyway. The doctor prescribes them to my mother for her weight. You want to try 'em?"

"Yeah, sounds like what I need. Thanks." I down the pills with a handful of water, "Thanks a lot."

"Better living through chemistry."

"Where the hell did you get 'em? Wait, you didn't steal these from your own mother, did you?"

"Never mind. Enjoy."

❦   ❦   ❦

"What's this all about, officer?"

I rolled the window down.

"Shut up."

Detective Degrasse peered at me from the rear-view mirror from where he sat in the police cruiser that had just appeared from behind me out of nowhere.

"Shut up, and step out of the car." The arresting officer grabbed me by the arm as he turned me around and pushed me hard against the car. "Put your hands on the car where I can see them. Move slowly. Do it now. Spread your legs." He kicks at my feet, "Wider."

The headlights of the oncoming cars formed star bursts, a kaleidoscope of color, the sharp edges coalescing to white, while the array of lights atop the cruiser turned the whole event into what seemed like an alien abduction. The cruiser door opened and closed behind me. The arresting officer pulled my arms off the car one at a time and cuffed my wrists, while Detective DeGrasse, who had exited the cruiser after I was cuffed, read me my Miranda Rights for the second time.

"…You have the right to remain silent…"

And silent I remained.

"Do you understand your rights as I've read them?"

"What's this all about?"

"You know what it's about," Degrasse said as the walked me back to the cruiser.

As an insult, they re-cuffed my hands in the front of me before sticking me the cruiser to illustrate they thought me more pathetic than violent.

"Comfortable? Watch your head, now," The officer said as he pushed me into the police car and I ducked inside the back seat. DeGrasse spoke to the officer in a low voice and shut the door.

The cops searched my car, pulled everything apart, then hooked it up to a tow truck.

Sixty-eight Chevy Impala Super Sport; where the hell am I going to get door panels for that?

Then, I remembered the three pills in my pocket, enough to nail me for a neat little possession charge. *Thank God they cuffed my hands in front of me,* I thought as I worked the pills into my hand through my pants, popped them in my mouth, and swallowed before anyone noticed. At least I could go to jail without going into withdrawal.

They removed the cuffs when we got to the station and made me lean against the wall to be patted down one more time. An uniformed officer asked me to empty my pockets. They inventoried everything in the metal tray: wallet with drivers license and credit cards, penknife, $120 in small bills, and eighty-seven cents in change. They also took my watch, my Saint Jude medal, the one I received from Mrs. Boil, and its chain.

Saint Jude, the patron saint of lost causes, seemed appropriate hanging from my neck at this particular moment. With Mrs. Boil long gone along with her prayers, off into the ether, off to Purgatory, or, wherever, I guess I was pretty much alone. The medal had never been off my neck since she had given it to me; Saint Jude fit my style.

They put me in a room with a table, three chairs and a fluorescent lamp. The light made me squint. I stood in the corner and watched myself sitting down in the chair. *Poor bastard, his luck sure has run out.*

In that moment I had no past or future, and no interest in how this situation would turn out.

Do what you want to him, but leave me alone.

After a while Detective Degrasse came in with another guy in a suit. No introductions. I did not answer their questions. After a few minutes of this, Degrasse made a motion with his head and the suit left. He looked at me for a minute, then began the interrogation in earnest. "You know, Vince told us everything. He's blaming it all on you, of course, saying that you got him addicted, that he's got a malpractice case against you, things like that."

Fascinating.

"That's what he does, you know. He gets young doctors like you to whore for him. That's his pattern." Detective DeGrasse looked down, leaned on his elbows, locked his fingers, tapped his thumbs together, and pursed his lips. He, looked up and cocked his head. "Hello!" he said and waved his hand in front of my face. "Did you hear what I said?"

"Yes."

"Did you know that? Did you know that slime ball did time in the federal pen for prescription fraud? That a doctor served time with him, and that the doctor lost his license?"

My ignorance accrued on my face but I still said nothing.

"That's what I thought. Well, here's something else you don't know: Your friend is in the next room, this room right here." He pointed to his left with one finger, and the fist of his hand bobbed like the head of an angry goose. "He's spilling the beans. And since he's a convict, he knows just how to spill them so they end up right in your lap." He paused for a moment. Dramatic effect. "So, you got anything you want to tell me?"

I looked down, "No."

"When did you use Demerol last?"

I shook my head

"What's going on, doctor? Do you have a problem? If you do, I can help you."

He deserved an answer, even a lie. He was only doing his job.

"No comment."

"Well, let me tell you how this is going to go down. I'm going to let you go." He made a face that said, *I could give a shit.* "You can go back to your apartment or wherever the hell else you want to go. You can go back to work and cut on people, for all I care. You're lucky I didn't find anything in your car, or you'd be spending the night in jail, which is where your pal will be spending his evening, and that piece of shit car you drive would be impounded—by the way, you can pick that up tomorrow any time after 9AM.

"Tomorrow morning, I'm going to take everything that slime in the other room is telling my partner and I'm going straight to the DA with it. Now, this DA is a prick. He will charge both of you with fraud and diversion. He'll charge you with trafficking. That's mandatory jail time in this state, if you're convicted." He was into it now, on a roll. "And he'll send copies of the investigation to the medical board and the judge advocate general for your army reserve command."

That startled me. He had done his homework.

"That's right, I know about the army; I know about everything. You may not have heard, but the Uniform Code of Military Justice rules have changed. You can be court-marshaled as a reservist even if the offense occurs when you're off duty. If you're convicted, which you most certainly will be, you will go to jail, get court-marshaled out of the army, and lose your license to practice medicine here in this state for ten years.

I believed every word he said. The information horrified and fascinated me. His invective struck me dumb and vapid.

"You sure you still have nothing to say? No? Well, you can go." He shook his head. "God help you."

I got up

"Oh, doctor, I'll tell you one more thing: That piece of shit in the other room is not helping you at all. He's not worth it, doc; he's not worth all that loyalty you give him. He'll hang you out to dry the first chance he gets. I've seen it before."

I made a move toward the door.

"He's done this before. You know, suckered the doctor, the whole thing."

"May I go now?"

He shook his head. "Go on, get out of here. I'll be seeing you again soon enough."

I believed every word he said.

❦   ❦   ❦

When I got home, I saw a red light flashing in the dark living room.

The answering machine.

The sickening sweet taste of the cough medicine that I gagged down before even considering whose voice might be recorded there drove me to drink a beer I didn't even want just to kill the taste. When the flashes in my head matched the flashing of the light on the answering machine, I sat down and listened to the message.

"Hey, buddy (Ha, ha)! Listen, I just wanted to…" I heard voices in the background, Snatches of commands and conversations, "I will, I will," Vince said, talking to someone else, "Now, just hold your horses, will you, goddamn it! You all said I could have this call, now how about letting me have it!" Back to me. "Rock? Sorry about that (Ha, ha). Look, I've got a little problem. You remember that medicine you prescribed me? What was it? Dramamine, or, Donnetol, or, Demitol."

More voices in the background, "What was it?" He said to the voice behind him, "Demerol?" More laughing, "That's right, Demerol…Yeah, Rock, it was the Demerol. Well anyway, I had the

Demerol with me, I picked it up, just like you told me to, and they pulled me over and found it in the car. They've gone and arrested me, and I need you to talk to these guys and straighten this thing out. You're supposed to call a, um, a Detective DeGrasse for me as soon as you get in and tell him that I was only doing what you, as my doctor, told me to do, okay? Thanks, Rock, I mean, Dr. VanSlyke (Ha ha). No offense, doc. I need your help, now, so don't let me down. I'm counting on you. Okay, well, talk to you soon I hope. All right," he said again to someone behind him, "All right all ready! I'm done. Jesus! Here." Then I heard a click and a beep.

Silence.

My decision came while sitting on the couch staring into space; it just came to me, just popped into my head: the final solution. Until I decided this whole mess seemed such a dilemma, but after, I just walked back to the bathroom cool as a cucumber and inventoried the medicine cabinet: one half bottle of Benelyn and Dilaudid left, fourteen Percocet in the shaving kit, a couple of Tylenol #3 in an aspirin bottle. My liquor cabinet held one half quart of Wild Turkey, two inches of single malt scotch, and some tawny port. The refrigerator housed four cans of beer and two wine coolers.

Not enough.

Demerol, something I.V., that's what I needed, but I couldn't go out for it, not with the cops watching. The drugs would help, but I would have to change my strategy. A towel, disposable syringe, alcohol swabs, a multi dose vial of two percent lidocaine with epinephrine, all these things I had.

The epi will stop bleeding. If I cut down to the artery, then thread a catheter into it to keep it open...

I love it when a plan comes together.

Back in the kitchen, I opened a beer and took the Percocet two at a time and managed to get them down without vomiting. Into a small cooler I filled with ice I threw the rest of the beer and the wine coolers, then carried it into the bathroom. Next, I poured the rest of the bourbon into a pitcher. I left the Scotch in the bottle. I could mix that with the cough syrup.

Too sweet…I'll never keep it down.

With all the booze arranged within arms length of the tub I checked the temperature of the water.

While the water-cooled, I finished the Percocet and two more cans of beer.

Got to work fast, before my hand-eye coordination goes.

Naked I walked back into the living room and tuned in National Public Radio on the stereo, soft classical music, and few interruptions. Aaron Copland's *Fanfare for the Common Man*. The state-controlled radio stations of the old Soviet Union played soft classical music to prepare the proletariat for announcement of the death of a high-ranking party official. Classical music seemed apropos. Something befitting a funeral. My mind wandered. The colored dials glowed beautiful in the dark.

The levers of a Russian spaceship on its way to Mars!

Snapping myself up sharply I thought, *It's happening. Work fast.*

Once in the bathroom again, I mixed the Dilaudid with the Scotch and set the bottle in the ice chest with the last beer and the two wine coolers. Three ounces of alcohol were enough to stop my hands from shaking, so I figured I'd be safe. Once in the tub, I drank the next wine cooler. The water steamed, stinging hot, but not hot enough to stop me from getting in.

Ready.

Strange as it may seem, with drugs and alcohol on board I felt focused. I concentrated better. Narcotics cleared my mind, helped me stay on task. The brain becomes accustomed to the chemicals. On occasion, the phenomenon led to a dissociation, or preoccupation, similar to a condition aviators in the military call "target fixation," when a pilot focused on hitting his target to the exclusion of flying his airplane. Boom! Flight surgeons like me diagnosed target fixation post-mortem during aircraft accident investigations.

I focused on my left wrist, the target.

I identified the anatomy easily enough. My own pulse pounded between the flexor tendons and the wrist bones as I examined the area.

The artery, right under there.

It's important to identify the anatomic landmarks first, before you start cutting, to fix them in your mind, because in a moment they will change. I picked up the syringe, pulled off the tear-away wrapper with my teeth, and congratulated myself for having been so clever as to heist these from the hospital whenever I could. I uncapped the needle, with my teeth, then let the cap drop back into place before I set it back down. I ripped open the alcohol swab and wiped off the vial of lidocaine. I did the same with the hemostats and the skin of my wrist. Why all this attention to sterility? Force of habit, I guess.

After a moments rest I felt wide-awake, but dreamy. The steam rose from the tub like a fog over a marsh. I nodded and roused myself again.

Getting a little too dreamy. Decision time: Should you do the cut down first or drink the Diluadid? Split the difference: unwrapped the catheter (clever man to have a drawer so full of medical goodies!) Insert the catheter into the radial artery. Ready? Okay, pick up the syringe and inject the skin over the ventral aspect of the wrist over the artery between the radius bone and the palmaris longus tendon. Feel the sting? (Wince). The anatomy disappears in the area infiltrated with the solution, under the weal, like a bee sting. Stop. Let the medicine soak in, otherwise, operate from memory. Scotch and Dilaudid. What a combination: Bromton's Cocktail.

Dr. Bromton's concoction of narcotics and ethyl alcohol, administered for pain control in terminal cancer patients in the 40s and 50s seemed appropriate. My intuition pleased me. This disease, whatever its name, was about to become fatal, too. Then, my moment of clarity passed into nausea and nausea into determination.

Most wrist-slashers cut across tendons. Lacking a firm perception of anatomy, mutilators bend their wrists back, a maneuver that moves the tendons above the artery, protecting it from the blade. The worst injury most ever get is what is known in the business as a "spaghetti wrist" which results in a crippled hand. Pathetic. A far cry from passage to the beyond. The correct way to cut down on the artery, parallel to the tendons with the wrist flat or bent slightly forward, longitudinally, brings the blade down atop the artery.

The tissue of my wrist split like an overcooked hot dog, burst open before my blade. I learned to cut tissue, developed my style from a master, Doctor Wynnbeir. Deft strokes, Doctor VanSlyke. Deft strokes and steady, two cell layers at a time. Doctor Wynnbeir, the first physician colleague ever to call me doctor, trained at Hopkins, under a protégé of William Halsted, the father of American surgery. It's always the same; two cell layers at a time.

The epinephrine stopped any significant bleeding. For a moment I found myself back in the O.R. I looked deep into the incision.

N.A.V.L., I think, Nerve, artery, vein, lymphatic...

"Eighteen gauge angio-cath please. Let's have it. Move! I'm losing this exposure, Let's go, people..." The sweat ran into my eyes. I turned to confront the scrub nurse, but of course, I found myself staring into the commode. I laughed so hard I slid down in the tub and cried. After a second, I saw the catheter on the toilet seat. I picked it up and looked at the incision.

My eyes blurred from the tears and sweat. Rubbing them with the back of my hand only made them burn even more. My wrist, even held up close to my face, seemed a blur. The blood vessels in the wound confused me. Which one pulsated? Then, all at once, I found the artery. With the catheter positioned and stabilized, my hand propped against the side of the tub, I stabbed the trocar into the vessel and watched the wound fill up with blood. The trocar slipped from the catheter and the catheter slid the rest of the way into the artery. The palm of my hand filled up with blood as if a nail had been driven through the palm.

"It is finished," I heard someone say, but it must have been me.

Lying back in the tub, I finally relaxed.

CHAPTER 26

*A*fter I take the Dexedrine, Mike stands next to me holding my shoulder as I vomit again. When I finish, he gives me two more pills and makes me take them.

"There's always more where that came from."

"You sure this stuff's safe?" I hold my gut.

"Hell yes! I told you, my mother used to take it to keep her weight down. She used to get it from her doctor. That's how I found out about them. I copped a couple from her a few times when I was a kid and got buzzed off my ass. The stuff's great for lots of things.

"My mom got them first when she went to college in the sixties. She told me the nurses gave these things out like candy. Campus heath service gave them to students to help them cram for tests, or finish papers. Now, with the fucking Republicans in office, that shit stopped. I know for a fact that the air force uses it for flight crew-members that fly more than sixteen hours at a time. My father told me. He was in the air force."

"No shit. That is fucking fascinating, but I still feel like I'm about to die."

"You'll feel better in a minute. Trust me."

So, I do…and I do.

❦   ❦   ❦

First, the bright light, then the pain in my left arm, then the cold.

Squinting the light out of my eyes, squeezing them as hard as I could, and covering my face with my right forearm did little to ease my discomfort. It was reflex, a pathetic defense against the light, bright as an atomic fireball. After a moment, I lifted my head from the edge of the bathtub, glanced about, then rested it again. Only the parts of my body that jutted above the bloody water, my knees and my chest, like abstract alabaster statues on a red velvet mat were visable, like bones in a bowl of duck blood soup. When I moved, I saw that I, myself, floated in that soup. The bath water had turned to burgundy wine.

The bent catheter floated by.

What the hell is that doing there?

My wrist, swollen to twice its normal size, came out of the water, right at me, when I crooked my elbow. The gash in the skin, three and a half inches long on the soft underbelly of my forearm, oozed clotted blood. The edges of the wound, wrinkled and macerated from submersion, looked pasty white and friable. The incision gaped, gawked at me like some toothless, sardonic smile.

Shivering, I scrunched down under the water for warmth, but the water had turned cold. My hand felt like a club. The numbness frightened me so badly that I did not want to think about what had happened, what I might have done to myself, or why.

Then, I awoke for real, sat bolt upright and examined the wound. The old blood clot I expressed with my thumb and forefinger confirmed there was no active bleeding. The radial artery had most likely clotted off, but I knew that the collateral circulation from the ulnar artery, the one on the other side, would take over until the wounded vessel could re-cannulate. The wound appeared clean from soaking all night.

Suture it later, at the sink where you can get some proper lighting. Just rest a moment; let your heart slow down, let your head stop spinning so that you can think this through.

My shivering rippled the cold water. A couple of ounces of blood could make a room look like a slaughterhouse. In water, a couple of teaspoons of blood could look like a bathtub full. Even a little blood can make a real mess of things. With my eyes closed, I fumbled for the drain-lever with the ball of my foot until the bath began to drain. The gurgle and hum of the water and the need to support my own weight motivated me to keep going. The slippery fixtures squeaked under my toes until I managed to turn the hot water on and refill the bath. The steamy waterfall tumbled from the spout, splashed in the soup and swirled around me. The warmth wrapped me up like a liquid blanket. It kept me safe.

Looking around I inventoried the room.

Booze, drugs, paraphernalia. Party? No. I didn't party. Suicide attempt? Maybe. Okay. Why? What's the motive? Every murder has a motive. Violence doesn't happen in a vacuum. Then, what was going on? What went wrong? Okay, forget why. Just forget that, for now. Focus on your mistakes. What went wrong? Why didn't it work? List.

1) I took the narcotics, which lowered my blood pressure and stopped me from bleeding to death.

2) I must have cannulated the vein instead of the artery. Veins are a low-pressure system and will stop bleeding when the blood pressure drops.

3) I should have picked either an overdose or exsanguination. You can't have it both ways.

Oh well. Live and learn.

My analysis helped me understand the facts at least, what went wrong. When the spots before my eyes cleared, I decided to stand. I adjusted the temperature of the water and turned on the shower. I stood up and stuck my face in the spray. As I touched my injured wrist, I heard pounding, like a knock at the door, only in my head. It was fear. Fear was the only thing that could knock that loud.

And still I did not know its name.

CHAPTER 27

❀

$\mathcal{A}$s a fourth-year medical student, I think of myself as already graduated. A doctor. Graduation, the ceremony, still a whole year away, is no worry. Graduation, I know is automatic. A done deal; I'm just going through the motions. The actual degree is just a matter of timing. The only question is where to do my residency. Medical students, picked for residencies like football players are picked for the NFL draft, don't know where they will end up. "The Match," as it's called, sounds sophisticated, but it's a draft just the same, just like the army draft of the nineteen sixties and seventies. Oh, you get to make a list. Sure. You get to choose a hospital. You might even get what you ask for, but the whole thing's a toss up.

The Match takes place in March.

As a senior elective I decide to do a rotation overseas, in Great Britain, in March. Brilliant. Orthopedic surgery at the orthopedic hospital in Oswistry. I scrape together enough money, write a letter to the university, make my travel reservations and zoom, I'm in London for a month.

"Are you an American?" an English gentleman asks; he is intent on buying me a drink.

"Indeed I am!"

"Well then, young fella, let me buy you a drink!"

"You're so very kind. How 'bout a bitters?"

"I said I'd buy you a drink. Now, if you'll have a real drink, then I'll buy. If you're going to drink that swill, then you're on your own,"

"Well, then, I'll just change that to a bourbon."

"Bourbon it is for the fine young American lad!"

And bourbon it is, everyday, for a month.

I go to "theater," the British version of an operating room, for about four hours in the morning, and clinic once or twice a week in the afternoon, and I drink everyday. I see the inside of every pub from London to Manchester.

Then I get the phone call.

"Rocky, Rocky? This is Mike. I can hardly hear you with this echo. Can you hear me?"

"Yes, yes, Mike, I can hear you. Go ahead." I am standing in the hall with one ear covered.

"Rocky, I've got some bad news. You didn't match at Brown or any of the other hospitals you listed. You've got to get back here right away, or you're going to be shit out of luck next summer. You won't get a job in surgery. You have to be here to interview personally or you're fucked."

One minute I am drinking before a portrait of Margaret Thatcher—they all call her Maggie—At the Stoke-on-Trent Conservative Club—the next minute I board a train for London/Heathrow. One minute the club president toasts my health and gives me his tie as a remembrance, the next minute I'm a beggar looking for a handout. A doctor without a residency. A free agent.

"What the hell were you doing in England?" The dean says to me, incredulous. "Do you know what an embarrassment you are for the medical school? To have a graduate without a residency is a terrible embarrassment. Now we will have to see what we can scrape up. This is unheard of! I hope you got whatever it was you were looking for out of your system. You must remember, your life is no longer your own."

Jesus.

❦   ❦   ❦

Once out of the tub I am warmer, but woozy. The pounding outside got more insistent. Wrapping my wrist with a sloppy, gauze
dressing made me look made-up for a monster movie. Creeping out
to the front door with a towel wrapped around my waist, I peeked
through the peephole and saw a distorted head three times normal
size, getting larger, then smaller again with each approach to bang
again on the door. Vince, his face red, breathed heavy. His anger
bathed his upper lip with sweat. He appeared anxious, fearful, and
furious.

Something inside me told me to abandon him out there, to cut
my losses and figure this thing out on my own, but the pounding
made me feel nauseated, it shook my soul. Something deep within
me told me. *No good can come of this visit.* He banged again, and I
opened the door.

"Hey, Rock!" His face changed in an instant from that of a frightened, angry man in a keyhole, to one of a vacuum cleaner salesman,
the Vince I knew. "Where have you been?" he asked as he pushed
past me.

I closed the door.

"Hey, did you get my message? Why didn't you call me back?
What the hell happened to your wrist?"

"Cut myself shaving"

No reaction. "Hey, look, we've got problems. These fucking cops
blew this thing all out of proportion. Have you talked to the hospital
yet?"

"No."

"Well, be careful. They're apt to tell you to go in and give them a
statement or something."

"Statement? What kind of statement?"

"How the hell should I know? You know, a statement about, oh, you-know-what." He put his fat fingers to his lips and sushed me, "But, they're fishing. I wouldn't talk to them until you absolutely have to. That's my advice."

"What about work?"

"I wouldn't worry about that now. If they call, tell them that there's been some kind of family emergency. I don't know—tell them you cut yourself shaving, ha-ha-ha. We'll figure something out. Maybe we'll put you back on active duty. That worked pretty well, didn't it? Ha! We sure got 'em there, didn't we."

"Yeah, but what about—"

"Look, what we need to do is to get us some stuff, you know, and get somewhere where we can prop up and think this thing through. You know what I mean?"

My mind began to wander. "Overdose or exsanguination. It's got to be one or the other."

"What? What did you say?"

"Nothing, never mind."

"Did you hear what I said?"

"Oh, uh, yeah. What?"

"About the stuff. You know." He makes a motion like he's injecting something into his arm. "The stuff."

"Oh, right. Yeah, let's do it."

"Are you okay?"

"Oh, I'm fine, really. Just let me go get cleaned up."

"Hurry up."

Back in the bathroom I locked the door. Vince talked in whispers on my telephone. A disposable suture kit I'd stashed with the rest of the stuff I'd filched from the hospital lay under the sink. Never know when you might need one of these. I dug it out and opened it. Once I doused the wound with disinfectant, my hand began to sting. I felt better. A surgeon can't be too careful with his hands. To suture the gaping wound tight, I taught myself to tie the knots one handed, right there at the sink, an easy enough process, if I held a hemostat between the fingers of the hand I worked on to steady the suture. Seven knots I tied that way, watching the wound close with each progressive stitch. After I got dressed, a long-sleeve shirt hid the bulky surgical dressing.

❦   ❦   ❦

We pulled up outside the drug store.

"Let me go in this time. It's one we've been to before," I said.

"What do you mean?"

"I said, let me go in. I'll tell them I'm the patient representative so they won't ask for any I.D. If they call me, they'll just get my machine. If they call you, you describe me and tell them it's okay. Besides, the last thing you need right now is to get caught passing a bad script."

He spent the ride rehashing the Gestapo tactics of the law enforcement authorities and how they had mistaken him for a repeat offender.

"You know, you're right. I guess it would be better."

I took the script and left the car, stepping onto the darkness, the apron of the cool twilight, fresh but threatening, like black ice on the highway. To put some distance between me and the car and him I quickened my step. When I entered the store, a bell rang over the door, a real bell on a strip of curved metal, not a mechanical tone set off by the disruption of a magnetic field. Fluorescent light spilled into the darkness behind me. Vince watched through the Cadillac window as I walked in and went to the back of the store.

At the pharmacy counter I became the consummate professional. "I'm Dr. VanSlyke. Let me speak with the manager." A young girl in a white smock typed away at a computer keyboard while her gaze darted from a CRT to some papers on the counter.

"Pardon me young lady, may I speak to the manager, please?"

She flipped to another sheet of paper without looking up.

"Excuse me, miss?"

She glanced up and than back to her papers. "Just a moment."

I took one look around the store and back at the girl. "Miss?"

"Just a minute."

Bang! I slammed the palm of my hand down on the counter so hard that I startled myself with the sting. "Get the manager—now."

"About what?"

"I'm afraid, young lady, that I must insist on speaking to the manager."

"About what?"

My face reddened. "About filling a prescription."

"I fill the prescriptions. Give it here."

"I rather speak with the manager."

"What's it for?"

"The manager, please?"

"It's for narcotics, right?"

"Miss—"

"It's not going to work. I'll—"

"Mindy!" A thin round-shouldered man with wire-rim glasses and a severe spinal curve that doubled him almost all the way over stepped out of a back room. "Is there a problem?"

"Mr. Smith, this guy—"

"Ah, Mr. Smith," I said, all smiles, "I'm Dr. VanSlyke."

"Mr. Smith, this guys trying to—"

"That will be all, Mindy," the old man said through pursed lips. "Please go in the back and finish checking in that new stock."

The young woman glared at me, then spun around on her heels and disappeared in to the back. The old man turned to me and smiled. "Please forgive Mindy. She's been her all day. How may I help you?" he said.

"I am Dr. Rocky VanSlyke." I slid my credentials across the counter to him. "I've just received a call from the authorities informing me that someone passed forged prescriptions on my pad. I'm meeting a patient with renal colic, and rather than send him out with a prescription before I know what's going on, I thought I'd fill the 'script for him myself and check for any forgeries while I'm waiting. May I see your hard copies?"

He took my license and the script from me, lifted his glasses which hung from a chain around his neck and examined the documents. He looked up at my face and back down again. "Well, this is a little unusual, Dr. VanSlyke. I'm not used to having to open my records on such short notice."

"I know this is an imposition. I won't remove anything. I just want to flip through the scripts I've written that might have been filled here and check the signature."

He eyed me. "Well, that's just it, doctor. I'm not sure that I recognized your name. Also, your address is on the other side of town."

"I understand. Actually, I've just opened an office down the street. The patient lives in South Philly."

"I see," he said holding his glasses up again.

"Is that the Bowl of Hygia?" I pointed to a plaque on the wall behind him, desperate to change the subject.

He turned and looked over his shoulder and then back at me. "Why, yes. Yes, it most certainly is."

"Well, well. I'm impressed. I don't think I've ever seen one."

"There aren't too many around."

"And, are you the recipient?"

"No, no, actually my father was. This was his store. He started the business. I followed in his footsteps."

"Big shoes to fill, aye, Mr.. Mr.."

"Smith."

"Yes, of course, Mr. Smith. This is Smith's Pharmacy! How silly of me."

"Not at all. It's an old store. We Smiths should have been gone from here long ago. How is it that you know about The Bowl?" He gestured over his shoulder with his thumb.

"Well, you're not going to believe this, but my father was a phar-macist, too." I looked down at the floor and shuffled my feet. My cheeks burned as I fought to make my humiliation play like humility.

"Really?"

"Yes indeed." A lump grew in my throat. "And one of his greatest regrets was never having received that honor before he died."

"Oh, I'm sorry. Not too many do, you know. It's a very prestigious award."

"He lived a full and happy life." I choked on that one, but it had the same effect as true sadness. I glanced at my watch. "Mr. Smith, I hate to, but…"

"Of course, doctor. Let me get my records for you so that you can review them while I'm filling this script for Mr.. . Mr." He looked down at the script, "Buddy. Buddy? Oh, yes Mr. Vincent Buddy. We've filled this for him before. Kidney stones, was it?"

"Yes, indeed! I'm impressed again!"

"Well, we're a small operation, you know. It's easier for us to keep up with our customers."

"You're too modest, Mr. Smith. Yours is a dying breed."

"Yes." He turned red. "Yes, maybe you're right, doctor, maybe you're right."

After a moment, he retrieves a Rolodex from the back room. "Well, I'll be. I guess we have filled a few schedules twos for a patient of yours, a Mr. Buddy. Looks like, for Demerol."

"Yes, that's him. Vincent Buddy."

"Hm, well, they all look okay to me. Have a look if you like."

I reviewed his record just to make it look good. At least two-thirds must have been written in Vince's handwriting because I did not rec-ognize the signature. "Well, everything looks okay to me," I said, forcing a smile. "That's a relief." Turning to the plate-glass window at the front of the store, I kept an eye on Vince while cursing him under my breath. He glanced at his watch and fidget.

"Doctor, will that be all?"

Mr. Smith handed me a white bag, stapled shut.

"Well, now that you mention it, I could use a half a dozen or so disposable three cc syringes with twenty-two gauge needles. Would you have any?"

"Well, only five cc. Sorry."

"Five cc. will be fine."

He bagged them up the same as the medication. That will be twenty-six dollars and fifty cents for the Merperidene and twelve dollars even for the syringes, I'll give you the hospital discount on those, for a grand total of thirty-eight dollars and fifty cents, plus seven percent sales tax, that comes to forty-one dollars and twenty cents."

"Here you go" I handed him a fifty. That much dope had to be worth ten times as much on the street.

"Thank you and, here's your change and receipt. Dr. VanSlyke, it was so nice to talk with you. Please stop in again when you can do so under more pleasant circumstances." When he paused, we looked straight at each other, and then he went on. "I mean, sometime when you don't have a patient waiting."

"Oh, of course." I smiled, "Thanks for your help." I took the bag and headed for the door. When I got there, I saw Vince leaning forward with his head on the steering wheel. I turned on my heels and went back to the counter. I checked my pocket to see how much money I had. I spotted a few twenties and stuffed them back in.

He looked up at me after a moment and said, "May I help you?"

"Mr. Smith, do you think you could call me a taxi? My brother-in-law dropped me off and he seems to have left me."

"Why certainly, doctor."

"I think I'll wait at the burger place down the street and grab a bite while I'm waiting. Do you have a side door?"

"Why yes, yes we do. Right this way, doctor, right this way," and he pointed. "I'll call right away."

"Thank you."

CHAPTER 28

On graduation day, I am stone cold sober. My medical diploma waves at the crowd after I receive it, like it has a mind of it's own, like all the other kid's diploma's do. My diploma waves as if someone in the audience watches me receive it, someone who sweated out an investment of precious time and hard-earned money in my education and now cranes to see if I acknowledge him or her, but there is no one out there among the faces. I hear someone yell, "Attaboy!" and I pretend the salute is for me. A few waves of my fists over my head brings a laugh and a cheer, but I know it is a charade.

Afterward, I shake hands with a few names from the class rosters and faces from the yearbook. Everybody looks happy. I am grabbed to complete candid pictures of the ceremony, someone for my classmates to say, "And, who's that on the end? No, that's Kenny Stevens right there. Who's the guy over there on the right?" Someone for my fellows to ask about during class reunions and wonder how they missed me during all those years. I stand around, even at graduation, after four years, trying to fit in.

Mike spots me and invites me out to dinner with his family. His folks flew in from his hometown for the occasion. They look at him during dinner with much pride.

"Hush, now, and listen to your brother," his mother says to his younger sister whenever she says "Mom?" It happens whether Mike is speaking or not. She apologizes twice during the meal for having to, "Take her medicine," before she sets about rummaging through her purse for the triangular pills I recognize so well as Dexedrine. Mike rolls his eyes at me whenever she does this. I look down and smile. I am embarrassed for her and for him, but I don't know why. I watch her as she moves her food around on her plate instead of eating. Once, when she catches me watching her, she sets her fork down and smiles.

His father drinks Scotch and lots of it. He says nothing at all until Mike asks him to tell me about what it's like to be a flight surgeon in the Air Force. He dismisses the request, leans on his elbow and waves his glass back and forth in front of me with his bottom three fingers extended, like a pontiff giving a blessing. "Let's not talk about that now," he says, but it comes out, "Less nod talk a bow thad now." And then, "I'm proud of you, son," which sounds about right.

Mike will move to Boston for a residency in radiology.

"Great hours. Great money."

After dinner we promise each other we will keep in touch, promise to look each other up whenever we visit each other's town. But, of course, we don't. After dinner, his mother holds up his diploma.

"That's my baby." Then she spills her drink.

Enough time passes to make him a stranger to me again. The next time I see his name in print is four years later. I read about him in the alumni newsletter, a name in a bold box labeled Class of 1984. "Michael B. Moran, M.D., Class of 1984; wife Amanda, two children, Michael, J. 3, and Melissa, 2, chair of the Roger C. Lipitz Research and Policy Center for Integrated Health Care in the Department of Health Policy and Management of Johns Hopkins Medical School, died suddenly." A feeling passes through me when I read the newsletter, a moment of recognition, of pride, then it's gone. His parents and his wife must feel something like this, too, I muse. For a moment I wonder if I should cut the box out and save it.

I throw it away.

Outside Smith's Rexall Drug Store, the darkness followed an adjacent street behind an abandoned gas station. I cut through and walked the half block to the burger joint. When the taxi arrived, I gave the cabby the directions.

"That old hospital? What a ya, sick or somthin'?"

"No, I'm a doctor." I looked behind me to see if we were being followed.

"A doctor! What's there some emergency of somthin?"

"Something like that. Just don't get pulled over."

Outside the hospital, we talked again. I asked the cabby to drive a little farther, past the emergency room, to the back entrance. It would be too busy at the ER for me to pass unnoticed. After we stopped, while he made change, I clipped my I.D. badge to the pocket of my shirt. With a big tip and a little wave, I left him and walked inside.

The receptionist looked up when I passed, but she looked back down again and buzzed me through the secured doors. The double doors to my left led to the ER Their world, I knew, would be in chaos. By force of habit, I hesitated. Then I remembered the bag I carried, turned and headed for the back staircase leading to the on-call room.

I listened for a moment for anyone, a nurse or a lazy resident, who might skulk in the stairway, then I dashed up four floors to the residents quarters. I punched in the three digit code that granted me access to the restricted area and stepped onto the floor. A few more steps and I entered my on-call room. With the key still standing in the lock, I disappeared inside and shut myself in.

CHAPTER 29

*M*y first three months as a resident are pure misery. I live on adrenaline and caffeine, panic and fear. Every time the beeper goes off, my heart rate doubles, becomes irregular. My chest pounds from the palpitations and I have trouble breathing. On one occasion, my pulse rate is so fast that I cannot count it. I feel light-headed much of the time. Someone always screams at me, some doctor, patient, or nurse who knows she knows more then I do. Fear that a patient will die too soon who shouldn't and leave me alone to explain, or that some patient won't die who should and keep me up all night. That kind of fear is with me every waking moment, which is to say, most all the time.

This is when I start with the pills.

"You look like shit."

"I feel like shit."

"Here, try one of these," Vince says.

"Give me half."

He gives me half.

He gives me the other half.

He gives me two...

My heartbeat so fast I had trouble breathing.

I haven't been like this since I was an intern.

My breath whistled through my teeth like a cold wind through a crack. It rolled over my palate. My chest heaved. My stomach rumbled. The diarrhea came before I gave myself the first shot.

The commode, the drug and the syringes were with me. I felt safe and alone.

After my bowels emptied, I washed up, walked to the bed, and gave myself a shot. Two hundred milligrams. I should have passed out, but I didn't. The pillow on the bed in my on-call room drifted up to cushion the back of my head as I closed my eyes.

I expected sleep, but it did not come. Instead, my thoughts stood at attention as my psyche held inspection.

"Where you from, soldier?"

"Georgia, sir, I mean, that's where I grew up."

"First time behind enemy lines, son?"

"Why, yes sir. It sure is."

"You scared, soldier?"

"No. I mean, no, sir."

"You're a fucking liar, son. You'll do just fine here. Let's move out…"

Sitting up, stark straight, from the dream I checked my vital: one point eight grams.

It might still be enough, I thought, but I'm going to have to figure another method of administration.

The individual shots would not do it; not enough volume in at one time. I'd needed an I.V. bag, on hundred cc's, two hundred fifty cc's at the most, to mix the Demerol in, and maybe some potassium. Then, I could give myself enough all at once, through some I.V. tubing, to get the job done.

I got off my bed and tested my legs. Things came to mind. *Young surgeon dies at local hospital—overdose suspected. Are hospitals push-*

ing doctors too hard? Details at eleven. An object lesson for the residents who followed. That's the room. Right there. That's where he did it. Nobody suspected a thing. I remember reading somewhere about an anesthesiologist. They found him sitting in a chair in the doctor's lounge, as if asleep. His hands rested comfortably on the arms of the chair and his head drooped forward a bit. The only oddities were the four converging black rubber straps hanging from the back of his head. They held a black rubber mask in place. The cause of death was deemed accidental. He wasn't trying to kill himself, he was trying to get some rest. When he turned on the nitrous oxide, the laughing gas, he forgot to give himself any oxygen.

There were three places I could get I.V. fluids fast: the O.R., the ER, or the ICU. I could get some from the floor, but someone would spot me for sure. I didn't have much time, I knew, so I took the elevator down to the O.R. The doors opened to the dark and quiet hall. I listened for a moment to be sure the hall was empty before I stepped out. The I.V. fluids were kept in the supply closet to my right. To get there, I had to pass the nurses' desk.

"Hey, doc? Where you been?" The old soldier.

"Jesus, you scared me." I covered my lack of ease with a startle, "You won't believe it," I continued after catching my breath. "Fort Meade."

"Fort Mead, huh? Military Intelligence? I'm impressed!"

I put a finger over my lips to quiet him, "You know how it is. I could tell you, but…"

"Yeah, yeah, yeah, I know the rest. Boy, do I know it! It's in your dossier, anyway. I'll look it up later."

"Look, do you have any Ringer's Lactate in small bags?"

"We might have. Let me look."

"I've been all over this place looking for some." I followed him to the cabinet, making small talk. "Just couldn't find any. Everybody says they're out"

"Yeah, well, it's a little unusual. The small bags are only used in pediatrics resuscitation. With all the shit in this stuff, the mineral or what have you, hell, you know what I mean, anyway, with everything that's in here, as soon as you mix it, the medications will precipitate out."

"Wow, ah, wait a minute, that's right. I don't even know if they are computable." I stopped for a moment and squeezed my lower lip. "Um, then, maybe I should think about this a minute. Maybe I should use some normal saline instead."

"If you're going to mix it with anything, that's what I'd do."

"Let's do it that way."

"Here you go, doc. Who's the patient, so I can charge this to his account?"

"Oh, shit, I don't even know."

"Oh, well, that's OK. What's the unit?"

"Surgical ICU"

"Do you happen to know what bed?"

"Jeez, I don't. Second or third from the right over against the back wall…"

"Doc. Man, you got to get some rest or something. You're gonna kill somebody! He laughed.

"Don't I know it."

"Okay, well, I'll figure something out."

"Cool. I appreciate it."

"No problem."

❦   ❦   ❦

Back in the room, I opened the door. I moved quickly and quietly so no one would see me. After locking the door behind me, I saw something that looked like a firefly dart back and forth in the room, the trace of a burning ember. I flipped the overhead light on and found Zack sitting in the chair at the foot of my bed with his feet up on the desk.

"I thought we weren't supposed to smoke in here."

"I've really got to quit these things." Zack turned the cigarette around in hand. "Hey, partner, where you been?" When I didn't answer he said, "How 'bout a smoke?"

I went and sat hard on the edge of the bed. When he took the pack out of the pocket of his scrub suit and handed it to me, I accepted one, lit it, and took a drag.

"Something you'd like to tell me, maybe?"

I shrugged. "How'd you get in?"

"You left the key in the door."

"Jesus."

"Yeah, well, I said the same thing when I found this." He held up the bloody syringe that I'd used to inject the Demerol.

My hands shook as I hung my head.

"And, let's not forget about this." He held up the vial of Demerol between his thumb and forefinger.

After a quick glance up, I put my face in my hands.

"Says here...let me see..." He read from the label on the vial. "Says here that this medication is prescribed to, ah, Mr. Vincent G. Buddy. Isn't that the attorney guy? The one who works for the hospital?"

His head tilted as he took a drag off his cigarette and exhaled a trumpet of blue smoke out of the corner of his mouth. "So," he says, "what's up?"

"You're not supposed to be smoking in here."

"A, you already said that, and, B, you're not supposed to be shooting up fucking Demerol."

My mind went blank. Good intentions bounced back and forth across my mind like two mirrors in a hallway, facing each other, appearing deep, but creating a flat illusion like 50,000-watt radio waves over the shallow edge of my conscientiousness.

And, now, the greatest hits of the 60s, 70s, and 80s...Be a good boy. Don't lie to Mommy. Tell Daddy the truth...

I looked up.

"Rock? Listen, Rocky?" He sat forward, his face close to mine.

I started to cry.

"Look, you need a friend, okay? Don't say anything more. I know what's going on. I don't care what it is, but I want to tell you something about myself. "You see this?" He picked up the Demerol. "I used to shoot this stuff." I watched him nod his head at me. "Yep. I got kicked out of my first residency for stealing the stuff from the ICU. I took it out of my patient's I.V. and replace it with sterile water. Do you understand what I've said? I'm an addict. I depended on this stuff, but I haven't used any in a long time, almost three years. "Rocky, my God, your killing yourself." There were tears in his eyes. "They've been looking for you."

In a flash, I saw it end.

Hot lights melted. cold steel froze. Latex gloves snapped. The blood I remembered in the palm of my hand turned to hot tears. Like a voice crying in the wilderness, I heard a moan. Maybe mine. Maybe not. I felt a hand on my shoulder and, for a moment, I thought Zack might be Vince.

"We've got to get you some help my friend, before you get yourself arrested and tossed in jail. That ain't gonna help a goddamn thing." He took another drag of his smoke. "I know where we can get you some real help. A place where they specialize in treating doctors like us."

A fragile quiet filled the small room. Sighs of relief mingled with my tears.

"You have no idea. You have no idea how close…"

A knock at the door shot through me.

Don't answer it. There's no one out there I want to see.

The pounding continued, louder and louder, so loud I thought it must be a battering ram beating down the door.

Zack stood, crushed out his cigarette in the ashtray and tucked in the shirt of his scrub suit.

"They're here."

He did not explain who "they" might be, but it seemed clear it was not the cops.

"It will be okay." He looked down at me then looked back at the door. "It will all work out. Come on, it's time."

The relief, before Zack even opened the door, of hearing those few disjointed sentences from another human being is indescribable. Later, after I'd been placed in the hospital, I thought of how we'd traded, Zack and me: his cigarettes for a piece of my pain.

"That's what people do," a therapist of mine would say later. "They find something in common—an illness or a disaster—then they trade."

My pain diminished a little when Zack and I traded. That brief conversation in my on-call room turned my nightmare to nostalgia. The opportunity to destroy a version of myself, one created from drugs and pain, for the boost of my ego, with the sacrifice of my soul, a version who kept me hostage to the past, to its constant hunger for pleasure or pain, blessed me even in its paradox.

Zack blessed me.

As the author of my release from the bondage of personality he blessed me, the way Mary Shelley blessed Doctor Frankenstein with the privilege of watching the destruction of the Monster, the way Bram Stoker blessed Count Dracula with the spike.

Who could know more peace?

On my first night in the detox ward, one man in a yellow robe and paper slippers shuffled up to me as I faced the metal doors, afraid to go any further after the portals locked behind me.

"Hey, asshole. You got a light?"

"I don't smoke."

"You're fucking beautiful." He shuffled away, "Just beautiful."

Epilogue

"There will come a time when you believe everything is finished. That will be the beginning."

—Louis L'Amour, novelist

I wasn't afraid anymore.

My world shrunk to a few comfortable walls, a small outside recreation area, AA meetings, and a quiet calm that washed over me like a slow motion wave, slower then the Demerol, but with a similar sensation. No more cops. No more hospital. No more Vince. My former life became the few rays of fluorescent light that drifted from the hallway into my dark room each night. My memories jitterbugged before my eyes as the iridescent beams danced on the folds of the quivering blanket I wrapped around me to keep my soul from shivering away. In drug treatment, your body aches from the physical withdrawal, and your mind races.

The others like me in treatment, the doctors, lawyers, nurses, pharmacists helped me to understand. Once I would have distrusted these people on principle; other professionals were not to be trusted; I manipulated them and depended on myself more, but that seemed so long ago. Now I was one of them and happy to be so. Together we all figured things out, put the pieces back together, or comforted each other when the pieces could not be found. In my case there were plenty of pieces.

Vince was arrested.

The cops offered to drop the criminal charges against me if I would testify as a states witness at Vince's trial. I agreed, of course. I was finished and the police knew it. They knew the hospital would fire me and the medical board would take my license. The humiliation of testifying was better then the shame of going to jail. Late at night, when I couldn't sleep worrying about all this, I imagined that Vince had assumed a false identity, skipped town, moved to Canada or Mexico, and obviated the need for me to testify. It was easier to fancy him crossing some border a thousand miles away, moving to Toronto, say, or Nuevo Laredo, somewhere more cosmopolitan with easier access to drugs, then to see myself climbing those three steps up to the stand.

A bunch of us arrived at the entrance of the main building each day fifteen minutes or so prior to the start of our group therapy. We clients sat around, socialized, smoked cigarettes, burned holes in our blue jeans and brushed the smoke from the air around our faces. We stood like silhouettes, hollow shadows with empty coffee cups saved behind our backs, somewhere to snuff out the smoldering butts.

"Can I see you over here a second?" My therapist pointed to a patch of grass five feet or so from where we all were standing.

"What's up?"

"Vince is dead," he said.

My mouth dropped. "Dead? How?"

"He shrugged," I don't know. A heart attack or something." He looked at me for a moment, narrowed his eyes to a therapeutic squint. "How are you feeling?"

"What? Oh, yeah, yeah, I feel, ah, I'm okay. Thanks."

The news wasn't enough. I wasn't satisfied with the explanation. I could not resolve Vincent Buddy with mere knowledge of his death, not without knowing a wooden stake was driven through his heart or a silver bullet had traversed his brain.

I never heard another word about him, not to this day.

Although, by convention, he was entitled to fill the chief resident spot at Liberty, Zack withdrew from the surgical residency that summer and, the following year started over again in psychiatry. To Zack, the experience of organizing my intervention, lining up the cops, the administration, and the treatment center, changed him. He wanted to work with addicts full-time. When the two of us were free at last, Zack became a good friend. I met his wife recently, just before they moved to Tucson. They were expecting their first child.

For more than a year after treatment, I was unable to do any but the most menial of jobs. I stacked boxes at a grocery store for a while and worked at the airport, loading and unloading airplanes. I stayed off drugs and alcohol, kept with AA, and did my best to be a good citizen. My AA sponsor had me get a library card and made me register to vote.

After moving back to Atlanta and starting classes part-time in the English Department at Georgia State, I began to write. I write now in the mornings. Short stories, poems about Karla. I may never practice medicine again, but maybe I will. It seems the board is about to give me my license again. Nowadays, what I do for a living doesn't seem as important as just living itself.

Not when I'm walking down by the lake, watching the geese fly.

Afterword

Joseph Molea, M.D. is a 1986 graduate of the State University of New York at Buffalo School of Medicine. After finishing a general surgery residency, he became certified by the American Society of Addiction Medicine and earned administrative credentials from the American College of Healthcare Executives. He is the Executive Director of a specialized addiction treatment center for professionals with impairment problems in Tampa, Florida. He lives in St. Petersburg, Florida with his wife, Heidi, and their three children. This is his first novel.

0-595-21843-1